More Advance Praise for *Ballet at the Moose Lodge*

"Caroline Patterson's stories in *Ballet at the Moose Lodge* explore the depths of love and longing, escape and return, hope and regret in the lives of women and their men in the Western towns she knows so well. Ranging from a forlorn young woman in Seward, Alaska, to yesterday's schoolmarms in a remote Montana hamlet, her stories express in vivid detail the dreams and nightmares of a wealth of characters. Like mini-novels in the Alice Munro tradition, these stories offer readers insights into the joys, terrors, and confines of small-town lives that matter."
—**Annick Smith, author of *Homestead (The World as Home)* and *Crossing the Plains with Bruno***

"Caroline Patterson, with *Ballet at the Moose Lodge*, gives us stories about broken-hearted on-the-street household disasters and high-country triumphs. Terrific storytelling!"
—**William Kittredge, author of *Hole in the Sky: A Memoir* and *The Willow Field***

"At once heartfelt and unflinching, Caroline Patterson's stories cover the wide world of hurt, hope, and uncertainty she finds in small, specific, often overlooked places, from juke joints to chicken pens, Montana to Alaska. She's as empathic and skillful a writer as any publishing today, and her book ought to be read."
—**Beverly Lowry, author of *Her Dream of Dreams: The Rise and Triumph of Madam C. J. Walker***

Praise for Caroline Patterson's anthology *Montana Women Writers: A Geography of the Heart,* winner of the 2007 Willa Gold Award for Nonfiction as well as a Silver Award in *Foreword Magazine's* 2006 INDIES competition

"*Montana Women Writers* contributes substantially to the northern Rockies' ever-growing reputation for literary excellence. The essays and poems suggest the diverse ways in which each writer understands her physical setting and its formative role in her identity and how Montana's spectacular landscapes and towns small and large stamp themselves upon narrators or characters. . . . *Montana Women Writers*—with its 'ongoing, fascinating discussion'—has earned a place on the shelf with *The Last Best Place* and other collections."
—**O. Alan Weltzien,** *Montana The Magazine of Western History*

"Many anthologies end up as bookends—less than ten percent of the selections read and very little knowledge of the editor's focus gained—but *Montana Women Writers: A Geography of the Heart* deserves to be fully read, each of the thirty-nine authors leading the reader to a better knowledge of Montana's literary legacy and promising publishing future. . . . [T]he anthology provides, as Sue Hart puts it in her introduction, 'the experience of Montana.' . . . History, rage, and hope—Montana as it is experienced by those who live in the demystified West."
—**Hilary Hoffman,** *Drumlummon Views*

"*Montana Women Writers: A Geography of the Heart* is a treasure to be mined and sifted, gems on every page. Vivid and intense, *Montana Women Writers* is full of pleasure and conflict, of escape and perseverance, about our ongoing romance with one piece of the great American West. More than all that, it is a collection of writings by women of enormous talent and influence, authors whose voices represent the loss and longing of all people questing for that place they might call home."
—**Kim Barnes, author of** *In the Wilderness: Coming of Age in Unknown Country* **and** *Hungry for the World: A Memoir*

"*Montana Women Writers: A Geography of the Heart* reveals a territory that's utterly compelling, the insightful and splendidly said work of thirty-nine women writers from Montana. What a wonderful collection, page after page—a handsome, open-hearted gift. This ought to be a Montana and western and national bedside book for years to come. Bless Caroline Patterson for putting it together."
—**William Kittredge, co-editor of** *The Last Best Place: A Montana Anthology*

BALLET AT THE MOOSE LODGE

Stories

CAROLINE PATTERSON

BALLET AT THE MOOSE LODGE

Stories

CAROLINE PATTERSON

DRUMLUMMON INSTITUTE

Helena, Montana

2017

BALLET AT THE MOOSE LODGE

Caroline Patterson

Drumlummon Contemporary Fiction Series, Volume 2

Published by Drumlummon Institute, Helena, Montana.

Cover image: Lucy Capehart. *Tutu*, 2016. Cyanotype on paper, 24 x 20 in.

ISBN- 0-9964183-1-8
ISBN-13: 978-0-9964183-1-7

Cataloging-in-Publication Data on file at the Library of Congress.

Drumlummon Institute is a 501(c)(3) nonprofit that seeks to foster a deeper
understanding of the rich culture(s) of Montana and the broader American
West through research, writing, and publishing.

The publication of *Ballet at the Moose Lodge* is made possible through
generous contributions from the many supporters of Drumlummon Institute.

Design: DD Dowden, Helena, Montana

Manufactured in the United States of America.
10 9 8 7 6 5 4 3 2 1

Distributed to the trade by Riverbend Publishing.
To order, write to P.O. Box 5833 • Helena, MT 59601–5833
or call (406) 449-0200 • www.riverbendpublishing.com

DRUMLUMMON
INSTITUTE

418 West Lawrence Street • Helena, Montana 59601
info@drumlummon.org • www.drumlummon.org

To Fred, for the long haul

PUBLICATIONS

"Resurrection Bay," *Epoch*, Vol. 39, Nos. 1 & 2
(nominated for a Pushcart Prize, 1990)

"Hunters and Gatherers," *Southwest Review*, Vol. 91, No. 2
(won 2007 *Southwest Review* McGinnis-Ritchie Fiction Award)

"Backfires," *Alaska Quarterly Review*, Fall/Winter 1992
(nominated for a Pushcart Prize, 1993)

"Bridge Night: A Fairy Tale," rosered.org, September 2012

"Good Bones," *Seventeen Magazine*, November 1993

"Etiquette," *Salamander*, Vol. 2, No. 2

"Scrabble," *Southwest Review*, Winter 1995;
Drumlummon Views, Vol. 1, No. 3, 2007

"Fruit in Good Season," *Epoch*, Vol. 51, No. 1, 2002;
The New Montana Story: An Anthology, 2003

"Memorial Day," *InterMountain Woman*, Spring 1996

"The Boy Scout," *Big Sky Journal*, June 2016

"Neighboring on the Air," *Terrain Magazine*, September 2012

"Wedlock," *InterMountain Woman*, Fall 1996

"For whom is a story enough?
For the wanderers who will tell it—
It's where they must find their strange felicity."

—EUDORA WELTY, "CIRCE"
The Collected Stories of Eudora Welty

CONTENTS

I

RESURRECTION BAY

"You are entering Resurrection Bay," the speaker booms as the ferry swings from open sea into the mountain-lined sound, and Abby Fischer sees a tiny town hunkered down near the edge of the water, smoke rising from a hundred chimneys, the broken tongues of docks jutting from shore, and the narrow road that heads north through town and over Moose Pass to Anchorage. Winter is two months away and the mountains are dark against the blue sky. Next to her, Charles is in a reverie. He nuzzles her neck with his beard, whispers, welcome to Seward. They turn to watch the eagles feeding at the dock, the people waiting in pickups, the police cruiser that stops them as they drive off the ferry. Hey pal, the cop says to Charles, you're comin' with me.

Abby drives down Main Street, and looks at the cluster of buildings. The people hurry along the sidewalk, their collars turned up against the wet wind. I have no history here, she thinks. She sits in the Seward Coffee Shop to wait for Charles. A guy across the counter stares at her face, then at her chest. If there's one thing she doesn't like about Alaska, it's men staring at her chest. She wants to get a pin that says, "So what. I got jugs." She orders a bowl of oatmeal and starts to make a list titled, "Getting Settled in Seward." One, she writes, and circles it. Get an apartment. Two, a job. The guy stands up. He's wearing boots stamped "Property of Whitney Fidalgo," the name of a cannery. He walks up, tells her her boyfriend is in the clink. Just like that. She looks at her list. Three, she thinks, bail out Charles. The cops want to question Charles about Rod, the guy Charles stowed away in the camper. Rod was stinking drunk when they loaded at the ferry terminal in Kodiak. Don't do it, Abby told Charles. Ah hell, Charles said in his compassionate voice, the guy doesn't have any dough. When the ferry crew found Rod passed out in the lounge, six hours later, he tried to give them two hundred dollars. They wanted to prosecute anyway.

The officer is nice enough, Abby thinks, but who isn't when they're accepting money? She wonders if he thinks she's an adventurer. Or a tree hugger. She wonders if he thinks she's white trash. Whatever he thinks, he says, your girlfriend's set you free, pal. He turns to Charles and smiles, welcome to Seward. Abby notices his back teeth are missing. Charles, who has a full set of white teeth, gives the officer his best all-purpose smile. Thanks, he says. Really, Abby thinks, it's all quite civilized.

* * *

Charles takes Marine Diesel class at the Alaska Skills Center. He makes fifty bucks a week for this, and every two weeks, big green checks that say "Government and Youth—hand in hand" arrive in the mail. We'll get a set net site, Charles tells her, then we'll fish all summer and travel all winter. It sounds good to Abby. Sometimes she has a vision of the two of them walking some kind of cosmic path, alighting and taking off, over and over again. Abby never moved as a child, and now, with Charles, she can go anywhere.

She takes Carpentry class. They're framing a dorm. She crawls to the attic space and lays on the sweet-smelling boards. Mountains of clouds roll by. She thinks of Greece. France. The Trans-Siberian Express. She thinks of someone, say Mrs. Boulieau, stopping her mother in the aisle of the grocery store, and asking what is Abby doing now? And her mother saying quickly, she's graduated from college, and then, shaking her head and smiling apologetically, now she's in trade school in Seward. Abby likes to picture Mrs. Boulieau's face as she says, Seward? Where's Seward?

The instructor asks her if she's done much carpentry. Actually, Abby says, I was a voice major. Tra-la-la, he says. He thinks she'll be better on smaller projects. She spends six weeks building a podium. She glues the plywood inside out. She can't miter corners. Once she pounds a bent nail right into the wood. Every day the class clown walks by and says, you still working on that thing? When she is done, the podium is too short, so she adds a border of two by fours. It takes two men to lift it. She transfers to auto mechanics.

Willy is her partner in Auto Mechanics. He ran a shop in Kotzebue until he drank himself out of a job, and he's here for rehab. He's twenty years older than most of the students. He watches Abby trying to wrench a carburetor out of a dinged-up Chevy, her braids hanging close to the fan. The corners of his eyes crinkle up, and he laughs.

Abby, he says, righty tighty, lefty loosey. Abby likes the way the words roll from the back of his throat. An Inuit phrase maybe that means what you force will not come to you. She jerks the wrench and smiles. The bolt will not budge. Righty tighty, lefty loosey. She thinks of her last recital, the ocean of audience, the way the notes rose from her diaphragm, thick and rich. The dark green of her plants, leafing and budding in their Eugene apartment. Things she can do. Righty tighty, lefty loosey. Maybe he is saying she is a very stupid girl.

. . .

Abby walks to town from their low-income housing, past the junk shop where Cas Witherby makes sculpture out of rusty pipes. Past the Breeze Inn, boarded for winter. Past the docks where a month ago groups of men watched a huge crane lift the boats from the water like dripping toys. Past a dry-docked halibut boat where a light flickers in the portal.

In the grocery store, she waits to feel the familiar rush of warmth for these women bundled against the cold and buying pockmarked bananas. The fluorescent lights starkly illuminate the two aisles of the store. There is one other customer and Abby smiles at her as they pass near the cereals. The woman simply looks at her. Abby feels small suddenly, and she looks at the withered tomato in her hand. She realizes that she is losing her sense of humor. This time she doesn't try to humor the clerk she and Charles have nicknamed the Great Stone Face.

. . .

It is October 12, and Abby can barely make out the ghostly white of snow on the tops of the mountains. Charles's buddies from Marine Diesel are over again. They come over a lot, sometimes even at nine on Saturday mornings. If Charles is gone, they just look at their feet and leave.

Abby brings them cold beers from the refrigerator. Everyone is talking about their cars. Abby gets right in there, talks about the Chevy she's working on. The conversation changes, when she talks, from loosey, goosey to formal call and response. Charles acts as if nothing has changed. Finally no one says much of anything and she goes to bed. She falls asleep to the ripple of their talk. Cherried out. Cyclone headers. Holley high rise.

She wakes up when Charles gets into bed. Hey, he runs a finger down her cheek, I hope you're not mad. She puts her arms around his back, feels the thick muscles along the spine. She could never leave him. Charles cups her breasts in his hands. Nice jugs, he says in his greaseball voice. She laughs and kisses him and remembers the first morning they made love, her flannel nightgown bunched up, Charles holding her, the flashes of rainbow on the wall as a crystal turned in the window. And the light. The golden light.

. . .

By the end of October, Abby wants to move back to Eugene. Charles reminds her of their plan. Only six more months, then a set net site. We'll haul 'em in, make big money, he says. We'll travel all winter. Abby misses things. Bookstores, movies, conversations, most of all voice lessons. They aren't far from Anchorage but the roads are so bad the truck doesn't work well. There is a movie house in Seward. They've seen *Pinocchio, The Bad News Bears Ride Again,* and *Coma*, which has been playing for three straight weeks. Abby feels her mind is rotting away. She gets stoned and goes to the Homemaker's Fall Bazaar, and the crocheted potholders make her want to cry.

Charles gets a job at night in the nursing home for crazy people. Sometimes, when he is on shift, he brings them by the apartment and they slurp tea and crow with delight at the brightly colored hot pads.

After work one night, Charles takes her on a picnic to cheer her up. He makes her shut her eyes until they get to Old Woman's Point. She hears him unzip the pack. She hears the clink of glass, the soft whap of fabric being shaken, the hiss of a lighted match. Okay, Abby, Charles says as he stands behind her and holds her around the waist, surprise. He has arranged a blanket, two candles, two pears, and a bottle of wine on the sand. He tells her, Buck up, Lucky. Lucky is his nickname for her. Pretty soon, he says, we'll be playing in the big time.

. . .

Thursday the Auto Mechanics class has Industrial First Aid. They watch movies of people being burned. Men with severed arteries, broken limbs, seizures. At three in the afternoon, they learn CPR. They practice in pairs on a Resusci Andy, a five-foot plastic doll with a mouth shaped in an O. Again and again, one guy breathes into its mouth, while another mashes the plastic chest with his hands. Two breaths. Five pumps of the chest. Abby and Willy are next. She cups her hand behind the neck to clear the trachea. She bends over and Willy kneels next to her. Someone yells, Smoke 'em Abby. She smiles, takes a deep breath, puts her mouth over the plastic mouth of the Resusci Andy and exhales. She expels so much air, her lungs hurt. The Resusci Andy shudders then gives a long, squeaky sigh. Everyone explodes with laughter. She laughs so hard, she cries. You got what it takes, Willy says. He is pumping the doll's chest for all he is worth.

. . .

There is a month of rain before the snow creeps down the mountain and hits the town. If Inuits have thirteen words for snow, Abby wonders how many they have for rain. Rain that drives against the plate glass window. Rain that covers her face like dew. Rain that pockmarks sand. She watches the clouds, the way they glide into the bay then gather force, growing larger and blacker. Sometimes she can tell what kind of rain it will be by the clouds.

It is the wind that scares her. Not the warm, sweet wind off the Japanese current, but the piercing Arctic wind. Sometimes, when she is alone on the beach and the Arctic wind blows in, she imagines she will be sucked out to sea and wrapped in stinking kelp. When she tells this to Charles, he buys her a warmer coat. He encourages her to make some friends, not to get too isolated. Charles, Abby thinks, no shit. And beneath the nylon and layers of down, Abby still feels the wind slice clean to her heart.

. . .

They show movies once a week at the old folks' home. Movies about animals. If there were anything else to do, Abby would not watch these movies. The home smells like antiseptic, floor wax, and urine. From down the hall, a woman yells, Mama, Mama. Abby sees Charles at the nursing station. He is talking to a woman behind the desk. She looks about Abby's age. She is laughing, running her hands through her dark, curly hair. She looks warm, happy, Abby thinks, and this thought makes her go numb. For a moment it feels like everything is stripped to the bone.

The movie is about caribou. An Inuit woman named Sally dances in front of the projector. The caribou migrate south underneath the shadow of her undulating arms. An old man wanders behind the screen, trying to open the doors. Let me out, he says in a flat voice, let me out. The caribou are mating. A woman slaps herself over and over. The caribou run south across the tundra, and their racks make a dry, clacking sound.

. . .

Ruby and Evan, their upstairs neighbors, are driving down south. Abby and Charles help them carry out boxes of shot glasses, a moose rack. Ruby turns to Abby, we're going to be gypsies, she says, sixty-year-old flower children. Maybe you should wait until spring, says Charles. Oh no, buster, she says, when you gotta go, you gotta go. Isn't that right, Evan? Evan looks at her and nods. Evan, she laughs, don't say much.

Evan's nice, Abby ventures when she and Ruby are alone. Evan's a baby, Ruby says. I'm tired of men who want mothers. She takes a long drag on her cigarette and the smoke billows out of her nose. What I really want, she says, is a father.

Charles and Abby wave as the white van pulls onto the road. I hope they make it over the pass, Charles says, it's supposed to snow. The van gets smaller and smaller, and the puff of black smoke and the blur of tires finally disappear as the car rounds the bend that heads over Moose Pass to Anchorage.

Charles and Abby go inside and sit at the kitchen table they found at the dump. It's 4:30 in the afternoon and the sun is setting. When it begins to snow on the tops of the mountains, Abby feels a chill clear to her bones. She turns up the heat. Charles has taken off his sweater and he's wearing a T-shirt. The clouds gather over the mountains, and the radio says, it's going to be a big one. Praise the Lord. The radio plays three hours of hymns out of the nine hours it is on the air. Abby is starting to hum them. The clouds are moving down the mountains. Big clouds, dark and heavy with snow. The windows rattle. The radio plays, "Battle Hymn of the Republic."

Charles watches the storm move in. Abby, he says, this is really something. Abby puts on two sweaters and crawls into bed. Underneath the covers, she can hear the wind howl. She wonders how long it takes to get cabin fever. It is only November.

. . .

Abby presses the on switch, and the slide tray clicks into place, and the lesson about starters begins. A cartoon drawing comes into focus. A woman dressed in a frilly apron waves good-bye to her husband, who waits curbside in his Model A. In the next frame, the man holds the starter crank, and in the frame after that, he turns the crank, a herculean effort, Abby can tell, by the sweat standing out from his forehead like a halo. The wife clasps her hands at her breast. The announcer asks: How can a twelve-volt battery produce twenty thousand volts? Abby knows the answer. She has seen this slide show three times. It's the power of the almighty starter!

Abby thinks about last night when she explained to Charles the reasons she wants to leave. The fact, she said, that she has not made any friends. The fact that there is nothing to do. The fact that she has no opportunity to sing. Charles suggests that she try taking walks. Abby is incredulous. Walks? Well, running, maybe, he says, it'll clear your head.

Abby picked up an ashtray with the two salmon leaping over the waterfalls. She threw it at Charles. Okay, she yelled, I'll go for a walk, and she slammed the apartment door behind her.

She walked down Main Street. Past the Seward Coffee Shop, the plate glass iridescent, chairs turned up on the tables, catsups filled and waiting. Past the grocery store with its wilted lettuce and rotten tomatoes and the silent clerk. She wanted to stay out all night but it was too cold. She crossed the street and walked home past the handicraft store the Homemakers opened for

Christmas. Past the window filled with Pyrex bottle bird feeders, crocheted caps made of Budweiser cans, homemade dolls whose stitched smiles are savage in the moonlight.

. . .

It's nearly Thanksgiving, and Abby writes in her journal that she's going to make an effort. She and Charles are riding to school in the dark. The sun doesn't rise until 9:30. She looks at the pink-tipped sky before she walks into the Auto Mechanics building. Okay, she thinks, it's okay.

She has been assigned a new partner, Mike. He has straight blonde hair and wears beaded moccasins up to his knees. He ignores Abby except when he needs money. At coffee break, she goes outside to see the sun, and someone tells her Willy is in the hospital spitting up blood. He's drinking again. Can you blame him, Abby thinks, then wipes the thought from her mind.

As part of her self-improvement plan, Abby walks over to the Methodist Church after work. She tried to sing once in their apartment, and in the middle of her scales, the new upstairs neighbors pounded on the ceiling. She has been singing into a towel in the bathroom, but she is afraid that she is ruining her voice. The minister told her she could sing at the church, but, he winked, you might have to sing for your supper.

The church is empty. She sits for a while in a pew and listens to the wind rattle the windows. She imagines the congregation: the stone-faced store clerk, the loud waitress at the coffee shop, the postman who repeats her last name whenever he hands her the mail.

Finally she unfolds her Xeroxed music, sets it on the piano, and begins her scales. Under the benevolent gaze of Jesus, she feels shy. Her voice is thin. The piano keys are stripped of ivory, and some of them don't work. It's okay, she tells herself, okay. She launches into arpeggios, and begins to forget.

When she feels alone, really alone, she starts to sing "Chi il bel sogno di Doretta" and her voice gets strong and she likes the way it echoes through the church. The way it fills the empty room. The way the wind sighs back. "Chi il bel sogno di Doretta?" and the snow taps on the windows. She wonders if Charles is home yet, "Il suo mister come mai, come mai fini?" A door opens somewhere, and in the middle of her reach for the high A, she stops. If it's Charles, she doesn't want to look concerned. She takes a breath and goes back three measures to the part where Doretta says once love matures, the young passion dies with understanding.

Someone coughs. Abby looks up from the music. A woman is standing in the shadows at the back of the church. Her parka is silver fur, the muff thick around her delicate face. The woman says, I heard you singing.

· · ·

Her name is Nina Ruskovitch. She is thirty, living with a real estate bigwig in town. They have a little house with door-to-door carpeting, a stereo, a blender: things Abby has forgotten about. It always smells sweet because Nina burns incense to feel dreamy. Her eyes are deep-set and she has a soft, high voice. She doesn't always listen to Abby. That okay, Abby thinks, I don't always listen to her.

Nina's planning her marriage to the bigwig. A glass chapel somewhere in California. A satin dress with a high collar or a sculpted neckline. She can't decide, and she shows Abby magazine after magazine of bridal dresses. Just pick what you like, Abby says. No, Nina says, as she flips through the latest *Bride* magazine, it has to be right.

When she gets home, the apartment is silent. Charles is working longer and longer hours. We need the money, he says, and she can't argue. But tonight, she has things to tell him and there's only the empty room, the moonlit bay, the click of the furnace as the temperature drops to zero.

Charles gets back around midnight. She is lying in bed, her hands flat against her sides. He pulls her braid. Hey, he says, there's dogs around the moon. When he crawls into bed, he wraps his arms around her. Sally, he murmurs, ran away again. Old nurse what's-her-name bawled us out again. Are you asleep, Lucky? Are you asleep? He turns over and falls into a heavy sleep, and in the bedroom window, Abby sees the moon faintly rimmed with red, blue, and yellow clouds.

. . .

Nina is teaching her belly dancing. Abby comes over after school, takes off her coveralls and puts on a leotard of Nina's. They stand in front of mirrors in two different rooms and Nina yells. Isolate, she says, feel your rib cage lift out of your stomach. Nina wears a sequined bra. Watch me, Nina says. Abby watches the way her glittery chest moves up and away from her stomach, the languid ripple of muscles. Nina used to dance at the Booby Trap in Anchorage, and she told Abby she had all the sex she wanted. Sometimes, she says, she misses it.

They practice isolations. Belly ripples. The Camel Walk. Abby likes the shimmery music they dance to, the sounds of some place far away, some place hot, some place completely different from Seward.

What are you doing here, Nina asks her when they're sitting around the kitchen table. Abby tells her about Auto Mechanics class, the set net site, the trips they'll take. Nina begins to flip through a magazine. Abby tells her that she and Charles are kind of like cosmic warriors. Nina looks up when she says cosmic, and offers Abby what she calls her caveman diet, nuts and coconut. Nina says Charles should provide for her. She says her man buys her pretty things. They have matching bathrobes. A girl needs pretty things, she says, there is strength in pretty.

. . .

13

It is three weeks before Christmas when Charles and Abby go walking on the beach. Charles has just told her they will have to stay in Seward for Christmas. But I can't stand it here, she says. It's so beautiful, Charles says and sweeps his arm out to indicate the mountains, the rolling sea, the broken dock. I'll show you a grand Christmas, Lucky. This nickname is beginning to get on Abby's nerves. There is nothing in the town, she thinks, on the scale of grand.

Abby sees a patch of snow piled in the center of a tall rock. She runs over to scoop up a snowball and screams. She has laid her hand on a dead seal. A baby seal with freckled, grey fur. Charles runs up and begins to examine it. Abby, he says, it's a fresh kill. Who cares, she says, let's go. No, Charles holds her arm, let's take it back. He grabs the baby seal by the tail and slings it over his shoulder. What in the hell are you doing? she yells. We'll tan it, he says, looking very happy with himself. It doesn't belong to us, she says and begins to cry, leave it here.

She sobs at Charles's back as they walk up the beach, and she hates his square shoulders, and the way he keeps walking. Finally she's just tired. The Tlingits say Kooshdakhaa, the land otter, walks the beach at night like a man. The stars look icy, and under the faint yellow disc of the moon, rocks and logs take shape as walruses and seals.

. . .

From the bedroom, she can hear the quiet puncture as Charles slits the seal's belly. He is whistling. She tries to read, but it's hard to concentrate with all the carnage going on in the bathroom. Abby, Charles says, this really isn't bad. She hears the soft tearing of the hide, the clatter of the knife as it falls on the floor. Charles shouts, Jesus!

When she reaches the door of the bathroom, Charles is holding his hand. Abby concentrates on his cut to block out the shiny guts, the whiskered nose, and the porcelain smeared with seal blood. Charles looks up at her, then holds out his finger. I need your help, he says. Please help me.

It's all she can do to touch the slick little body. And as she tries to turn it so Charles can cut off the rest of the hide, it slips out of her hands and she leaps up as if it's alive. Then after a while, it's not so bad, she gets used to the mess, the blood slicking her fingers, the wet flesh. As the raw smell of seal oil thickens in the bathroom, she and Charles kneel, side by side, scraping the fat from the hide. Charles kisses her neck, suggests she chew the fat from the hide like the Inuit women. She makes a face and sticks a piece of blubber down his shirt.

At midnight, the hide is clean and stretched. They put the naked little seal body in a red plastic bag, start up the truck, and take it to the dump.

. . .

The colored light bulbs sway up and down over Main Street, so small against the Arctic wind, the snow-covered mountains, the darkness, they bring tears to Abby's eyes. Or maybe it was the Sunday schoolers' nativity scene. Or maybe it was the practiced merriment of the minister as he herded them through the rehearsal. Whatever it was, she needs a drink.

The Northern is dim and warm and she walks up the narrow path between the bar and tables, looking for Charles. She can feel the eyes of the men at the bar, and it reminds her of those X-ray glasses advertised at the back of comic books. She orders a drink and looks at her watch. Tinsel glitters over the bar, and the moose head has on a Santa Claus hat. She wonders where Charles is.

Nina and the real estate bigwig walk in the front door. Abby waves them down. Charles will be here soon, Abby says, let's order a round. Nina is unusually quiet, and Abby and the bigwig talk over "I'm Dreaming of a White Christmas," which is playing for the third time. He tells her about the '63 earthquake, how the docks washed out and the ground split open and the mud shot up as high as the trees. How land was cheap when everyone moved to Anchorage.

When it seems they have exhausted their store of conversation, the real estate bigwig starts watching whatever Nina is watching at the bar. Something about Nina's nonchalance reminds Abby of all those afternoons she talked to Nina as Nina flipped through the pages of magazines. This nonchalance makes Abby want to hurt her.

Abby stirs her fourth drink, then leans over the table. I want to tell you guys a secret, she whispers, because you're my friends. Nina and the real estate bigwig look at her in mild surprise. Charles and I are going to be married, she says. She is drunk, but she can't believe she is doing this. Nina looks startled, and the real estate bigwig seems happy to have something to drink to. They drink toast after toast to happiness. In the blur, Abby remembers Charles, and her insides feel like hamburger.

Abby finally weaves home, and when she opens the apartment the stench of seal oil nearly makes her throw up. Goddamn seal skin, she thinks, and goes to the kitchen where the spotted pelt is strung over the oven door. It's still damp in places, and some fat still clings to the hide. The Christmas I tanned, she says to herself, the Christmas I fucking tanned. She walks from the kitchen to the bedroom. The blankets are pulled up. The furnace clicks on. The outside thermometer reads five below zero and falling.

· · ·

It's Christmas Eve and the preschoolers toddle up the aisle to put paper stars on the spindly pine tree. The Sunday schoolers come whispering, dressed in sheets, and a boy about ten stands at the back of the church and says, behold. In the front pew, Abby is waiting to sing. She turns her head and sees Charles in the pew behind her. He gives her a big smile and a thumbs-up.

The minister says a prayer for the Christmas season, and out of the corner of her eye she sees the grocery clerk, which for some reason sets off a flutter of nervousness. Finally, the prayer is over, the congregation looks up, and it is her turn to walk up the aisle. Her face is frozen, her hands are icy, and the piano hits the opening chords of "O Little Town of Bethlehem."

It's all wrong. The piano is out of tune. Her breathing is off and her voice is thin when she finally sings about the "hopes and fears." She can see her carpentry teacher, the auto mechanics instructor, Nina and the real estate bigwig, the way they look glassy-eyed, like she was some kind of background music. Even Charles looks worried.

She sits down while the minister discusses the meaning of Christmas. The room becomes distant, and she can barely hear what the minister is saying, angels, inns, someone was born, righty tighty, we call our savior, *lefty loosey*.

She walks up the aisle again to sing "Silent Night." Her voice is warming up. The congregation joins her on the last chorus and everyone looks dreamy and the church glows as the children file out of the door carrying tiny white candles.

Everything's drawing to a close. Charles is buttoning up his flannel jacket. People are shifting in their seats and a baby cries from the back of the church. They will go home now, Abby thinks, happy, they will go home and become families.

Abby, however, is not finished. Something about the grocery clerk, the way his lips moved in and out as he slept, the way the light flashed off his glasses makes something crack inside her. She wants to exact something.

She stares at him from the front of the church when the lights go up and announces she has a Christmas surprise for them all. The minister looks miffed. She doesn't care. Give me an F major chord, she asks the startled pianist. She hears her note and then in full voice begins to sing "Chi il bel sogno di Doretta." The room is stunned quiet, except for a wall of sound, her sound. The babies are startled quiet. The grocery clerk shakes himself awake. This beautiful dream, she sings, and she can feel the air fill her back, her lungs, her throat, where are you now? She sings about love's mystery, and the kiss of passion that dies as soon as it's born. People are looking at her and then at each other, and Abby thinks to hell with you all. To hell with your little faces, your windy churches, your X-ray bars. She sees Charles looking up at her, his face flushed with triumph. To hell with you Charles, she sings, with your Marine Diesel and your stinking seal skin and your set net sites, fini. Then his face gets dimmer, winking out, and she can't think. It is only *Ah! mio sogno!,* the high C, and the suck and rush and the promise of air.

HUNTERS AND GATHERERS

February first, Laura sent Peter, her ex, a postcard. "This is the biggest show in Kodiak: at sunset, the cars line up at the dump. Everyone cracks a beer, turns on their headlights. A black bear wanders by, licks a pair of Pampers with a tongue big as a pork chop, while two other bears hump near a pile of milk cartons. Horns honk, headlights flash, someone shouts, 'Go for it.'"

Of course, she'd never seen the bears humping, she'd never actually driven to the dump. She wasn't even in Kodiak anymore: she was in Anchorage, broke and jobless and looking for a place to live, but who wanted to write about that?

Still she liked to imagine Peter reading the card—the drift of regret across his face at her airy *joie de vivre*. To twist the knife, she considered adding a postscript, *I have taken a lover,* as if a lover were something delicious and disposable you could pluck off a grocery store shelf.

. . .

Laura sat on a chair crisscrossed by duct tape and faced the two men across the green linoleum table. "Laura MacElwain," she said and shook their hands.

The thick-limbed, pimply man hopped up to get her a beer. The other had chest hair that crawled up toward a beard that crawled up toward his eyebrows. He rapped his knuckles on the table in a slow, irregular beat.

They looked at her.

"Name's Vince," the pimply man finally said. "Babes call me in-Vince-ible."

"Dale," the hairy man said, as if he were crossing a great

distance. He rested one hand on his buck knife and jerked his thumb toward Vince. "And Vince is full of shit."

"He's jealous 'cause I got a way with chicks."

"Rules here are simple," Dale said as he watched Vince circle the room. "Rooms are sixty bucks. Everybody leaves everybody alone. And we all ignore Vince."

"Why?" Laura asked, thinking *sixty bucks.* She hadn't seen in the *Anchorage Daily* anything under $300.

"He's a pain in the ass," Dale said.

A door opened, steam rolled into the room, and a tall woman walked up to Laura as if they were alone, offered her her hand and said, "Diane." She sat at the table, her hair draping the chair, and began to paint the longest fingernails Laura had ever seen. "The guys won't bother you, and the price is right." She admired a torch-like thumbnail. "I live my own life."

Vince slapped a sandwich together, held it in front of his mouth, then turned to Laura. "Single?"

"Engaged," Laura lied. "I've got a job possibility at the Anchorage Museum, and two months' rent."

"She's okay by me," Dale said. He wandered off down the hall, where Laura heard the opening music to *Magnum PI.*

"Gloria," Vince whined to the scraggly canary blinking in a cage near the table. He fed it a strip of bologna, and nodded in Laura's direction. "She's not single."

Diane lit a cigarette and took a long draw. She looked at Laura, her eyes flat. "It ain't paradise," she said slowly, "but it's good for a temporary layover."

· · ·

If people asked her, *why Alaska?* she would say *adventure,* but she meant escape. Escape from that morning in March when she lay across the Indian bedspread, watching Peter at the window. He turned and said, "I'm scared." She sat up, pulled her robe tight. "Relax," she said. "It'll pass." This had happened before in the last two years, and she would stroke his back until the flesh rose under her fingertips and he sighed and once more they had lives together.

"No," he said, looking out at the bowl of blue sky. "You and I. We are not working out."

Shock tripped down her backbone. She noticed his bookcase was out of order: Dostoyevsky filed before Chekhov. As she dressed, Peter came toward her, mouthing words, and she had a wild urge to laugh at a tear dangling from his nose like snot.

March, she trudged the numb streets past couples flinging Frisbees on the common. April, she read for orals until the texts about !Kung hunters and gatherers and Nuer ghost marriages swam before her. May, she was sick of it. She leapt out of bed, singing "Compared to What" at the top of her lungs. She cut her hair and read books about Robert Marshall, who wrote studies of Inuit life from his cabin in Koyukuk and played Schubert's *Unfinished Symphony* as he drifted to sleep. He was someone who found a blank space on a map, and went there.

When she graduated, she flew to Alaska. She wanted to work as an anthropologist, observing rituals, family relationships, and tribal customs. By January, she had worked as a salmon-egg packer, a motel maid, and a waitress. She'd seen some customs all right.

In Anchorage, she bought a used car, and as she drove out of the lot, she looked at the skyscrapers hunched over Knik Arm, the Chugach Mountains hovering over the broad plain of houses and streets that stretched south to the waters of Turnagain Arm. This is it, she told herself. This is where I start over, like those old novels about girls from the country who have their hearts broken, then rush to the city to conquer the world.

· · ·

Laura filled out a job application at the Anchorage Museum.

Under "Job Desired," she hesitated. She knew she should write "secretary," but as she looked around the hushed reception area, decorated with scrimshaw and baleen, she could picture herself a young Margaret Mead, rushing off to the Arctic, her oversized parka bulging with notebooks. She'd work among the Inuits—watching village dances, touching the round, dimpled faces of the children—and at night, she'd diagram family relationships, the male and female symbols dancing across a page washed by lantern light.

The receptionist looked at Laura's application. "We're not hiring anthropologists right now," she said, curving her lips into a smile. "Come back next week?"

Instead she hired on as a temporary secretary in a movie distributor's office. The job involved sending endless telexes from Anchorage to Seattle, "Yes, *Avalanche*. Check sent January 15. No, *Atomic Cafe*." Laura was so broke she ate concession samples for lunch—licorice, jujubes—then she wandered downtown to watch people in restaurants and to write little poems about hunger.

A week later, she got food stamps. At first she bought meek portions of beans and rice. She dreamt her father stood in line behind her, mouthing the words, "scum of the earth." Then she got more daring. Tomatoes at a $1.50 a pound. Nectarines. Huge, glistening steaks. As she pulled out her coupon books, she glared back at the clerks and silently dared people to whisper.

• • •

It was the ugly time of winter, when the snow was mealy and layered with dirt and gravel. After work, Laura drove the wide streets home, past neighborhoods of trailers and clapboard houses, temporary and decaying, past ragged Sitka spruce rising out of the muskeg like specters. She tried to picture those laughing Inuit children, but she saw only the tires ahead of her, spraying slush through the five o'clock dark.

Vince was bustling about the kitchen, readying himself for a date. He opened his arms to Laura. "What d'ya think?" His hair was slicked back off his face, and he was dressed in shiny pants and a shirt printed with vintage Cadillacs.

"She'll never know what hit her," Laura said.

"We're going to dinner, we're going to the movies, and then...," he lowered his voice, "she'll meet the real Mr. Vince."

"Whoa," Laura said as he walked out the door. "I hope she's ready for *that*."

It was nighttime, the time of day she dreaded, when her life seemed to loom before her, formless and empty. It's so unfair, she thought, for twenty years everyone gives you elaborate directions—stop, yield, S-curve ahead—like one giant game of *Chutes and Ladders,* then suddenly they hand you your life back with little graduation cards that say, "Welcome to the Rat Race—Ha, Ha."

She thought about writing Peter a "fuck you" letter, but it seemed pointless. She thought about reading the book her mother sent, *How to Get What You Want Without Really Trying.* She imagined dancing at a topless bar, her breasts brushing men's mouths, and the way they looked hungry, and the way they looked vacant.

Instead she wrote home: "Mother, my roommates are great—Diane was head of her class at Vanderbilt—and we go to movies, take long walks. The museum's hiring in spring, and I've got a great-paying job at a lawyer's office overlooking Turnagain Arm, where Captain Cook turned around when he realized there wasn't a Northwest Passage."

• • •

Laura propped her elbows up on the bar separating the kitchen and the living room and watched Diane's fingers work the pasta dough. It was Friday night and Diane was back from the Brooks Range where she spent two weeks with a fox trapper she met at the Monkey House, a bar featuring a cage of sad-faced rhesus monkeys.

"What was it like up there?" Laura said as the dough softened in Diane's hands.

"Cold as a witch's tit. We landed on the river and had to shovel into the cabin." Diane rocked gently back and forth as she kneaded. "Kneading's important, Laura, you got to work the dough till it starts to get stiff."

Laura watched as the dough split, flattened, became round again. "But what'd you do every day?"

"Oh, checked the traplines, fed the fire, cooked, and went to bed early to save wood." Diane took a hit off the cigarette pinched in her flour-whitened hand and looked down at Laura. "It's hard work."

"But I mean wasn't it weird with a guy you really didn't know? A guy you met at a bar?"

"I had a feeling about him. I never go with a guy unless I have a feeling," Diane said.

Laura tried to remember if she had a feeling about Peter. She sure as hell had one now.

"Of course, I probably won't see him again," Diane said. "I rarely do."

"But doesn't that make you angry?" Laura said. "Doesn't it make you feel used?"

"Of course not." Diane poised the knife and began to cut the dough in slow, neat strips. "I think of it all as temporary. As a body to keep me warm in winter."

· · ·

She sat at the kitchen table trying to compose a letter to Peter. "Dear Peter," she wrote. "You stupid fool." She crumpled up the paper, took out a new sheet. She wrote "Peter," then she couldn't think of what to say. "Was broke. Got job. Was hungry. Got foodstamps?"

When Vince walked in, she blushed and ripped up the paper.

"I gotta go to this dinner," he blurted. "Wanna come? Please?"

She knew she shouldn't, but the prospect of another night alone daydreaming about some Arctic village was dismal. And there was a plaintive quality in his voice she'd never heard before. "What the hell," she said. "I've got to eat."

She knew she'd made a mistake when Vince returned to the kitchen in a peacock blue jumpsuit. "Hey," he said in a cloud of mouthwash. "Ready for the high life?"

As she stood in the doorway of the Holiday Inn ballroom, she felt like she been in a long hibernation, but she didn't know what she'd awakened to. Men in bursting suits and their wives with swooping hair and blue eye shadow wandered around a room decorated with orange flags and signs that said, "Price Slashed" and "Screaming Deal." The guy who sold her her car downed a martini and looked quickly away from her.

As she sampled bear roast, pickled whale, and mountain goat stew from the "Anchorage, You're Fair Game" buffet, Vince introduced her to people farther and farther down the table and she saw them look at her smooth hair and high-necked dress, and their eyes said, *outsider*.

When they presented the "Top Salesman of Anchorage 1979" award, Vince wasn't even close. On the chart ranking all the dealerships by sales, Vince Spiker at The Lemon Orchard came in seventh to last. Disappointment flashed across his face. She touched his hand and said, "I'm sorry."

He shrugged. "I guess," he said, digging into a third helping of caribou ragout, "I need work on my closing."

Later that night, a voice in the kitchen woke her from a deep sleep. A chair scraped the floor, bird food pelted into a dish, and a voice said, "So that's the deal, take it or leave it."

The bird chirped.

Laura pulled the covers over her head to muffle his voice.

"Gloria loves me. Don't ya? Gloria?"

. . .

There, scattered across the kitchen table with a flyer for a
moon boots sale, was the letter. She stared at the neat curves
of his handwriting, and the return address: Virginia (so he'd
gone home), and the postmark dated February 5. Dale walked
into the kitchen, saw her, and tiptoed out. She shook her head,
picked up the letter, and carried it back to her room. Her limbs
seemed to move in slow jerks.

"I'm probably the last person in the world you want to hear
from, and I don't blame you for that. I was awful, Laura, and
every day I look down at the faces of my students (I'm teaching
at the Williamsburg Boy's Academy) and I know it again. I hope
you'll someday be able to forgive me. We were doing something
on ballads, I was doing that Robert Service, "Northern Lights
have seen queer sights," etc. (a silly thing, isn't it? But kind of
charming, too), and it made me miss you. Not that you're a
queer sight. Far from it. But you're really up there doing it."

She waited a good two weeks before she answered. When she
finally sat down to write, she couldn't decide what to say. That she'd
been in the Brooks Range with a fox trapper, where temperatures
dropped to 40 below? She wrote (and hoped it sounded "dashed
off") a card saying she was working for a movie company in
downtown Anchorage, where Inuits lined the streets, where planes
flew in daily from the interior, where temperatures dropped to 50
below, and daylight was as long as a three-martini lunch.

. . .

Each morning, she walked from the city parking lot through
streets full of plastic cups and sprawling drunks. Past
Woolworth's where she could now afford to buy chicken legs for
lunch, past the Booby Trap with its stained neon sign of a big-
breasted woman in a martini glass.

It was Monday and a week of this lay before her, a week of
coming and going in the dark, the cars puffing out exhaust like

old men, the drivers barely visible behind frosted windows. A week of walking into the office and seeing Debbie, the office manager, open the safe, turn on the telex machine, start the coffee. Laura envied how she knew the exact dimensions of her world, and moved comfortably, almost sensually within them.

Debbie raked back her white-blonde hair and checked her watch when Laura came in. She swished over to set some typing in Laura's in-box. "Mr. Mulroney wants this out this morning." She looked at Laura's coat as if it were in their way.

Laura sat at her desk and looked at the basket full of telexes to be sent, letters to be typed. The telex machine rumbled in the distance. She felt tiny.

As she typed, "Dear Mr. Vardis," Mr. Mulroney was yelling at the phone. "For Christ's sake, we want adventure up here, got that, a-d-v-e-n-t-u-r-e, not this touchy-feely crap. What do you think this is, *California?*"

She had four telexes to send, and even though pushing the send button to Seattle, Los Angeles, sometimes even New York gave her a certain pleasure—she liked to imagine a mail clerk somewhere saying, "It's from *Alaska*"—she was thinking about Peter teaching or her friends getting advanced degrees, their lives moving right foot, left foot, and here she was, small as a dot, punching out messages like "Yes, *Conan the Barbarian*" or "No, *Magic of Lassie*."

That night as she lay on her bed and blew smoke rings at the ceiling, she thought it was okay packing salmon eggs, slinging hash—somehow it was all an adventure, but it was February now, and the world seemed to sink around her. Everything seemed remote, impossible. Where was the part where someone stepped in and said: This is how to get what you want. And, by the way, what is it you want?

A perfect circle of smoke touched the ceiling. She stubbed out the cigarette and fell asleep with her clothes on. She dreamt she was in an Inuit fish camp with Robert Marshall. They were watching the red-bellied silvers swim into the honeycombed fish traps. She reached in and touched the slippery back of a fish caught in the trap and felt its powerful thrashing. She wrote that down. "Powerful thrashing." Then Robert touched her hands, her face, her hair with his rough fingers. "They get caught in a web of sticks," he told her, his eyes very blue. "The Inuits thank the fish who give them their lives." He kissed her first on the neck, and shivers ran down her back like minnows. Then, as he lay on top of her, his anorak flapping over his head like a halo, Robert Marshall whispered, "Check sent December 20."

. . .

"Good Morning, Anchorage," the radio chirped. "It's a balmy fifteen degrees and we're taking bets on breakup. When do you think the mighty Yukon will flow again?"

Laura turned it off, and dressed quickly in the dark. Before she left the house, Vince called to her, "You make me coffee?"

"Fuck you, Vince," she said and shut the door.

At work, Debbie leaned over the telex machine, and watched Laura type. She talked about her husband, home from the Slope, as the lines of type inched out of the machine. "Watch your dollar signs, Laura, Mr. Mulroney gets hopped if they're missing."

Debbie reached over and punched in an "n" that was missing from *Pinocchio*. She looked behind her to see if Mr. Mulroney was still in his office. She got to the point. Her husband's brother, Barry, needed a date.

Which is how Laura found herself sitting next to a large ruddy-faced man at the Alaska Rendezvous. A crowd jammed the rickety bleachers. A family in matching parkas sat in front of her. A few rows down, some Inuit men laughed in a slow, lilting way and huddled toward one another.

Barry had an easy confidence about him that said he was no stranger to women, but there was something frank about the way he looked at her. "Lucky you," he said, extending his hand. "I'm your blind date. A roughneck."

She laughed, and said, "Well, you ain't got yourself such a prize either, pal. Laura Cantype from Small World Telex."

He laughed and looked at her as if she were the only person in the bleachers. "Well, I bet you're damn good, Miss Cantype."

She downed her coffee, and the whiskey spun pleasantly through her head.

. . .

They were in time for the dog pulls. Last year's winner, Animal, was hitched to the sled of 200-pound weights. When the timekeeper's arm came down, the part-boxer, part-husky leaned against the weight of the sled, his forelegs bunched with strain, and the crowd jumped up and started yelling, "Animal! Animal!" their faces blazing, as if Animal were all that stood between them and spring.

The sled shuddered and inched forward.

"Who do you favor?" Barry said, looking at his program. "Animal? Or Brutus, the part pit bull who's later?"

"Animal," she said, and smiled. "Girls like animals."

"Is that right?" He cocked his head.

"Well, let's say they're better in the harness."

He toasted her with his thermos cup.

They heard the swish of runners on snow, and a sled pulled into the middle of the arena, then arced slowly around the field, the dogs barking and pulling with sheer joy, the musher leaning back on the sled, and as they glided past, the dogs' coats rippled like water.

When the sled pulled up to the podium, the musher threw back the fur-lined hood, and her blonde braid tumbled down her back. She turned her strong-jawed, pink face to the crowd and waved.

Laura stood up for a better look.

Barry stood up next to her. She could feel the heat of his body and his fingers caught hers.

As the announcer droned, "Winner of the Alaska Iditarod, folks. This little gal braved 40 below weather, drifts tall as a Kodiak—" Barry held up a steaming pretzel, and she bit into it. "You have salt on your face," he said. She laughed as his fingers brushed off the grains. He held up the pretzel again.

"Wait a minute." Laura put her hand on his arm and turned to watch the woman as she moved from dog to dog, quieting them, her movements swift and sure as she checked the lines and harnesses, her hands moving across them like Braille.

. . .

Barry sat heavily on the side of her bed. He seemed to fill up the entire room. She sat next to him, and his hands ran up her back, and Laura helped him unsnap her bra. She wished his lips weren't so loose, but she liked the long, ropey muscles up his spine. The phrase "taking a lover" drifted through her, and a part of her felt deeply thrilled, as if she had crossed into some new territory. This place where you talked until you got into bed. You didn't analyze or discuss or pull apart all that happened, you just did what you did and you left. No past, no future. Get in, get out.

Barry came quickly, his eyes rolling up to the ceiling, then collapsed on top of her with a groan. He rolled to the side, but she could still feel the burn of his skin. "Dear God," he said. "You have beautiful tits."

Beautiful tits, she thought.

He opened an eye and asked, "What are you thinking?"

"February," she said. "It's February in the world." As she lay there, tangled in blankets, flushed and musky, Laura told him about Vince and his canary, Mr. Mulroney and the telexes south, and what it was like those nights driving home through the slush and grey, and as she talked she felt as if something were coming loose, melting, like those icicles that drop from the roof in a thaw. She turned over and looked at him. He was softly snoring. She shut her eyes and as she drifted off, she heard the muted bells of *Jeopardy*.

"Testing," an echoey voice boomed through a microphone and into their sleep. "Testing." An amplifier squawked. "One, two, three."

Barry sat up, "What the hell?"

"Beats me," Laura said. "I've never heard this before."

A G-chord was struck, an amplifier whined, and someone started to sing, "White Birrrd."

She could hear a door open, and Dale's voice. "Jesus H. Christ, Vince."

Gloria squawked.

"Well," Barry said, putting his clothes on. "I'd better get going."

As they walked by the living room, she glared at Vince. He didn't see her. He was singing something about a golden cage, his face close to the microphone, his eyes half-shut, and he seemed to suck each word like candy.

At the door, Barry said, "This is a weird scene." He said good-bye and walked down the driveway. A melancholy snow drifted down. His car started as Vince's voice rose in a crescendo, "On a winter's day, all alone...."

. . .

Laura pulled the covers up over her head.

What is happening to me? she thought. She used to consider herself a careful person. A person of intellect. Jesus, she thought, the most intellectual thing I do now is decide what to eat for breakfast. She remembered working on her thesis, the dusty stacks of government reports, trappers' diaries, and missionaries' letters she read for news of the Shoshone Indians, and, every night when she clicked on the light, the tidy pleasure of it all, the note cards, the note file, and finally the writing. What happened to that person? Who was this person who got drunk, slept with strange men, typed, "Yes to *Creepshow*, No to *Humongous*"?

It was Saturday morning, and she was waiting for Vince to leave the house. She heard him whistling in the kitchen, then he asked Diane if she'd made him coffee. "Eat shit," Diane said.

Laura stared at the ceiling. What she needed, she thought, was order.

She took out the journal her mother had given her for graduation, cracked the spine, and wrote, February 27 on the blank first page. She began to diagram their household. A hunting and gathering society. Two males, two females, all unrelated. Lived in same household; earned separate incomes. No sexual relationships could be determined except one man wanted to make it with both women. Food sources: packaged macaroni and cheese, bologna sandwiches, pizza, Diet Coke, beer. Religion: undetermined, possibly TV.

Laura tore up the diagram, and went into the kitchen. Diane was standing at the table, holding a piece of paper. "You lucky thang," she said, laughing.

Laura, the note said, release me from my golden cage.

"All I can say Laura is this," Peter wrote, "when I got your letter, I knew I wanted to try again. I don't know why I think you'd consider this, or what you think about me, but would you? You don't know how many times that awful morning in March has come back to me to haunt me, and I pray to God I could undo it all, unwind it and start again. I think I've conquered those old fears, which had more to do with faith than you, and I wonder if you'd think about it. The woman who teaches history and anthropology is leaving, and I took the liberty to suggest. . . . All I can say is think about it."

Part of her wanted to get on the plane tonight. And she could see him as she walked down the off-ramp, his hands shoved in the pockets of his tweedy coat, and the way he'd look at her, discerning, passionate, and the way he really *knew* her. And a job, a real job, bringing Boas and Leakey to fresh-faced boys. But she couldn't see that part. Somehow the vision stopped after she got off the plane.

. . .

Laura jerked the car into second and stomped on the gas as she drove home from work the next day. Debbie told her she was too slow on the telexes. Mr. Mulroney yelled for hours on the phone, *"Wooden Clogs?* You've got to be kidding me. Who the hell's gonna watch a movie about wooden clogs? Why not high heels? Sneakers? Who's buying this shit, some fairy?" He slammed down the phone, called her into his office, and told her she'd better start getting there on time. She nearly gave notice. Then the flowers came. Six blue carnations with a note signed, *White Bird.*

. . .

She was going home to set this straight. She drove through the dusk, saying, "Listen Vince, we're roommates. Period. No notes. No flowers. And for God's sake, *no songs."*

She drove out of the downtown where the lights were coming on, and the sidewalks flashed red under the neon naked ladies. Men wandered down the slush-banked streets, dipping into bars, coming out again, dipping into others. Sometimes when a door opened wide enough, she could see a girl on the runway baring her ass to the crowd. She drove down the strip past the car dealers and mobile home sales to the Mountain View exit. She edged into the intersection and was starting to turn, when the car quit.

She turned the key again. Pumped the gas pedal. Nothing. The cars behind her honked, then slowly began to pass her. She put her head on the steering wheel.

This was it. She was going to get on the plane tonight and just give up. Forget it. Fuck Alaska. She was sick of winter, sick of trying. She'd call Peter from Chicago, and say, "Guess what?"

Finally a man hitched her car to his and towed her to a gas station. The mechanics said they'd try to fix it, but as they looked under the hood of her car, they started snickering and one of them asked her if she knew what a dead horse was.

When she called the house for a ride, Vince answered.

She watched with relief and dread as his mud-splashed Camaro with the coat hanger aerial drove up.

"You must be soo tired," he cooed as she got in the car.

"I'm okay, Vince," she said flatly. "Thanks for the ride."

"Can I buy you a drink? Something to soothe our ruffled feathers?"

Suddenly Laura was very tired. "Look," she started, but she couldn't think of anything to say.

"Don't try to talk," Vince said. "It's been a big day." He gave her a sidelong, goopy look. Laura thought Vince in love was one of the most awful sights she'd ever seen.

"Vince, can we go home?" Laura said finally.

He brought her instead to the Lemon Orchard. "I thought you might want to see the place I work," he said.

She looked dully out the window.

He drove up to a little yellow shack in the middle of an ocean of cars. "This is my office. This is where the deals are made." He got out, unlocked the office door and reemerged with a huge ring of keys. "I can get you a Chevy, a Mercury, a Cadillac Seville—"

"Vince," Laura said each word slowly. "*Please.* I'm hungry. My feet are cold."

Vince headed out toward a Chevy pickup. "I can see you in a pickup," he said. "Cowboy boots, tight jeans, hair in a ponytail. Those cowboys'd line up to buck *your* bales.

"Or maybe an Audi—" He said, sailing on toward a yellow car with a missing right fender and a window sticker that said "Price Slashed."

"*Goddammit, Vince,*" she yelled, skating across the icy lot after him. "No cowboy's gonna buck my bales! And I'm not thinking about a Chevy or an Audi or for that matter a sleazy-ass car salesman!"

"Why not a Cadillac? Drive what you strive for, I always say." He was putting the key in the door when she caught up with him. She stopped suddenly and slid into him, her face inches from his. He looked down as if he had been expecting this. "Here we are," he said.

"Vince," she hissed as she backed away. "*We* are not 'here' as you put it. We are not *anywhere*. We are standing in a car lot on a Wednesday night in freezing weather because you will not take me home. I do not want a car. I do not want to get to know you."

"Leather interior," Vince said. He opened the door and got in.

She stood looking over the shiny tops of cars in the lot, then she sighed and got in. "Look, I'm sorry I said that about you being sleazy, okay?"

"This is where I go when I'm down," Vince said, fiddling with the radio. A staticky rendition of "Muskrat Love" came over the air. "I think, here I am in this big old Cadillac. I'm pulling out of my five-bathroom house to go off and put some more money in the bank. Or maybe I'll buy something else—what?—another boat? A bank? Or take my glamour-puss to a supper club where we'll have three lobsters with caviar on top." He turned the wheel back and forth, switched on the wipers. "I don't even like caviar."

She touched Peter's letter in her pocket and took a shuddery breath. She could go tonight. She'd step off the plane, and there would be Peter with his wavy hair, and he'd kiss her and ask her for stories about the North Country. She'd settle in a little apartment near the school and wear nylons under her jeans and wind her hair in a bun, and the boys would look up at her as she talked about New Guinea or Africa, places she had never been. Her life would march quietly on: grad school, a job in a junior college, the tasteful wedding, then children chirping in the backseat of a Volkswagen. She'd tell stories about dog sleds and Inuits, mountains and caribou, and as she talked, she would look across the table into Peter's eyes and see the temperature dropping.

And here? What would happen here? She didn't know. Her nose began to run. She sniffed.

Vince plunked his arm around her. She hiccupped, then relaxed into the warmth. They stared out at the cars receding into the red-hued darkness.

The wipers swung right, left, sweeping off a dusting of snow as taillights rocketed past on Spenard, the round red lights signaling turns and stops, then dissolving into watery streaks that shot on into the dark like comets. She thought for a minute she was going to turn her face to his and kiss him, just for the hell of it, when he turned and whispered, "We could do it in the back seat."

. . .

They did not do it in the back seat. Vince drove her home, and when they arrived, dishes were left on the table and the back door was open as if someone had left in a hurry. Dale's TV was on, his bedroom door open. As she and Vince walked out the back, Laura could tell by the catch in her chest that it was below zero and falling.

Dale and Diane were standing out in the yard looking up in the sky, Diane hugging her sweater around herself. Laura could see Dale looking at Vince and her, taking this in.

"My car died," she said. "Vince picked me up at the garage."

Diane pointed and said, "Look."

Laura stepped across the yard in Dale's footprints carved in the crusted snow and looked up. Above the city, above the strip, the car lights, and the Chugach Mountains, great streaks of color spread across the sky.

"Fucking beautiful," Dale said.

"It's like a floor show," Diane shivered.

"A gas puddle," Vince said.

Aurora borealis, Laura whispered to herself. As she watched the colors pulsing above her, she wondered, and here? What would happen here? Maybe she would go to that Arctic village. Or fall in love with a kelp fisherman. Or write about some frontier city where neon naked ladies blinked on and off under the towering stillness of mountains, then go to sleep each night listening to Schubert's *Unfinished Symphony.* She didn't know, but that was the adventure: not knowing.

She inhaled a stinging gulp of air, and looked up through the clouds of her breath. It was clear now. The full moon was low, and the stars were bright and heavy. All around her, tiny, charged particles rose up to strike the gases of the earth's formless atmosphere. She watched a patch of white spread from the mountains to the pail of the Big Dipper. Around it, red and green clouds shimmered. The lights weren't the bold, clear colors she'd imagined, but muted, as though she were seeing them through a veil. A blue streak slashed across the sky, then disappeared. She looked for the blue. It reappeared over the North Star, and began to gallop the sky.

WEDLOCK

When I was thirteen, my cousin Carla padded down the stairs of the Shoshone Home for Unwed Mothers in Kellogg, Idaho, long and lean in her flowered smock top and moccasins, and I was disappointed. For the past two months, when I thought of her, I didn't think of her wheat-colored hair or tilted eyes. I pictured her belly, huge and lumpy as a sack of groceries. I looked again. Nothing.

"Ted, Gloria," Carla said to my parents in a flat voice. There was an awkward silence, punctuated by the distant dinging of a TV game show, when the events of the past two years seemed almost palpable, and even Carla seemed to pale a minute before the weight of things. Then my mother put her hand on Carla's arm, and pointed to a sampler. "Carla," she said, "do you cross-stitch?"

"God no," Carla said and flipped her hair over her shoulder. "I can't sew worth a damn."

I laughed. My mother pinched her lips.

Dad looked over his glasses and smiled. "Now I know how you ladies like to chat," he said in the take-charge voice he used with his insurance clients, "but Carla and I have business." "Business" meant that he paid Carla's bills since her parents had disowned her. He put his hand on Carla's elbow and steered her into the kitchen.

The red plastic couch made a farting noise as Mom and I sat down. We started to laugh, but I stopped, thinking Carla would hear me. Mom pulled her knitting out from a suitcase-sized purse, and as the needles began to whisper and clack, I stared at the piano, its blackened keys like missing teeth, and the sampler that said, "For tomorrow is another day." I tried to listen to them talking in the kitchen, but their voices were muffled by a droning refrigerator.

Suddenly, as if on cue, several doors upstairs opened, and out came the girls. Nearly a dozen of them. They came down the stairway and passed through the hall, their steps slow and heavy as if they were moving through mud. One girl walked like a crab, her limbs crawling under the weight of her enormous stomach. Another girl, pear-shaped and spotted with acne, gave me a hard look, and I decided she was thoroughly bad. A girl with a heart locket and a ponytail tied with pink yarn smiled at me, and I stared a long time after her, wondering, did her boyfriend make her? Did she become someone else in the back of the car?

My mother kept patting my hand, Morse code for "don't look, don't look," and to demonstrate she kept her eyes on her knitting. Finally, she suggested I go outside. It was not a suggestion. I went outside.

. . .

The Shoshone Home for Unwed Mothers was not the shadowy old place I'd imagined, with turrets and wind whispering in the corners of grey rooms, "how, how could you?" It looked disappointingly like an abandoned ranch in the foothills of the Bitterroots. The fields were filled with weeds, and in front of the peeling ranch house, three trucks sat on blocks, their windshields smashed in web-like designs.

I walked around the house for a while, whacking the dried bushes with a stick, then hopped in the driver's seat of the most dented-up truck, the only one with wheels, and turned the steering wheel to the right, the left. I shifted forward like I'd seen it done, and imagined rough hands touching my waist, my breasts till my neck flushed. Propping myself on the stick shift, I looked up in the rear view mirror through half-closed eyes and said, "Kiss me."

The stick shift snapped, then went slack. I shut the door and slunk away.

Back inside, the doors swung open and shut as girls moved from the hall to the TV room to the kitchen, and I imagined the truck, loosed from its restraints, coming through the front door and hitting them, knocking them down, one after the other, like bowling pins.

The hall emptied again and my mother smoothed the white tissue paper of the present she brought for Carla.

"A girl can always use a nice red cardigan," she said, brushing the bangs out of my eyes.

I waved her hand away from my face and asked, "Just out of curiosity, what happens when a stick shift breaks?"

"Classics, Susan, are a wardrobe's building blocks," she answered.

"I mean would the car just start rolling?"

"Take your wool sweater, your basic oxford cloth shirt," my mother said, winding up. "They never go out of style. I bet Carla will have this sweater by the time you've graduated from high school. If she takes care of it, college."

"You're not listening to me!" I hissed. "Would it just go out of control?"

My mother turned as if I'd just spoken. I could see her eyes focus on me before she said flatly, "Transmissions? Ask your father about transmissions." Then a cheek muscle twitched and her voice was sharp, "Look, you just count your lucky stars."

"Okay," I said. "I'm sorry."

She tucked a stray hair back in her French roll and sighed. "Carla's doing her best under the circumstances."

Every time Carla was discussed, the conversation always had to do with circumstances. She was always cheerful considering, doing well despite, or bearing up under the circumstances. And they were always veiled conversations, the grownups straining to look over me, as if I were taller than they were. Circumstances, I figured, stemming from the day Carla came home from school to find her mother dead in the basement. She was twelve. Her father, Jerome, turned to religion and the pursuit of Communists. Carla fought. She fought her stepmother Iris so ferociously she was finally sent away to her grandparents' farm in Big Timber.

I envied her. Even though her grandparents made her go to church twice a week and they were as dry and bitter as the soil that barely supported them, she had one great advantage. They were nearly deaf. "I lie in bed and wait," she wrote me, "till I hear Wilson's truck. Then man we're off. Wilson's got a black pickup now."

We ate dinner that night at a dark restaurant shaped like a miner's hat and perfumed with chicken grease. My family and Carla sat with three other pregnant girls at the scarred counters.

I sat next to Carla, and said, easy like I'd practiced, "How's it goin'?"

Carla slowly pulled apart a chicken wing with her long, pink fingernails. "B-O-R-E-D," she spelled, something I copied for months. "This place is a prison. No cigarettes even. Did you bring some?" she said, looking at me with interest.

I looked at the counter and whispered, "I'm out."

She gave me a sidelong glance and pointed to herself. "I've got plans," she said softly.

"Escape from the Home," I said. "It sounds like a movie."

Carla laughed. She looked around, then whispered, "Wilson and I are getting out of this dump just as soon as he fixes his truck."

"Where to?" I said. My parents wanted Carla to give up the baby, dump Wilson, and go to the Montana School of Beauty.

"I dunno." Carla shrugged. "We're just going to drive." She looked at me. "Listen, don't tell your parents."

"You kidding?" I said and my voice went too high. I looked at her, then down to my chipped plate. "Does he write you?"

"He's crazy about me," Carla said. "He sent me this." Under the counter, she passed me a blurred snapshot of a pickup. Lounging against the side was Wilson. All I could make out of his face was his grin, and a black space between the front teeth. I looked up to make sure my parents weren't watching. On my right, Mom was talking to a frizzy-haired girl. "When I had Susan, I lived on Tiger's Milk. You know, molasses and brewer's yeast." The girl looked like she was going to be sick. "High in iron," Mom said and patted her hand. My father took a hearty bite out of a chicken leg, and grease dribbled down his chin. The girl next to him concentrated on her string beans.

I snuck a look at the back of the picture. "Baby," it said, "I'm coming 4 you."

. . .

The summer I visited Carla at her grandparents' ranch, she had a different boyfriend. His name was Steven. It impressed me that he called himself "Steven" not "Steve." I figured it was a sign of quality, along with his dark complexion and Mustang convertible. He worked at a gas station in Big Timber and had a shirt with a name patch that Carla wore to parties or around the house when she rolled her hair in orange juice cans. I envied her. She was Steven's girl, and she painted her toenails pink.

My visit lasted for two weeks, but the time stretched on like I was under a spell. By day, Carla's grandparents were like gruff fairy tale stepparents that had to be outwitted.

Nights, we were on our own. As we lay in Carla's bed and waited for Steven's car, we listened to the cottonwoods scrape the roof. To pass the time, we talked about hairstyles or people we knew. Carla was forthright about her opinions, and she gave me advice about my looks that made me flinch. There was so much, she implied, that I could do.

"Get yourself some of those pink rollers at the dime store, kype 'em, even, "she said, "and we'll roll up your hair. It'll look great."

"Okay," I said and vowed to do this night after night until my hair became the same fall of curls that spilled down her back. Finally, from the distance, we heard the crunch of Steven's tires. We climbed out the window onto the roof, shinnied down a nearby tree, and walked the quarter mile to Steven's car. My heart was pounding.

"Steven," she said and leaned close to kiss him.

"Hey, babe, wanna ride?" This was their little joke. Then he'd look over at me and nod. "Susan."

I always felt honored to be included in these rendezvouses. No matter that I had to be dragged along, or that I spent a long time in the back seat trying not to watch them kiss.

Steven drove fast. You could drive as fast as you wanted then, and Steven put the accelerator on the floor. As we sped down 191 as far as Melville, Harlowton, or White Sulphur Springs, I sometimes hoped my parents would forget me here. Other times, I'd just listen to the tires lick up that oiled road, smell the dry wind, and I'd wonder if we'd die out here on a railroad crossing or a blind curve like in those teenage songs. It never occurred to me that those teenage songs never mentioned somebody's little cousin.

Carla sat as close to Steven as she could. "Can't you get this piece of junk to move?"

He looked at her and laughed. "We're going 90. Wanna get out and push?"

Carla tossed her hair and I could see the glow on her cheekbones and the way her eyes sparkled as she leaned forward into the wind, and said, "Let's go."

From the back seat, I sometimes imagined the car was her heart, racing into the dark.

The night before I left, Steven had to work. The day had been hot, scorching the ground, and the cattle stood stupefied beneath the cottonwoods. As the sun finally burned its way down, we laid in bed, fully dressed, sheets to our chins.

Carla said, "Let's get out of here."

I was tired. "Where?"

"Outside. I want a cig."

We climbed down the tree and snuck over to the pasture. The cattle stirred. Crickets chirped. Even the ground under our feet seemed to expand in relief from the heat. We walked a long way that night, silently sharing Camels and listening to the ringing dark.

When we reached an apple tree at the base of some foothills, we stopped. Carla looked beautiful in the bright moonlight, and suddenly I felt rushed to ask her for something I didn't know how to articulate. Instead, I asked how she met Steven.

She laughed. "I had this friend, Rosalie. We smoked together in the alley behind the school. One day, Steven shows up to take Rosalie for a drive, and the next day he calls me." She laughed, short and hard. "She tried to burn me with a cigarette lighter. Went around for weeks telling everyone I was a slut."

She took a deep drag on her cigarette. "But I don't care what Rosalie or anybody says about me." She paused. "I've been called a lot worse."

I knew she was talking about her stepmother. "Everyone knows, Iris is a witch," I said, tasting the sharpness of the word.

Carla snorted.

"Mom's a drag, too," I chirped.

"Yeah," Carla said and turned to look at me, her eyes narrowed. "But I bet she never made you take a bath in two inches of water to save on the bill. Or made you pee four times in the toilet before you flushed. Or told you just how much you cost her."

I didn't say anything.

"But I knew how to fix her," Carla continued. "One night I just looked at her and said, 'I wish you were the one I found in the basement. Not Mama. You.'" She laughed as if something were breaking in her chest.

The night seemed to shrink around us. Carla furiously rubbed coins together in her pocket as if she could conjure up something to change this. Finally she said, "You know something's wrong even if you're a kid. You think, Ma's sleeping. Or she fell. I don't know what I thought. I was only six. But there she is lying on the floor in a pool of blood and the washing machine is still going. So I sit. I sit there for hours like a fucking fool." Her voice cracked. She drew deeply from her cigarette and wiped at her cheek.

I had the nightmarish sensation of falling over the brink of something. I put my hand on her arm as much to steady myself as to comfort her.

"Let's walk back," she said.

"Okay," I said and my voice came from far away. I looked up at the sky jammed with stars and wanted to say a prayer. The only ones I knew were stupid.

• • •

In the months after our visit to the Home, letters from Carla were less and less frequent. When she wrote, she wrote about Wilson. "He's tough," she'd say. "He's gonna take me away from this dump." I hid the letters in the hatbox that held my Barbie doll.

I expected to hear that she'd run away. I pictured her living in Spokane, driving with Wilson to Coeur D'Alene Lake in a convertible, or slow dancing in the ballroom of the Davenport Hotel, Wilson looking dreamily into her eyes.

The evening she called we were watching Nixon speak to the press. Dad and I were seated in front of the TV, and my mother was cutting my bangs. Dad answered the phone on the third ring.

I didn't pay much attention until he said, "I'm taking this upstairs." His air of big secrets made me realize it was Carla.

He left the phone hanging deliciously at the end of the cord. As if she could read my mind, Mom put her hand on my shoulder to keep me in the chair, but before she cradled the receiver, I could hear the even notes of Dad's voice in duet with a distant, sometimes broken murmur. I thought I heard him say, "I thought we had things figured out, Carla. I thought we had plans."

When he reentered the dining room, Nixon was saying, "I am not a crook, I am not a crook." Dad watched his long, twitching face, then turned the volume off. "Carla," he said, "has had a baby boy. She's keeping the baby and marrying Wilson."

Mom looked at him, scissors dangling in her hand. "But what about the adoption, the Montana School of Beauty?"

"I know," he said, shaking his head. "I know."

"Oh, Ted, they don't have a prayer." My mother searched his face.

"Prayers," he said, "are something Carla will need lots of."

"Susan, thank God you have more sense than Carla." Mom shook the scissors at me. "Let this be a lesson to you."

I stared up at her through crooked bangs.

I jumped up, ran to my bedroom, and locked the door. I opened all the windows, even though it was spring and the air was wet and cold, and I got out my cigarettes. Sitting at the window, I lit up and started to write in my diary. "Susan likes to steal and she likes to smoke and she likes to ride fast in cars, especially over 100. She likes beer. No, she likes rum better."

My handwriting got large and crooked. "When she gets out of here, she's going to live in a city and be a hippie, paint her face, and march down streets, yelling—" In huge capital letters, a word to a page, I scrawled, "Susan has no sense at all!"

. . .

I couldn't imagine why Carla had decided to get married in Pinehurst. Inside the unpainted, wooden church, the guests looked as ancient and sad as the streets of town; even my parents looked old in the greying light. Jerome and Iris did not come. There was no wedding processional. There wasn't an organ in the church. There were only the sounds of trucks shifting gears on the interstate, the shuffling of feet, and wind hissing through Lost Horse Canyon.

At last some men walked in holding between them another man who looked like he'd gotten lost. I craned my neck. It was Wilson. His face was wide and freckled, his jaw was strong, but by far his most distinguishing feature was his nose, which was red and flat as if it had been broken more than once. I must have been staring, because when he came down the aisle past me, he leaned into my face and said, in a tang of whiskey and Listerine, "For better or worse."

Carla was standing at the back of the church.

My memory had washed her in the dusky colors of the summer nights we raced down 191. Her hair still cascaded down her back, and she looked wild and shy. But as she neared my pew, I felt like I was watching a candle struggle to stay lit in a breeze. I searched her face for a sign, a flicker of recognition, but as she walked by, her face looked drawn and her deep-set green eyes were impenetrable.

. . .

The reception was at the Trail's End, a local restaurant built in a log cabin with a neon martini glass and scantily clad barmaid. Inside, tissue paper wedding bells swung over a table covered with a red-checked cloth, and everyone sat down to glistening steaks and baked potatoes wrapped in tinfoil.

An old man with a face as red as his flannel shirt turned to me and held up an unmarked bottle of blackberry brandy. "Well, sweetheart, how 'bout a snort?"

I looked down the table at my mother. She was talking to a woman next to her, whose hair rose up in a stiff beehive. "We take a lot of vitamin C," Mom said, "but as summer comes on, I've started giving them kelp."

The woman tossed back her brandy and looked at Mom, head to toe. "Kelp," she said.

"Live a little," the old man said and poured me a tumbler full.

The liquor was sweet and thick going down. "Great stuff," I said through the fire in my throat.

"See what you're missing?" the old man laughed.

My father, a few seats away, was telling jokes I'd never heard before. "What's the difference between beer nuts and deer nuts?" he said to the table at large.

The men near him looked at their hands on the table, then with curiosity at the only man here in a suit and tie. I cringed.

"Beer nuts are a $1.39, deer nuts are under a buck." His face shone as the table burst into laughter.

"You're doin' just fine with this stuff, Miss Susan," the old man said, pouring me a second drink. "How old are you anyway?"

"Thirteen," I said thickly.

"It's amazing how soon they fill out," he said to himself.

I got up and walked stiffly to the back of the room. My body felt as bright and red as the neon barmaid's, and no less conspicuous. As I stood, dazed, before the two bathrooms labeled "Pointers" and "Setters," I could still hear him saying, "I mean they get breasts and everything at just about 12!" He saw me hesitating, and hollered helpfully, "Setters!"

Inside, I stared in the mirror, pinching my already-red cheeks when the door opened. It was Carla.

She started to brush her hair. There was only the crackle of static as she pulled the brush through, stroke by stroke, her movements slow and deliberate as if she were swimming.

For a moment, I thought she didn't recognize me. Finally I met her glance in the mirror, and her eyes shone, almost black. "You were a beautiful bride, Carla," I said.

"Pinehurst's prettiest," she said sarcastically.

"Where's the baby?"

"Probably bawling his head off," she said as she outlined her mouth in a lipstick named Pink Fiesta, which I would buy at Woolworth's the day I got home.

I dug in my purse for a comb. I was groping for something to say, something that would bridge the gulf between that hot, starry night on the ranch and this bathroom decorated with pictures of dogs.

Carla turned to me, and said, "Your hair looks like shit."

"Oh," I said. I opened my mouth, then shut it and looked in the mirror. My shoulder-length hair was pinned at either side of my face in bright blue barrettes shaped like rabbits. I was copying Sharon Rose, the most popular girl in high school.

"Here. Let me fix it for you." She removed the barrettes and started to rip through my hair, stroking faster and harder until my scalp stung. A brown halo stood out around my head. She stopped brushing, and started to smooth my hair with her hands, palms flat, starting at the scalp, her fingers spread like a comb. Carla's eyes lost their squint. I could feel the whisper of breath at my ear and the smell of brandy filled my head like perfume. When I looked in the mirror again, I saw Carla staring back at me, crying.

· · ·

Wilson and Carla's apartment looked like two freight cars strung together and stuck on top of a crumbling storefront. The windows were long and looked out on the streets of Pinehurst.

There was a lime green sofa propped up on one end with a car jack and Camel cigarettes on a mantle.

Mom stood next to me in the front room, eyeballing the windows as if she were measuring them. "Carla," she said, "Some curtains'll really cheer this place up."

Carla lit up and appeared to consider this.

One of Wilson's brothers danced through the room brandishing a whiskey bottle, yelling, "Got the Jack so git on back!" all the way to the kitchen.

My father laughed awkwardly and my mother's face froze as people started following him. I slipped out to see the rest of the apartment before we would have to go.

The long hallway smelled like fried meat and talcum powder. As I walked toward the door of the bedroom, someone lunged out of the room. It was Wilson.

"The only thing that concerns me," he said as he looked at my face, "is not waking up."

I shifted from one foot to another, then looked him in the eye. "Best not to," I said.

"With enough of my best man Jack," he said. "this mighty treefaller will fall."

I tried to laugh like I was the kind of person who poured whiskey on my cornflakes, but it came out too high and squeaky. He got quiet. I got nervous and said, "Are you settling in Pinehurst?"

He looked at me seriously and lowered his voice to a whisper. "There is no home, Susan, for the timber beast."

I looked at his wide face and the mop of reddish-brown hair on his forehead and said nothing. Wilson leaned close to my face. I leaned closer, thinking he was going to tell me something. Then he reached his arm around me, pinched my butt, and hollered "Yee-*hah!*" before he danced and swayed down the narrow hallway to the kitchen.

I slipped into the bedroom to hide my burning face. I hated him. I hated him for his flat-nosed face, for his freckled arms, for this mean little apartment, for marrying Carla.

The bedroom was small, just a bed, a vanity with a taffeta skirt, and a large closet. The bassinet on the floor was framed by dirty blue ruffles, and inside were stuffed toys that looked like a drunk's idea of animals. The baby slept with its rump in the air. I watched the tiny cheeks expand and contract and wondered how anyone could sleep through this noise. I leaned closer. The baby's diapers reeked.

. . .

There were footsteps outside the door and I dove into the closet. It was Wilson. He bent over the bassinet and put his large hand on top of the baby's head. The baby started to whimper and Wilson picked him up.

The kid looked tiny in Wilson's arms. The whimper became a soft cry. "You smell like a shit factory," Wilson said. He lay the baby across the bed and changed him, whispering, "No kid of mine's wearin' stinky pants," jamming the duck-shaped diaper pins through wads of cotton. Then he picked the baby up and started to rock him. Shifting from foot to foot, then dipping the baby back and forth, Wilson started to sing, "Each night be-fo-ore you go to sleep, ma bay-bee."

I sat in a pile of dirty clothes, stunned.

"Whisp-er a little prayer for me," Wilson was getting louder. The words were thick with alcohol, but his voice was surprisingly sweet. He held the baby away from his body and sang into the kid's face. The baby looked at him through filmy eyes, too stunned to cry. "Tell-ell-ell all the stars above."

A flush crawled up my neck and I knew I was going to be sick. As Wilson continued to sing, I bolted out of the closet and across the bedroom.

In the bathroom, I stared at myself, at my pale skin and the freckles that popped out, one by one, like brown stars. Mom came knocking on the door to make me gargle with saltwater. She was convinced I had flu. I just wanted to sleep. Over the shouting in the kitchen, the clinking of glasses, and a joke Dad was telling, I heard Wilson sing on, undisturbed, "Whisper a little pra-er for me, ma bay-bee."

. . .

Years later, Carla and I met again at my folks' house. I had been working at a bank in Spokane and was about to be married to a loan officer, when I realized, at a particularly formal bridal shower, that I had no desire to be Mrs. Darringer. I broke off the engagement, quit my job, and came home to nurse my wounds.

Carla had a two-week vacation from the sugar beet factory and she was taking her kids Danny and Desiree to Lake Louise. She had stopped by to say hi. While the kids wandered around the yard, Carla and I gathered around the kitchen table for my mother's tea.

Carla had the same slightly wild look, but there was a kind of heartiness about her that seemed new to me. While she and my mom talked about baking whole wheat bread, I looked at her hands, which were larger and redder than I remembered but strong, and her nails were polished a frosted peach. Her hands had the look of something I felt far away from—a kind of no-nonsense mastery of things—and I could imagine them diapering up babies, fixing the drain, brushing her hair, signing divorce papers.

I must have been daydreaming because when she turned to me and said, "You have the look," I started.

"The look?" I said, tilting my head.

"Aw hell, girl," she said, motioning to me as if it would make me understand faster. "You look snakebit."

It stung. "It just wasn't right," I said, swallowing down the quaver in my voice.

My mother started up from her chair like a shot. The subject of my canceled wedding was mined ground between the two of us, and she masked her disapproval with movement: she gathered teacups from the bookcase behind me, then flitted across the room to the cookie drawer.

"Well, I can tell you two marriages later," Carla said, shaking out a cigarette from a pack of Virginia Slims, "you made a damn good decision."

"Marriage is something you have to work at," my mother said from the refrigerator, her voice sharp. She wouldn't look at me when she brought the heart-shaped sugar cookies to the table.

"Gloria, some things only take so much mending," Carla said. She lit her cigarette and shook out the match.

I looked at her gratefully and laughed. It was the first time I'd laughed in a month. In that moment I felt like Carla had sprung something loose in me, that Carla had always sprung something loose in me and that I depended on it, my family depended on it, and that we owed Carla more than she would ever take from us.

"Remember sneaking out of your grandparents' house?" I said.

"Hell, we spent more time out of that house than in it," she said.

"I thought I'd died and gone to heaven, riding around in that Mustang."

"You had," Carla said and took a drag on her cigarette.

My mother shook her head as she set down an ashtray and said, "We had no idea."

"Of course," Carla said, "that was the point." Then she turned to me. "What about the chant?" she teased. "Do you remember the chant?"

"The chant?" I looked at her for a clue.

"You don't remember?" Carla said, but she wouldn't say anything more.

Then it came back to me. The last night I spent at her

grandparents' ranch, we walked the long way back home
through the newly plowed fields. The day's heat had baked the
dirt hard on top, hiding the loose dirt below, so it was fragile
and unpredictable as crusted snow. We were tired and sleepy
and the night seemed to shrink around the sound of our
plodding feet when I turned my ankle in one of the furrows.

"Shit," I said, and liked it.

A few minutes later Carla tripped. "Piss," she said and spat at
the clumps of dirt.

As we continued to trip and stumble our way across the
fields, I don't remember who started it, or why, but one of us
strung the words together and liked it and we locked arms and
started to chant, our voices small and clear, hammering against
the bleary stars, against the hugeness of everything, "Shit Piss
Fuck Screw" because we were young and nothing else seemed
to matter.

BACKFIRES

I left Bridger, the slurry bombers buzzing, the sharp smell
of purpose in that sleepy, stupid town. The papers called it a
tragedy. I knew they loved it. They brought their lawn chairs
and binoculars and lined up by the hundreds on the banks
of the Salmon to watch the flames run up the mountainside,
to hear the crackling thunder of trees. They cooked hot dogs,
drank beer, and some even left to cut fire line. Someone, they
whispered, someone *started* this fire. The next day, businessmen
wagged their heads over coffee, women kept their children close,
and I caught the 9:15 freight to Pasco.

· · ·

I'm one of the grey men: the men who fix things, sell things,
break things and you never notice. We move in and out of your
towns, drink at your bars, sleep at your motels, eat your food,
fuck your women, and you never see us. We live at the edges of
things, but close enough so you can't see our faces real clear.

I worked at some job, fixing small engines, and I kept to
myself. It was a medium shop, twenty men, and they were
always organizing picnics, softball teams, football pools. I went
to one or two so they wouldn't notice I wasn't at the rest.

I met her at the picnic up Wildhorse Canyon. I was standing
near a group of people at the bonfire. They were roasting hot
dogs, and the kids were burning up marshmallows on willow
sticks, and sticking the goo in their mouths. I was watching the
fire—I believe in fire—when I looked over and saw her, a blonde
woman about up to my shoulders, her hair curling away from
her face, and even though it was July she was more pink than
brown in her blue striped shorts. Everyone was telling dirty

jokes and laughing in a beer-soaked way, but she didn't. She didn't say anything. She just stood by that ass Tom Dobbins and picked the meat off a chicken breast, strip by strip.

Now you'll think, here's this guy staring like a baboon, but you're playing me cheap. For as soon as I saw her, I had her memorized, and the rest I discovered as I stood there, sipping my beer, just watching the fire. If you listen, you can discover a lot.

. . .

Now I don't usually have much to do with women. Not real women. Women are fire. Men are their kindling. I know this. I look at men, men I work with, men on the streets, and I can tell which ones have been consumed. I look at them from far away, nothing but charred trunks with legs, and I feel sorry. Wives burn husbands, mothers burn sons, sisters burn brothers.

I tried to stay away from the girl.

But one night, as I was driving to the Kwik Mart for beer, I saw her. She was driving a blue mustang with a dent in the back, and she drove by me, plain as day, her windows down, her hair blowing back, yellow and shiny. This time she had glasses on, and I didn't like that, but in the husky night she looked cool. I pulled a U-turn and followed her. I followed her to the mall, always keeping, you mind, a good distance, and I followed her home.

Or I thought it was home.

Imagine my surprise as I crept up to the window and watched her stand before a closet and reach for a hanger, the golden hairs crawling up her pink legs, the calf muscles round and straining, when who comes in that room but that shaking wall of flesh, Tom Dobbins. He pressed his face into hers. Don't go, he said. She wrapped her arms around his neck. Pretty, he said. Pretty as a princess.

The sound of his voice—whiny as a bad starter motor—shook me to my senses and I got out of there fast.

. . .

I started imagining her—coming out of the shower, her skin glowing and beads of water on her bush. Her and me walking down the street, never touching, and I'd say something to her and she'd laugh, toss her hair, and smooth down the front of her yellow dress. Once, I imagined I touched her skin and it was cool, cool as night.

I decided to follow her.

I bought a thirty-nine-cent blue notebook. Number one, I wrote, Dobbins's address. A drive on the north side took care of that: 145 Phillips. That was enough work for one night. I popped open a beer, and watched "The Night of the Grizzly."

That movie was fateful, because I remembered something so important I said it out loud: Stealth, Robert.

Now I didn't do anything silly like buying dark glasses because I knew I was my best disguise. The next night I waited near Dobbins's house till I saw her car. I studied an Idaho map as she walked from the car to his house, her dress blowing around her legs to break your heart. I read every word on that map. I read about dogwood. I read about potatoes. I smoked two packs of cigarettes, then I followed her home.

She lived in a housing development, a place where little rows of houses were scattered like toys on the lee side of Rattlesnake Mountain. It was built for the young and playful, with a postage stamp of a swimming pool, which made me bit suspicious. But I didn't think about fire that night. I watched her lock the door to her Mustang, and slowly walk to her house.

I got home past two, and I didn't get much sleep, but I walked into work the next day with a light heart because I had a jewel: El Dor West #13 and all that it meant.

. . .

Now you have to understand something. I didn't want to fuck her, I didn't even want to touch her. People don't always understand people like me, they think I want to break in and force myself on girls to call myself a man. They don't understand I just wanted her in front of me. I just wanted her near.

But I know people, how they grab hold of something in you, something they don't understand, and they twist and turn it and you have to leave town. So a month after I started following her, when my landlady says to me, cocking her head so I can see the corner of her false teeth, why Robert Michaels I b'lieve you have a girlfriend, want to tell Miss Childers? I cough and say, with all due respect ma'am, I'm here to pay rent, and I give her the money and move out the next day. And into the Montague Apartments—one of those dim apartment buildings where every once in a while you pass people in the halls and you're not sure if you saw them yesterday or twenty years ago. You're not even sure anyone else lives there, except once in a while you'll hear bedsprings creak or beer bottles break, but least of all you hear voices.

It took me forty-five minutes to move in my TV, a box of clothes, and a Cointreau bottle lamp I made in shop class as a boy. I'm more sentimental about that lamp than about my whole childhood.

Then I sat at a table I'd hauled up from the dump and opened my notebook. I looked at the things I'd accomplished— addresses mostly—little scribbles on lined paper, little scribbles that are my nights, my days, my dreams, my everything, and I asked myself, What are you doing Robert Michaels? You who have seen how women take their men and slowly, like spiders, suck the life out of them, what are you doing? I put the little blue notebook in the trashcan. Then I took a knife and drew the blade up my arm and watched a thin line of blood appear.

Then some other part of me took over, and I saw her, real as day, reclining on my couch in her blue-striped shorts, and I talked dirty to her, and she just looked at me cool and picked the petals off a daisy. Robert, she said, I'm feeling warm, Robert.

I walked the tracks that night, past the tennis club that looked like a giant balloon losing its air, past the bushes where the bums were drinking in their camps. While I walked, I talked. I was giving myself a lecture. Remember Robert, I said. What women do to men. They trap them in perfume and breasts and then, limb by limb, they burn them alive. I crossed the railroad trestle, walked into an abandoned camp, and decided to teach myself a lesson.

I gathered sticks, and laid them on top of a newspaper. I laid them in a pattern, small ones, then larger and larger—I like my fires neat—then I held my lighter up and lit the paper. As soon as the flame was steady, I said OK pal, and stepped in the middle of it.

Now you're thinking, here's this wreck of a man in the middle of God knows where standing in a campfire. But I have some sense. I didn't stay long enough to get real burned, although the corners of my shoes melted down so they tapped in a funny way at work the next day. No, I just stayed there long enough to feel the heat. This, I said to myself, is what women do. Then I kicked in the fire and walked back to my car.

. . .

It didn't work. If anything, it was like the fire released a flood of thoughts like those tree seeds that grow when they're burned. I thought of her constantly. I saw her in the mirror behind me as I shaved, I saw her in the streets, and I saw her in the back of the shop as I fixed the floats on a carburetor saying, *Robertrobertrobert.*

At least, I told myself, she will never know you.

. . .

I stared at the blue notebook I'd fished out of the garbage, and I smoothed out its pages and I saw her lips rounding around my name. I wanted to reach her. I wanted her *mine.* I went walking along the river past the old Milwaukee station where the well-fed got more well-fed, through a tunnel of bushes between the ditch and the river, to the Orange Street bridge where Willy

Williams shot a man and tried to claw the bullet out with a hammer, when it hit me: she needed a name.

It took me a long time to find one. I walked up and down each side of the Salmon and nothing came. I walked around the downtown, up the zigzag path on the mountain, and tramped the wide, green-lawned section of town where the rich people live. I watched their fat petunias waving, their cow-like children pedaling furiously down the sidewalks, and I thought: Rosie, Sarah, Miranda, Desiree. I walked through the campus drowsy in sun and considered Bettina. In Rattlesnake Park, among the bobbing joggers, I was stuck on Maria. I walked everywhere, but it wasn't till I walked up the tracks on the north side of the river, the tracks they still use, that it came upon me in a fury: Lovely. Lovely, I rehearsed, it's time for your bath. Lovely, could you get the door? Lovely, wake up, you're dreaming.

· · ·

Oh, what busy happy days those were.

Every morning I'd get up at 6:00, drive over to her house, climb high in the birch by her back bedroom window and watch her wake up. This was my favorite part of the day. I looked down at the rumple of blonde hair, pink limbs, blue covers, and felt light enough to fly. Lovely, I'd say to her from my perch, good morning, Lovely. When the DJ said 6:25, her legs finally came out from under the covers, until there she was, wet with sleep, in her shortie gown. I watched her as she rubbed her eyes, pulled her hair from her face, and yawned, and once I was so frozen with joy I lost my grip and nearly fell out of the tree. I watched her as she walked in this tilted, sleepy way to take in the milk, plug in her hair curlers, and make coffee. When she left for work, I shimmied down out of the tree, always keeping, you mind, an eye out for snoops.

Evenings, Tom Dobbins was there, sprawled out on her couch and bellowing. I considered at one point killing him but decided it would attract too much attention. So the nights he was there, I just looked at Lovely, then snuck off and drank. Every once in a while I got lucky and she'd be there alone, stretched out on the couch like Cleopatra, reading or painting her nails. I liked pink best.

In my way, I went with her to the library, to the bowling alley, to the grocery store, to the mall for her pretty dresses.

. . .

I had to be careful. It was late August, dog days, a time you don't want to be too happy. The air had that tight feeling of something about to break, and one noon, a fight even broke out at the shop between a forty-year-old mechanic and a kid who beat him at arm wrestling. I worked hard to keep invisible. I even developed a little song in my head, it's just me I'm Mr. Grey, that I'd sing in my head in the back shop among the ignition motors and solenoids until even my song made me happy. Then I practiced just keeping blank.

At lunchtime I'd walk by the State Farm Insurance office, where she worked, to see if I could see my Lovely. Once I even went in, but when I stepped into the carpeted office, the air-conditioning blew a prickle up my skin and the receptionist looked up at me strange, like what was I doing there, and a voice in my head said *Whoaa, Robert.* Lovely wasn't there, thank God, and I beat it.

. . .

August 25, Lovely and her slob took a raft trip on the Salmon. The night before, I hid in some bushes underneath her window and got details from that old fool Dobbins who was sitting on the bed, his stomach lapping over his underwear, and shouting at a map.

A highway followed the river, so I decided to join them. In my own little way, of course.

The day of the trip, I went to the supermarket to stock up on beer, me, Mr. Grey, and as I was walking down the aisles, among the fat women with their carts loaded down like small barges, their children crying with animal faces, I was thinking of Lovely cool in glacier water, all wet and yellow and beautiful and I hoped she didn't get too much sun—when a grocery cart smacked into my side and almost knocked me over.

Shit, I said, and looked up—oh God why didn't I run?—and there she was. My eyes locked right onto hers, and it was like looking eye to eye with a rose. There she was, pink skin and all. She didn't say something dirty and look at me cool and pluck petals from a daisy or unbutton her top slowly or toss her hair and say in a low pearly voice Robert, Robert. She hurried around her cart and over to me, saying, Oh! I'm sorry, I'm sorry.

Something turned over in my gut, and I turned to head down cereals. She followed me, saying, Did I hurt you? What's your name? I'm so sorry! and then she reached out and put her hand on my arm and that's when I felt the heat of her palm shoot through me like liquid, like lightning, like wisdom, and my heart squeezed up through my mouth, and I turned to face her and I shouted, "Stop!" She looked at me and that's when I saw it. I tried to look away but her face was painted with the look that said you poor, poor man, life has knocked you down and left you in the gutter so you drink the filth like milk. The look that said Robert Michaels you are a sad little man. The look that said you are a fool. I started to run.

I drove up the Salmon to Hanging Rock Canyon, and I tried to pretend it hadn't happened. As I waited for Lovely and Dobbins's raft to float by, I laid out on the ground in the sagebrush and knapweed and tried to fill my mind with those early pink mornings, just the two of us and the birds singing. I watched them float by and I still saw her cool, rosy skin and blonde hair, and Dobbins, who looked like a beached whale. Lovely, my chilled maiden, I said to myself, Lovely.

But driving down the canyon, it came back to me—her long fingers on my arm — the soft hand, palm, her woman's fire. And, over and over again, that look, you poor sad man.

At the campground at Rainbow Bend, I was struggling.
I wanted to keep it the way it was, my perfect mornings, my
noontime visits, my evenings, my Lovely. But it was all brewing
inside, twisting my guts. Then I saw them swirling down the
river, coming toward me with the current, the water roaring
you poor poor man, the sound thundering against the canyon
and gut-punching me till my wind was gone, and I knew in the
deepest part of my heart I'd been tricked, burnt by this woman's
fire like the bastards I'd laughed at, those charred-up men that
lay themselves like kindling on women. They were my brothers.

My heart ripped open. I knelt down and cried until the
sound of my voice carried up the river, until I was exhausted,
until I lay in the dirt like a washed up worm, and slept the sleep
of the dead.

. . .

I never went back to the shop after that—I couldn't bear
the sight of the men who'd given themselves to women and
smiled, and the ignition motors where I'd sung my little songs.
I lay in my iron bed and drank. I drank as the cars rattled in
the streets and the dogs barked and the people on TV opened
and shut their mouths like fish. I drank as the day was born
and I drank as it wilted. I drank until the ceiling became the
floor and the mud-colored tile heaved up and swallowed me,
and the night ghosts thickened up the room and I cried out
Lovely, Lovely, and she'd be there, pink and yellow, saying with
cruel cool, *Robert, my sweet Robert,* the points of her teeth
flickering in her mouth like flames and I knew again I'd been
tricked. I yelled at her, threw bottles at her, and sometimes I
just plain burned.

I'd feel that touch on my arm, that burning, scouring touch,
and I'd split open.

That morning I heard the sweet patter of rain, and the
musky smell of wet dirt rose up from the streets and into my

grey apartment, and I knew something. I knew she had taken something from me that kept me blind so I could go on living, and I knew what had to be done.

. . .

I was very calm. I had many things to take care of.

I drove by the State Farm Insurance Company that night, 3:00 a.m. to be exact. I got out of my car with a bucket and paintbrush and walked to the glass door. No one saw me do it—I am a careful man—but as the traffic lights flashed yellow, I made up a pail of the thickest, blackest mud you've ever seen and I painted an X right across the door.

Then I drove to her house, balancing the pail of mud between my knees. As the paintbrush was stiffening, I crept to the back door so quiet the dogs couldn't hear me. The first thing I did was to mark her door with a huge X so's people would see.

The next thing I'm a little embarrassed about, but it had to be done. I went to the darkest part of Lovely's yard. Walking past the birch pinched my heart—where every morning I saw Lovely wake up, her long legs coming out of the covers—and I would have fallen apart but I remembered how she tricked me, how her eyes said you poor, poor man, and I stood in the corner by the lilac bushes, thick with leaves, and I unzipped my pants and held myself. Bitch, whore, cunt, I stroked myself, and I thought of her painted with red cheeks and black eyes, and I thought of her glowing, molten insides and the men moaning and writhing inside and I thought of her trying to swallow me—her latest victim—and I came over her marigolds and roses.

. . .

I hiked up Snowdrop Mountain and looked carefully for the right place to begin, and I found it, like you find most things, coming home, an old camp along the Milwaukee tracks that, judging from trampled-down bushes and the bottles of Thunderbird, had been recently used.

The rest was like going back on a long path you've made and undoing it. I moved out from the Montague Apartments as soon as I'd made my plan, and I took my cardboard box of clothes and my Cointreau lamp to the dump and watched them crash into the stinking pile of broken refrigerators, chairs without legs, and rusted out car bodies. I whispered good-bye to the crows that dotted the hillside. I've always like crows.

I got gasoline and matches, and I planned where I'd off my car. I marked September 8 with an X on a little calendar in my car. I chose that day because the frog-faced newscaster said it would be hot. I am a careful man.

. . .

A man gets the jitters before something big in his life, and the day before the fire I was so nervous I spent the whole day driving out every exit from town, running down the plans in my head. The only thing that calmed me was thinking of Lovely, defeated. Ha, ha, I laughed to myself. Outdone.

September 8 dawned just as it should. The sun burned over Snowdrop Mountain and the air hung heavy. Children whined, flowers drooped, and the town had that cornered feeling of too much heat and a winter ahead. It was perfect.

At 3:00 p.m. I parked my car in the lot of a grocery store, and I slowly walked over the bridge to my site. I wanted to remember everything right before—the faces of the people at the little picnic park by the river, the tapping sounds of the football players in a distant field, and most of all the face of the mountain that would defeat Lovely. There it was, with its little rock ledge halfway up, covered by spruce, tamarack, and willow, the dried-up spring, my Snowdrop Mountain.

I waited in some bushes until it was dark, then I walked to my site like I was walking up the aisle in a church. I had thoughts about Lovely in the early morning with her rumpled-up hair and her round pink arms, and then I remembered the look, the touch, my knowledge. Women destroy, I whispered.

At the hobo camp, I put kindling on top of the Idaho map that was my first night with Lovely, and I lit the whole pile with a wooden match and put a couple of hot dogs on top for effect. The fire sputtered a bit, so I dragged over a branch and set it on top. The branch lit up like the Vegas strip, and in minutes the bushes caught. I left when the trees at the bottom of the mountain started smoking, and walked back to the car, exhausted. I drove out a nearby freeway exit to relax.

When I came back to Bridger along the old highway, you can imagine my pride when I looked over and saw that bank of orange-red flame along the river, the huge sparks that flew up the hill lighting tree after tree like sparklers, and I smelled that tart wood burning and knew it was going to work. It was my grandest moment, my hand on the wheel of the old Ford Pinto, looking straight into the mouth of my finest creation, my fight against the woman fury Lovely.

I went to my hiding place, I won't tell you where, and I watched the wind push the flames uphill, lighting tree after tree like birthday candles. As the clouds of smoke billowed down the mountain, I watched the fire trucks come and the little black-jacketed men scurry out with their hoses. I watched the police cars rush up with their sirens blaring and the policemen burst out of the doors, put their hands on their hips, and look up. I watched people scamper off to call other people, and I watched the slurry bombers buzz closer and closer with their singing whine and they spread their red dust and I watched it fail.

They came in droves that day, the cars, the bicyclists, the motorcycles, the trucks, and they pulled up with the river between them and the burning mountain and they set up their camps and they stayed all night to watch my creation, these people who ignored me and colored me grey, they came and they watched.

Then I drove to her house, left the note, rang the bell and hid in the bushes. She walked out and opened the envelope, her long, pink fingernails slicing the top flap, and started to read the note. I had the feeling a man gets when he knows this is the moment that is beyond his control, and I took a drink of vodka and held my breath. She looked up at the mountain for a long time, so I couldn't see her face, and I thought I would burst until she finally turned and I saw the look of pure horror, then the pink dimming into grey, and then came defeat that was almost exquisite, and I knew I had won, and I had to leave town. She looked down at the note and then she slammed the door.

The fire's for you, I wrote, who fooled a poor man once.

· · ·

And that's when I left. As I crouched in the boxcar waiting for the yard bulls to pass, I took a long sweet breath and looked at the tiny people, poor, poor people, huddled on the banks of the Salmon, the sad charred men and the women who ruined them. I looked at Snowdrop Mountain, the orange, red, and purple tongues of fire, the blackened trees standing like corpses, and I thought about all the things a grey man can do.

II

LAKEFRONT PROPERTY

"Definitely a scraper," Leslie Broadbent said to me as she peered at the red-shingled cabin. She paused. I paused. Gulls made their tiresome cries overhead as we studied the water from the deck of the cabin. Waves slapped the rocky shore of Flathead Lake, the largest freshwater lake west of the Mississippi—a fact that was catechism for all Montana schoolchildren. Motorboats zigzagged white trails across the blue water, sailboats listed westward.

"I mean, look at it, Anna." She touched my arm and the two us turned back to look at the cabin. "It needs paint, the deck looks like hell, the windows are single-pane, and God knows what they'll find in the attic: it if isn't squirrels, it'll be vermiculite."

"You'll have to remodel," I said. "No doubt about it. The paint, the deck—they're gone." Accentuate the negative I'd learned with clients like this. If you didn't, they suspected you were withholding something. And if you were withholding something, they wanted it.

What was I going to say anyway? That she didn't have to do this? That she could learn to adjust, love the fact that the cabin was weather-beaten, that it had a history, that it was like a hundred places at this lake, built on long weekends by locals on hopes and prayers. And that once, places like this—with toilets instead of outhouses and siding instead of logs—were the fancy ones. The tire swing was gone. So was the ponderosa, though aspen and a few straggly tamaracks remained. Gladys and Harold had given me this house but I'd put it on the market immediately, seeing it only as a way to spring me into my future: the move to the big town of Missoula, a realtor's license, a new me.

Of course, I'd never say any of that. I was the real estate agent and the fact that I stood to make a cool $60,000—six percent of $1.2 million from this cabin perched on the edge of a glacier-carved lake—made my words dry up and blow away like dandelion fluff.

And, let's face it, the cabin *was* shabby: peeling paint, crumbling stone fireplace, and gardens dense with bindweed and Scottish bluebells, gardens where gladiolas once stood like frilly swords next to the bushes of yellow and red roses and blue delphiniums that grew six feet tall, where Gladys worked weekends while Harold, with his flattop, mowed the lawn each week in exactly the same way, starting on the left and going around, then finishing off by mowing diagonal strips across the lawn. Afterward, I joined them on the porch where I sat on an old chair that smelled of mildew and pine, where Gladys brought us iced tea and Harold told her it tasted like goddamned Kool-Aid, that if she had any sense she'd buy some decent cheddar cheese, not that Kraft shit. "Harold," Gladys would say and hold up her hand like a traffic cop. "Warning." And he'd stop, go silent.

"Remodel or start over," Leslie nodded. She looked down at her hands—as if they were calculators—then back at me.

You could leave it alone, I thought. I spent a lot of time here, swinging on that tire swing, sailing out over the blue glittering water, watching the lazy trails of rich people in motorboats trailing water skiers, imagining the lake monster rising up and gobbling them up like Cheez-Its, one by one.

But these people never left things alone. Outliers—lawyers and doctors and the people who worked remotely (whatever that meant) from Chicago and Los Angeles and points west—bought property, rolled in, and remade the world as they saw fit. I've sold them acres of forest, cabins, old family homes—only to return to find ragged stands of old-growth tamarack tamed into tree parks, meadows turned into prize-winning, drought-resistant gardens full of "native" plantings I'd never seen before. Then there were those who moved in, bought massive four-wheel trucks and cowboy hats and Appaloosas and decorated their houses and lawns with stuff we used to throw away—harness ropes, rusty plows, worn-out tools—as if they were teaching us what being Western was about. I—we—sold them everything, pocketing the dollars, and buying package trips to Hawaii or our own second homes in more remote areas where we bait-fished and drank beer.

"Hard to say what you should do," I said. I pressed the pads of my fingers together. "It's really up to you, Leslie." *Invoke the personal when closing the deal.* "We could look at more properties. There's a beautiful cedar-sided in Wood's Bay."

Leslie took off her glasses and squinted out at the water rolling to shore.

She looked good: her tanned skin unlined, her eyes a laser-like turquoise as she turned them on me. We were the same age, but her life as a sports medicine doctor had been much kinder to her than mine: hardscrabble waitress-cum-secretary-cum-real estate agent. Her husband, Marty, a dentist, had a head of golden-brown curly hair and a broad chest I wanted lay my head on. He was rumored to have played nose tackle for the Detroit Lions; she raced for the women's national Nordic team. The two of them looked like something out of an advertisement for expensive athletic wear. They had identical twin girls dressed in organic children's clothing.

My husband, an English professor who didn't get tenure, had a remodeling business. The two of us scraped by each year, hoping to add on to our crackerbox house to accommodate our growing family, but we were the classic cobbler's children: while Ben remodeled kitchens and basements for other people, our kitchen had cracked linoleum and sticky cupboards and an unfinished basement creeping with hobo spiders. Charles was six and had been sent to the principal's office twice in first grade; Hannah, at three, had learned to scale my husband's bookcases. The four of us, I like to think, had a motley, country kind of charm—we looked like an ad for the state-run health insurance for children—which in fact we subscribed to after real estate bottomed out in 2008.

"Of course," I paused, waiting for Leslie to turn to me. "You could look at it a different way."

Leslie's eyes narrowed, appraising me. "How?"

"You could see this as a kind of country cottage and just grow ivy so no one could see rotten spots."

She threw her head back and laughed, an actual belly laugh. "Then I could write stories about a rabbit named Peter and an evil gardener. And drink a shitload of tea."

She turned back to the lake. "I don't know what my problem is. I mean, it's not the money. And look at that view! And the kids? Marty? This is what we've all been working for, right? I mean, it's just another $100,000 to make it livable, right?"

I had to make this sale. Business had been slow, and I had a family to feed. It was time to spin the fantasy. "Do you see Marty, out on the lake, in a new motorboat—one of those Sea-Doo jet boats, you next to him, the spray reaching out behind you?"

"Marty and his boy toys." Leslie shook her head. She looked dubious.

I felt her mentally calculating the cost of a dock, motorboat, jet skis, water skis.

I took another tack. "Think of you, Marty, and the girls, waking up to the sound of the lake lapping, trees whispering, that handsome husband of yours so relaxed. But I don't know, Leslie, are you the country type?"

"Well, at least Marty would be in my bed for a change," Leslie said. "That'd be a plus."

"The smell of coffee," I persisted. "Seagulls. A warm fire after a cold swim."

"I'm thinking about it," Leslie said.

"And just lying there in the morning, hearing the lap of the water, the cry of the gull. Seeing Marty at the helm of that motorboat, facing into the wind."

"Well at least it would give Marty something to think about besides his dick."

"You'd be next to him," I purred. I had to keep her away from Marty and his dick or the sale would go dark. I had a family to feed. "You'd be next to him, sunset over the lake, the two of you sipping cocktails on that warm July evening."

"Marty and toys." Leslie shook her head. She looked dubious.

I felt as if I could hear her weakening as she struggled against that other calculation: her toys and his toys—and *whose turn was it anyway?*

"It *is* lakefront," I said. This was the moment to press in, lightly. "Of the last five places, Leslie, this one has the best beach. You're often paying either for the land or the house. And look at this: you have a view of Wild Horse Island, a serviceable dock, neighbors that you can't see, and that water. That blue-green water. Cleanest lake in the world, according to the Flathead Lake Biological Station. And the monster, of course, is thrown in for free."

"The monster?"

"The Flathead Lake monster, of course. Supposedly a giant sturgeon that lives hundreds of feet down in a lake trench and comes up only between April and May. It's rumor, but kids love it. Big, bulbous head. Slithery body, about forty feet long. The captain of the lake steamer that first saw him at the turn of the century said he had big, dark, glittery eyes."

. . .

The dream of starting over.

That's what I sell.

After years of knocking around, I found my heart somewhere between square footage and buy-sell agreements, earnest money and disclosure agreements. I loved the deals: the choreography of the sale, the push and pull, the pressure and the patience. I loved the dance of offers and counteroffers, concluding with the final, formal meetings at the title companies and that teeth-chattering moment when, everyone dressed to the nines, a bored title agent—the gatekeeper—turned page after page of the contract, pointed, and said, "Sign here" or "Initial here." I loved the money, the 4 percent, then 5 percent, and then—as I got a name—6 percent. And then the life of the house transfers. One life in the space begins and another ends. Real estate. Real. Estate.

But what I loved most were empty houses. Walking into houses, empty, clean, stripped of pictures, books, calendars, sports notices, trophies, wedding pictures, just blank counters, floors, and windows. I loved how each home spoke to me—from a 6,500-square-foot executive home to the 1,800-foot bungalow. I was the recently promoted executive with the country-club wife and athletic children who leaped from room to room. I was the newly divorced mother with her week-on, weekend-off family, and ready stash of white wine. I was the newlywed couple, starting out together, fucking on the bare wooden floor.

Empty rooms speak to me: Give me your newly married, your divorcees, your families on the skids, the young juvenile delinquent who'd fucked up in high school, gotten pregnant, had to give up the baby, and had to start her life over, and let her know she could come within my four walls and *here you can be reborn.*

. . .

I lived in this house with Gladys and Harold when I was sixteen. They took me in when my mother kicked me out. I was pregnant. My father was long gone. I thought Harold was bizarre, with his incessant lawn mowing. Gladys belonged to the house: she baked, cleaned, shopped according to the days: Monday, laundry, Tuesday, shopping, the days turning for her in a comfortable wheel of chores. Why in the world did they want to take in a foster child? *The Lord didn't bless us with one of our own,* Gladys would tell me as she sat on my bed at night, smoothing the covers over my growing stomach, ignoring the fact it was past midnight and I was drunk. Harold, who knew exactly what was going on, said, "Get upstairs, I don't want to know what you've been doing, but I don't like it, you're breaking your mother's heart." "She's not my mother," I'd say back. He'd look at me, his eyes two black stones. "She is now," he'd say, then turn back to the television and turn up the volume.

Harold survived the Bataan Death March. He had a purple heart to prove it and a deep and abiding hatred of anything Japanese. It was the kind of thing I shrugged off as a teenager— until later, I looked it up, saw the pictures of the gaunt Americans, the Japanese firing squads, the corpses curled like fetuses by the side of the road. Sadly, I didn't understand this until long after Harold was dead and I couldn't say to him, *you survived this?*

What Harold did talk about was the mysterious weather systems on the lake—how a body of water that large created a weather system all its own. He told stories about deaths on the lake related to weather: the college professor who went out on his sailboat and was found, dead, later that day. The two accountants who were found, face down in the water, after canoeing from their island cabin in mid-March, the dog swimming around and around the upset canoe and their floating bodies. The outfitter who was out with a client, reeling in 26-pound lake trout when a wind came up and flipped him and his clients and dragged them into a 260-foot lake trench.

People look at that water and think fun, Harold would say. *But the lake has mysteries.*

The monster? I would say back to him with a laugh. *Everyone knows that's a myth.*

I'm just saying it's dangerous, he said. *This lake has a life of its own and you're a fool if you don't respect it.*

It was Harold who picked me up the night the cops busted our kegger at Kerr Dam, most of the Polson junior class down at the police station, drunk and crying, parents crying with them, or hiding smiles under their hands. Not Harold. He paid my bail, took me out to the car, and said this, "Get your shit together. This isn't just your life to fuck up anymore, kid. You got another to think about."

Driving home, I focused on his profile in the dark—all angles and planes. I was drunk. I was furious. But I couldn't say anything to that profile.

Instead, I thought, the best thing is for me to die. It was the solution to the mess of my life. Lift up the lock, open the door, roll out of the car, and die. Simple. Clean. Done.

Harold's eyes peered at the dark two-lane road ahead, lit only by the occasional reflector, as we wound across the wide meadow at the south end of the lake.

We passed the ghostly limbs of cherry orchard after cherry orchard, the closed lakeside stands, the cabins, the rocky cliffs. I told myself, jump. I put my hand on the grooved notches of door lock. Slowly I pulled the lock up.

Harold didn't appear to hear me.

I put my hands on the silver door handle. The metal was cool. It was easy, I told myself. Lift the handle, open the door, and fall out. My body would roll out onto the dark pavement, my skin scraping, the child bouncing in my womb, the brakes screeching and smoking, and as these images tumbled through my head, we hurtled forward in our smooth metal capsule, our tires nicking the asphalt. I studied the lake, where a stray moon had silvered the water, and just as I turned my gaze back to Harold, to his thick hands curled around the sculpted white steering wheel, I saw a movement in the water, a dark body undulation in the spangled water. I whipped my head back to look at it, but it was gone.

The dotted lines blurred. I put my hands together and touched my belly.

He didn't say anything more, just kept his eyes on the road, watching for deer that were known to float out suddenly on the road.

. . .

Several weeks later, Leslie invited me to lunch. I bought a new outfit: I wanted to look sharp. I stood on our mildewed bathroom tiles as the babysitter tried to keep the kids from pulling out all the toys on the mushroom-colored carpet, putting on the silk pants and top and swiping on grey eye shadow, hoping to transform myself from the lake-town girl into someone more sophisticated. I wasn't sure my credit union plastic could accomplish this.

When I arrived at the riverside restaurant, waiters in black swooped from table to table. Leslie was in expensive jeans and a tissue-thin cotton top. As I sat down, I felt lumpish and overdressed.

"You look so nice!" she said. "I should have dressed up."

I mumbled something, thinking *Overdressing: the character flaw of the lower classes.*

We ordered: I had a loutish cheeseburger; Leslie had chicken salad. We watched an osprey through the window as it rose from a cottonwood and dove down into the Clark Fork River, fastened its talons on a rainbow trout, then rose, the fish wriggling in its grasp. The restaurant exploded in applause.

"Supposedly the talons have barbed hooks," I said. "To keep the fish from slipping out of their clutches."

"Amazing," Leslie said. "You know so much about the local fauna."

"I guess," I shrugged, "that's because I am local."

Leslie suggested the champagne. Veuve Clicquot. When the waiter brought the narrow sweating flutes, she held up her glass. "Let's toast to the lake."

"You're buying the cabin?" My heart leaped. We can finish the basement! Recarpet the living room! I tried to take a breath. *Cool. Cool as champagne,* I told myself.

"Damn right," Leslie said. "Peeling paint, bad deck, and all." She smiled at all of this. "Let's drink to it, Anna!"

Ching, ching went the glasses.

The champagne was light, dry, exquisite. "Amazing!" I said. My face felt like a two-by-four. Why? I was making a pile of money. Leslie, whom I so admired, was my new friend. What was wrong with me? I studied Leslie: her perfect teeth, the light brown of her eyes, and willed myself to be happy. "Leslie, that is great news!"

"We swam nude off the dock. We hung out on the deck, long after the sun went down. I have to tell you, Anna, it was the best time the two of us have had in years." She set down her glass and touched my arm. "It hasn't been easy for us."

"I'm sorry," I said. "Marriage isn't easy, is it? My husband drives me crazy. How long have you been married?"

"Ten years, two kids, two medical degrees, one affair," she set down her glass. "I guess we're some kind of statistic."

"Fifteen years, one miscarriage, two kids. That's me." I circled the rim of my glass with my pointer finger.

Leslie sipped her glass and looked at me. "But I believe in new beginnings, how 'bout you? I mean, what are you going to do, just throw in the towel? I think this will be a great thing for us. We need some calm. We need time together, all of us. A new start. Do you know what I mean?" Leslie set down her glass and looked at me. "A brand-new, shiny start?"

"I'm all about new beginnings," I said and held my glass up again.

Ching, ching went the glasses, and with that, a blossoming, and we drank until our babysitters were calling us.

. . .

Several months after the sale, Leslie invited Ben and me for a weekend at the cabin, without the kids. That afternoon, as we packed in our bedroom, I pulled on a new pair of slim pants and a linen tunic, Ben, who rarely noticed anything, said, "Are those new?"

I blushed. "Well, yes."

"You bought new clothes for this weekend?" Ben said. "Isn't this kind of weird—going for a weekend in your old house with this client?"

"It's okay, Ben." The old house was a skin I had shed and it didn't bother me to see it again. "It's nice to see the old place fixed up. I don't hang onto the past." To Ben my past was like one of the hundreds of novels he'd read, a contemporary version of the old marriage plot, only this one set in a shabby, red-shingled house where the character realizes her plight in a charming denouement and moves up by marrying the English professor.

"Why are you dressing up for these people?" Ben came up behind me, put his arms around my waist and turned me around to look at him in his flannel shirt and scruffy jeans. "Are you in love with Marty and Leslie Broadbent?"

"Of course not!" I said to the sting of his words. "I just want to look good, is that such a crime?" I kissed him on his stubbly lips. *The mustache again,* I thought. Sigh.

"What do you see?" he said. He turned me toward the mirror. I looked at myself. There I was: medium height, short brown hair, zaftig, freckled, not the slim, sleek version of myself with no past, no complications, just laughing, turning away from the camera just so.

"A mom. Overweight. Tries too hard," I said.

"Anna!"

"Well, that's what I see."

"Try harder, babe. There's a lot more there," he came up behind me, kissing my neck, my shoulders, his hands cupping my breasts. "A lot more there."

. . .

The lake place was transformed. The outside repainted, the yard landscaped with boxed plantings of wheatgrass, lavender, and native geraniums. The deck had been rebuilt and refurnished with teak deck furniture, and inside, there were yards of white carpeting. Jealousy wasn't the color green—it was the deep-red leather armchair that made my heart hurt. I felt all the bad dreams of my childhood had been rescripted by Pottery Barn. Then Leslie took us upstairs. "I'm going to put you up in the guest room. I hope it's okay. Bathroom's across the hall."

The room was a deep apricot, with a pastel-colored quilt on the bed and an original painting by a local artist of wild horses and naked women. Simple, lovely. A bouquet of wheat stood by the bed.

It was the same room where Gladys had woken up screaming one night and I'd run in from across the hall only to meet Harold at the doorway, his face ashen. "I don't know, I don't know," he said. His hands were shaking, tears coursed his cheeks. "She just woke up, saying her lady parts are falling out. Talk to her, please, Anna? I don't know what to do."

In the bed, Gladys had her arms wrapped around her legs, and she was crying as she rocked, rolling her white pin-curled head from side to side. The sight of Gladys—sturdy, invincible, implacable Gladys—crying was like seeing the sun go black. I had to steady my voice.

I wanted to run out the door, down the highway. I wanted the sweet sound of gravel crunching under my feet. I turned and walked out of the room, down the stairs and through the dark kitchen, past the counters that Gladys had wiped down each night, past the dishes washed and drying in the dish rack, the coffeepot waiting for its morning brew, the broom hung on its hook and the dustpan next to it and the shoe scraper next to the door, waiting for the dirt of each shoe that came into the house, the kitchen floor waxed and gleaming, and on top of that order—the helpless sound of Gladys's voice. I put my hand on the round brass knob of the back door and was about to turn it, when she cried out, *"Anna!"*

I put my hand on my stomach and waited. In two months, I would deliver a child.

"Anna!"

I ran back up the stairs. I held her. Harold came out of the bathroom and looked at me. I looked at him. "She has to go to the hospital," I said. "Now, Harold."

I wrapped her in a blanket. Harold carried her downstairs and into the backseat of the Oldsmobile, and I drove her to the emergency room. As I drove the dark highway, watching for deer, Gladys moaning in the seat behind me, he prayed in the seat, out loud, *Dear God, take me, take anyone, but not Gladys,* until we reached the St. James Hospital in Polson, where they performed emergency surgery. A burst ovarian cyst, the surgeon told me, painful, but easy to fix. A month and a half later, Gladys was back in her garden, spading up the weeds between her gladiolas and delphiniums.

That night changed everything between the three of us. Harold took me aside and told me that I had earned his "purple heart" in courage. Gladys and I, who had had a strained but polite relationship, relaxed with one another. I learned to play her card games—Hearts, Canasta, Double Solitaire—while she recovered in bed, the two of us laying out the cards decorated with orioles on the bumped quilt. She learned to tolerate my rock 'n' roll. I ate the custards and rice puddings she made for

me. And when we were back at the St. James Hospital, two
months later, as I was delivering the baby, it was Gladys who
came with me, who helped me through labor, holding my hand,
tears rolling down her cheeks, then running for the nurse to
tell them to give me an epidural, Gladys who told me to push
when it was time, Gladys who kept the nurses from bringing
me the baby so I wouldn't become attached, who made the
arrangements with the adoptive parents, who stayed with me
during the days my milk dried up and weathered my storms
of tears, until several months later, after countless suppers and
movie nights and games of Double Solitaire in the red house by
the lake, she said, "Anna, you're a young woman, it's time for you
to get up and out of this house and get on with your life."

"Anna?" It was Leslie. "Everything okay?" She peered closely
at my face.

I drank oak-barreled, granitic Malbec with just a hint of
raspberries.

Ben was next to me, pounding down locally brewed IPA,
followed by a shot of whiskey.

The men circled around the living room, Leslie and I
wandered the house, admiring things, Leslie laughing. "I think
they're getting along, don't you?"

The four of us lounged on the deck chairs, eating sushi and
salmon burgers and drinking wine and a microbrew called the
Flathead Lake Monster—an IPA advertised to "come up out of
nowhere and getcha." As we talked about schools and mutual
friends, I found myself imagining Leslie wandering around
this house: looking out the window at the gardens replete with
hundreds of daffodils, hyacinths, crocuses, lying in the living
room with the gas fire breathing its blue-hued tongues of flame,
reading *Anna Karenina* for the third time, her hand trailing off
the white sofa, padding barefoot (it was a house where everyone
took off shoes) to her large bed underneath a skylight that

revealed a canopy of ponderosa pines with large spiky arms that seemed to hold up the sky.

When the sun was headed toward the bare hills on the western horizon, Marty said, "Let's go for a boat ride. C'mon, everyone. Sunset booze cruise!"

Leslie packed drinks and the goat cheese and roasted red peppers and red wine, beer, and Scotch in the picnic basket. Marty was at the wheel, his curly hair flying back, his brown arm resting on the side of the boat, Leslie on the seat next to him, and Ben and I in the back of the boat as we sped out from the dock, the shoreline growing more and more distant, my heart bouncing as the boat hit the chop. It was a warm night and the lake was beautiful: there were billowy sails of boats by Dayton Bay, motorboats plowing triangles in the water, jet skis, like bees, buzzing the bays, and everywhere white diamonds against the blue water.

We sped across the lake to the northeast corner of the lake, cruising to Bigfork, then directly east. Marty, I could see, had a plan.

Leslie shouted, "He wants to show you the trophy homes."

After we covered acres of water, the breeze tangling my head, Ben's hand on mine, Marty slowed as we reached the shore.

"Take a look at these!" he shouted. "Try these on for size. This one—"

We cruised by a house shaped like a bird.

"This is the Osprey Nest. It was designed by a Polson architect. It is made of cedar and steel beams and is approachable only by foot. It is an osprey-watching cabin."

Next up was a giant twenty-six-bedroom log home, with a bronze statue of an elk, pots of red geraniums, and a large sauna in the back. "That belongs to one of the Endicotts. One of six places. They come every two years." Marty smiled back at us. "Amazing, isn't it?"

Ben pointed to a small dot along the western shore, barely visible in the dusk. "See that island?" Ben shouted. "I had to sign a nondisclosure agreement not to tell about the shooting range or the trophies of endangered species from Mongolia, South Africa, and South America. So here I am," Ben put his hand behind his head, grinning. "Disclosing."

"Fuck ya," Marty said.

"Go for it, Ben!" I stood up, my sundress sailing out behind me. "Tell 'em about the tree!"

"And you know what was up in the highest tree on that island?"

"What?" Marty shouted.

"A heart carved into the trunk. CP + FH. It had probably been there one hundred years. And they cut the tree down."

"They're assholes." Leslie turned to shout back at Ben. "We're all assholes. Think of that monster looking up at us, thinking, those assholes in their toy boats, I'd just like them to go the fuck away." Then she turned around, closed her eyes, and tilted her face up into the wind.

Marty smiled and cut the motor to cruising speed. Leslie poured us tumblers of scotch as we sat back to watch the sun glow on the Mission Mountains to the east, the rounded grassy hills of the Salish Mountains to the west. For a minute, everyone was quiet, as a kaleidoscope of oranges, pinks, and purples sank from the sky to the mountains, the water slurping the sides of the boat.

Marty broke the silence by pointing out some more places: de Soto's place, 16,000 square feet, a large clapboard home with sweeping lawns and an empty swimming pool. And a new place, supposedly built by a Scottish baron, with a turret and a shake roof that looked like it had been laid out by a drunk. "They're so rich they haven't even been here yet."

This seemed hilarious to all of us, and on the strength of that, Leslie poured another round of drinks.

Water flickered, light, dark, light, dark. It was one of those moments in your life when everything seemed to converge: the rocking, the red sky, the summer evening, the four of us, together in the boat as the sun was sinking. "This is perfect," I sighed.

"Let's make it more perfect." Marty revved the engine. My eyes couldn't seem to leave his arms, the sure competent way they held the wheel, his muscles flexing as he turned the wheel, the water fanning out to the side of the boat, all of us clapping.

Leslie, Ben, and I fell back in our seats, laughing.

"Marty!" Leslie cried.

"Marty, are you sure this is safe?" Ben said. "It's dark. You sure you know where you're going?"

"Hey, I got radar."

Ben cut his eyes at me, dark slivers in the dusk.

"Ah, Ben," I said. "Relax. It's Marty. He's done this a hundred times, haven't you, Marty? Right, Marty?"

"A hundred times two," Marty looked back at us. "We call it night running."

Marty turned in a complete circle again, straightened out the boat, and floored it. The water glistened, oil-like, the cabin lights on shore a constellation we headed toward as we sped through the silky darkness, like some kind of water gods on the wave-chopped lake, water like wings beside us, coating us in spray as if it could wash me clean, wash away that night I lay with the Kootenai boy—his dark hair falling around me, his eyes two bright coals, the boy I loved.

"Anna," Marty said.

He shouted something, but it was lost on the wind.

I climbed over the seat to hear what he had to say. I drew up alongside him. He turned to tell me that the 7,000-square-foot brick home with wine cellar and pool room on the shore belonged to the owner of one of America's largest computer companies. Our faces were inches from each other. I saw myself in his eyes—a cheap little Montana girl—and I kissed him and he kissed me back, a kiss so deep I could feel it to my toes.

Something hit the boat. Slowly, it seems, the boat jerked, rose up in the air—I remembered thinking it looked like it was holding its nose up—then it flopped down and slid forward. As it slid forward, the four of us fell back against each other, the picnic basket opening and goat cheese flying, a wine bottle spilled, glasses and paddles tumbled to the back of the boat accompanied by an ear-splitting screeching noise. I looked over and saw the dark outline of a picnic table. How could a picnic table be out in the lake? Then the outline of bushes. A tree. I looked down. We were sliding up a slab of rock, the fiberglass scraping and squealing, all of us shouting. Then it stopped. We went quiet. Our boat had ridden up the slab of rock from the lake to the beach and in front of us was a sign, the white script barely visible in the dark: *Welcome to Wayfarers State Park!*

"You fucker," Ben shouted to Marty. "You goddamn fucking idiot. You could have killed us, driving in the dark like that."

I remember thinking, incongruously, that that was no way to thank your host.

"Fuck," Leslie was laughing uproariously. "Fuck. I'm covered with sundried tomatoes."

She was: her slim tanned body speckled with wrinkled tomatoes, like red leeches.

I leaned over and kissed her smack on the lips. Then I laughed so hard that it turned into crying. I was drenched. I was shaking. My ears roared. I heard, in the distance a sound like a tail slapping the water.

Then like a cartoon in reverse, the boat, with all of us in it, slid slowly backward, past the picnic table and the metal grill for cooking hot dogs, and the signs saying "No overnight camping," and the metal box for the day-use fees, the fiberglass shell shrieking and scraping until the boat plopped back into the water.

. . .

The funny thing? After Ben and I divorced, I upped my game over the next few years, buying and selling massive log homes that crouched like lions in the mountains and lakefronts of Montana, whispering the language of offer and counteroffer, rustic and repurposed, until I had the money to buy the lake place back. I knocked it down and replaced it with a Cape Codder with sweet dormer windows. I kept the landscaping, the planters filled with native plantings I now knew the names of: verbena, lupine, dogwood. Sometimes in my bedroom, where I hear my children playing video games below, I lie on my queen-size Tempur-Pedic and look up through the skylight that frames the ponderosa branches against the blue sky, and watch their wide spiky fingers that wave in the wind, and the sight of this world, contained, fills my heart with the word: *wild.*

THE BLUE EGG

The older woman, the photo researcher who'd hiked across the Continental Divide six times, was fired first. As she walked out of the conference room of Fritz Newspapers, she shrugged her shoulders and said, "I guess I'm retired." The second was the blonde who looked like an aging flapper. When she limped out the door, she sniffed, and said to Madeline, "These people would fuck their grandmothers if the company said to."

Madeline was a weeper. Worse yet, she was a hiccupping, apologetic weeper. As her manager held her arm and helped her walk the hallway to her office, she cried and said, "I'm sorry, I'm so, so sorry."

"Why are *you* apologizing?" he said. "You should be mad at *us*."

This only made her cry harder. Madeline imagined herself going out in a blaze: telling the publisher of Fritz Newspapers what an idiot he was, a bean counter who measured people and news in a dim tally of spreadsheets and columns, a language more real to him than the human tragedies churning off the press in the warehouse below. The publisher liked to reward the employee of the month not with a restaurant gift card or a free parking space, something actually useful—but instead, with something that was free—with a carton of poop-speckled eggs from his chicken coop.

The manager frowned with concern. "Things have a way of working out," he said.

"Not for me they don't." Madeline hiccupped. "For me, things have a way of crashing and burning."

"God shuts a door and opens a window," he cooed, handing her an empty box labeled with the Fritz Newspaper logo: Your Story is Our Story.

"God slammed my head right into the fucking patio door." Madeline glared at him.

"You're angry," The manager said softly. He stood, hands dangling, studying his shoes, polished to a high gloss. "Of course, you're angry."

Identify the employees' emotions, she thought. Surely he'd learned that at some management workshop. *Comfort, don't engage. Use soothing tones. And keep them moving, at all times, toward the exit.*

When they reached her office, Madeline burst into a fresh round of tears at the sight of her daughter's third-grade drawing taped to her office wall. There was Tara, as Hannah Montana, Leo, her son, as Little Richard, the two of them holding guitars, smudges of brown marker freckling their ovoid faces. Next to it, the snapshot of the family farm in Malta, the falling-down barn, the clapboard farmhouse, the fields in a distance, where, as a child she stood, chin high to the wheat, and watched the heavy-headed plants wave in the wind, like water with its long and languorous currents.

Right now her life looked pretty much like that old barn: the shingles, helter skelter, barely covering the rafters, the boards clinging on the frame by rusted nails.

. . .

What she remembered most about that day was the publisher's right arm. Slender, hairless, and deeply tanned—despite the fact it was March in Montana. Brad placed his arm on the table and spread his fingers on the polished wood, the perfect half-moon cuticles disappearing as he curled his fingers into his palm. The Rolex knock-off, the little hand on the eleven, the big hand on the fifty, the nervous second hand. Tick. Tick.

He turned his head to her, tapped his fist, once, twice, on the long table milled from an old-growth Douglas fir and given to Fritz Newspapers to settle an overdue account.

Words floated out from his mouth: She was going to be let go. She was the one he hated to tell most, but she was going to be let go. She had done so much, written so many great stories, her articles so interesting, so timely, so punchy.

Punchy? She thought. *Jesus Christ, you're firing me and you're telling me my articles are punchy?*

Next to him was the human resources man, with his sallow face and long fingers that made little flourishes in the air as he spoke—the gestures he'd made two months ago during her performance enhancement when he told her she needed to write three feature stories a week and not piss off the advertisers. It was simply, he said, a matter of organization. He understood this because, in his own life, he had to learn when there was cake at office birthday parties, he had to think ahead to bring forks and paper plates.

Writing a feature story, she pointed out, was a bit different than office birthday parties.

Of course it is, he said. Of course it is.

Her lack of organization, she realized, had more to do with the fact that in a year her husband had had a heart attack, her daughter, a tonsillectomy, her son, a broken arm. The other women being fired that morning had similar problems with organization. The older woman, a photo researcher, was due to retire. The blonde receptionist was a week away from hip surgery.

Fritz Newspapers: Our employees are our greatest natural resource.

She remembered reading this on the company website, under the employee pictures: a smiling woman on the telephone headset, a cheerful black man operating a printing press. Dinosaurs, she would think later, as the company stock plummeted to fifty cents a share, dinosaurs, all of us, watching the meteors hurl toward Earth and saying, "We are the dinosaurs! We are number one!"

But that morning as the human resources man said something about her cobra, she simply stared at him.

"Come again?" she said. The only COBRA she could comprehend was the serpentine kind.

He started to go into the thirty days this and thirty days that, when Brad's tanned arm came down and touched the hand of the human resources man. "I don't think that she can hear this right now."

The man went silent and sat up straight as a second hand.

Her throat tightened. She was about to give Brad points for his humanity, when he glanced at his watch and paused.

He looked around the table.

"Oh, my gosh," He said. He jumped to his feet, his chair falling back against the wall with a thump. "I have Rotary."

. . .

Rage came later. She ranted at lunches bought by sympathetic friends. She refused to sign her termination agreement, enjoying the panicky calls from the human resources man, polite, then vaguely threatening. She tried to enjoy this new time with her children who'd wondered why she'd suddenly arrived home two weeks ago, in the middle of the day, with boxes of books and files, and pictures they'd drawn in her office. She shouted from soccer sidelines until her son asked her not to be so loud. She baked elaborate dinners, but after a meal of Chicken Marbella and twice-baked potatoes and arugula salad, her daughter said, "Mom? Can we ever have tacos again?"

At cocktail hour, she told her husband about the stories she'd broken: stories on the EPA violations at the Helena cement plant, the pilot Cromwell Dixon, who crossed the Continental Divide in a 1916 airplane that was nothing but lathe and canvas, then died two days later at a Spokane county fair. Every outrage, every fiery death: hers.

As her rants grew louder, her husband's eyes grew duller. The week she told him the CEO of Fritz Enterprises got a 1.6 million-dollar raise the week she was fired, he handed her a glass of wine and said, gently, "Move on, Madeline."

A month later, he wasn't so gentle. "Jesus," he said as she was beginning to wind up at cocktail hour. "Jesus," he said. "I can't listen to this anymore."

She cried and told him he was an asshole, but she knew he was right.

Move on, her friends said at lunches where they now split the tab. Don't go up against a company that buys its ink by the gallons. She contacted a lawyer about an unfair dismissal lawsuit, only to find Fritz Enterprises had engaged most of the law firms in town, so it was a conflict of interest for them to represent her. The one lawyer who could, said, Madeline, my best professional advice to you is that these lawsuits are expensive, rarely successful, and drag on forever. In short, he said, "Move on."

She made an honest effort. She wanted to rediscover that bright, hopeful personality that had taken her from the ranch girl with a braid down her back to a professional reporter with clothing that bore men's names. That drive that propelled her from the girl that bumped along country roads on school buses to speech tournaments, who killed a chicken each week for Sunday dinner to this new self who devoured espressos and Sunday *New York Times*. She'd rebooted her life once based on the idea that hard work, education, and enthusiasm equaled success.

Now, at fifty, what did she have? Just a mule-like determination. And rage. Deep, glorious, rose-red, burning, boring rage.

Each morning she drank a swamp-like mixture of bananas, spinach, lettuce, cauliflower, kale, romaine, and zucchini and tried not to gag. She figured if she was strong enough not to throw up, well, that was something.

She took a temporary job, taking care of an older woman, who lived in a single-wide on the family ranch. As she drove back and forth from Helena to Jefferson City, winding through the deep rock canyons of the Elkhorn Mountains, she began singing along with a CD a friend had given her, Natasha Bedingfield's "I am unwritten, Can't read my mind, I'm undefined."

The woman had dementia and seemed to think that Madeline was her only daughter, a barrel racer on the rodeo circuit. Each time Madeline walked in to cook breakfast and lay out the woman's medications, she cried out, "Hang up your boots, Ruth! For God's sake, they'll scratch the floor wax." Madeline didn't have the heart to point out that she wasn't Ruth—that her daughter was the one who's left her stuck here in this trailer with no-wax linoleum.

When Madeline set down a breakfast of bacon, eggs, and toast in front of her, the woman looked Madeline up and down and said, "Ruth, you look like shit. Get out there, get yourself a new man."

"I got fired," Madeline said.

"You gotta fix that," the woman said. She picked up a piece of bacon, studied it. "You need to crisp 'em up, Ruthie. Crisp 'em up."

"What do you mean, 'crisp 'em up'?"

"Kick 'em in the balls, that's what I mean," the woman said through the mash of egg and bacon in her mouth. "One whack, sister, they're out of commission."

"I thought you were talking about bacon."

"Of course." The woman looked at her, indignant. "Of course I am."

. . .

Ancona, Barred Plymouth Rock, Rhode Island Red, Single Comb Brown Leghorn, Speckled Sussex. At the heart of Brad

Kyle, accountant, and now CEO, with his tanning bed tan and fake Rolex, was an eastern Montana farm boy in love with his chickens. Brad handed out eggs at the weekly meetings he called "stand-ups"—because to sit down was to encourage lingering. The human resources man handed out raffle tickets and the winner won a dozen eggs from Brad's prodigious layers. Blue eggs, brown eggs, white with real tufts of feathers and shit. Madeline was ashamed of how much she wanted to win one of these stupid boxes of eggs, but her number was never picked. Brad, proud of his bounty, handed out the cardboard cartons as if they were a sign of his virility. And, according to rumor, there were more than just hens in his life. There were stories about the young blonde secretaries, and a second family tucked away somewhere in Idaho. His nickname around the company was "Larry," after the *Hustler* publisher.

. . .

Who was it said revenge is a dish best served cold?

. . .

She found his house easily enough. It was perched in the hills east of town. A large suburban box for his wife and five kids with a trampoline and snowmobiles baking in the sun—the kind of house her daughter would love with its multitude of bathrooms and brand new everything instead of the old fixer-uppers Madeline tended to buy that stayed old and didn't get fixed up but were some expression of the life she hoped to have with a gracious staircase and large living room and wisteria draping the front porch.

The only exception to its suburban blankness was the chicken operation, tucked in a fenced-in coop in the side yard near the driveway, bobbing heads, yellow legs, horny scratching feet.

And it was a real chicken coop. The kind her grandma would have. Not one of playhouse chicken coops for the well-heeled, in-town farmer so they could fancy themselves living off the land on eggs that cost twelve dollars apiece, once you figured in the feed, coop, heat lamps, fencing, and vet, and the cost of the executioner—because, of course, no one could bear to kill their own chickens. It didn't have little sashed windows and brightly colored stairsteps with a drawstring door where the children could sweetly herd the chickens to bed and then pull down the door while everyone's pastoral fantasy could sleep again for another night.

This was a farm boy's coop: plywood, two-by-fours, chicken wire, and a sheet metal roof.

She had to give Brad Kyle Montana points for style.

She pulled her beat-up Subaru into the driveway.

She dialed his number.

As the phone rang, she looked as his house, baking in the July sun, the windows reflecting back the blue sky, the flat sage-covered hills, waiting, as she was, to watch a body cross the living room to pick up the phone. Where was everyone? She looked at the other houses, so many square boxes perched on the Scratchgravel Hills, large Suburbans and trailered snowmobiles looming in the driveways. This was the measure of success: a home with nobody home. Playthings with nobody playing. A kitchen where nobody cooked. It was as if, she thought, we have become a nation of people who measure success by the spaces we build and do not occupy.

And why wasn't she home? What were her kids doing this very moment? Tara, most likely, was in the basement, watching reruns of Hannah Montana. Leo was playing Lego Star Wars on her computer where she should be editing that house painter's novel she'd just taken on for extra money.

Honestly. What was she doing? She was a fifty-year-old woman with a husband, two children, advanced degrees and here she was, sitting in the driveway of her former boss's house, plotting revenge on his chickens?

"You have reached the Kyle residence," said Brad's voice on the answering machine. "Oldsters Brad and Tami here, and Austin, Audrey, Ashley, Aiden, and Amy. We're out having fun! You know the old drill—leave your message at the—*beeep!*"

. . .

She shut off the car. She'd act like a housekeeper, water the lawn, a few flowers, then go over to the hen house as if she were feeding the chickens.

She put the hose on the sick-looking geraniums on the side yard. She spread a few rainbow-colored arcs of water across the lawn.

As she walked to the coop, Madeline could see the hens moving in slow circles, feeding on the grasshoppers whirring the air. The leghorn's obscene red wattles wiggled. The Speckled Sussex was off by herself, in a corner, cross-hatching the dirt. She was a black and white speckled bird with finely shaped head, rounded chest, and long, yellow legs. The bird seemed to be aware of Madeline's gaze, and drew its head back and gazed right back at her before it went back to tining the dirt in front of it. When the Barred Plymouth Rock eased up next to the Speckled Sussex, she spread her wings and flew at Plymouth Rock in a fury and the two hens' guttural cries wobbled the air. Speckled Sussex held her corner. Plymouth Rock daintily crossed the cage to the opposite side.

Speckled Sussex was the one.

Let Brad come home and see what it was to have something die in the midst of an ordinary day. She pictured his smooth face, horrified, at the sight of the Speckled Sussex, limp on the floor of the coop.

Madeline lifted the latch. The hens flapped their wings and cackled, running in circles.

Speckled Sussex backed into the corner. Madeline walked across the straw and stood over her. The hen looked up at Madeline as if for a cue, eyes blinking, flat, the bumpy lids extending then retracting over its eyes.

I know things, she said to Speckled Sussex. *I may be old but I know things.*

She put her hand on the neck of the Speckled Sussex and held it, firmly in the dirt.

The neck, so spindly under that fluff of feathers.

She looked around, found a small stick. She drew the stick slowly back and forth in front of the chicken. *Don't be afraid, little chicken. It's just me, Madeline, hypnotizing you.* The hen's head followed the stick, as she drew it, back and forth, back and forth in the dirt.

The air thickened, the clucking of the other chickens seemed to come from a great distance.

You'd die for the cause, wouldn't you?

Back and forth, back and forth. Madeline withdrew her hand from the chicken's neck. The hen's head continued to move as if it were still following her stick.

She picked up the hen and held it, its feathers soft against her stomach, its head still swaying from side to side. Madeline put her hands around the hen's neck.

Just one twist and that would be it. One hand turns one way; one hand, the other. The *snap.*

The other hens, the red hen, the white hen, the salt-and-pepper hen circled around her, their heads jerking, their strange depthless eyes focused on her. In the silence, she could hear grasshoppers rasp, cars whine on the highway. Those eyes, opening and shutting, opening and shutting, dull and timeless as the story of the two cocks fighting to the death that inspired the Greek Army to defeat the Persians.

She put her hands around the hen's neck and imagined the dry crack of the bones and that other sound, the click of wood on wood as the door of the conference room shut behind her. In the flat reptilian stare of the Speckled Sussex, the encoded knowledge, that she would kill the chicken, and eat it, and that was the way of things, and somehow, this hen was patiently submitting to this ancient fate.

She put her hands in her lap. The chicken stood on her legs, blinking, then laid its head along Madeline's neck.

Madeline stroked the hen's long shiny feathers.

Her face was wet.

She thought she heard some neighbors calling.

She couldn't get up.

The other hens roosted in the straw around her.

She looked down at her lap. There was a blue egg in it.

. . .

She had some explaining to do. The neighbor was shouting, lady, your lights are on! Her car battery was dead. Brad came home and she had to explain why she was parked at his house and why she had to use his phone to call her husband for a ride home. At least it was worth seeing Brad's discomfort at the sight of her in his large beige-carpeted house. "How are you getting along?" he'd asked. "Oh, just great, Brad!" she said to him as he stood, next to his wife, who smiled woodenly, their backs against yards of shining, white counters.

That night, after her kids were fed and her husband had gone upstairs after she'd explained for the fifth time why she'd been in a chicken coop at her ex-boss's house, she sat on the front porch, perfumed by wisteria, the sweet smell of longing. As she watched the sky deepen to topaz, she remembered the egg: how warm it was, how unexpected, how delicate yet solid the weight of it felt in her hand as she picked it up from her lap and how she knew the beginning of everything was contained in that cerulean color of blue.

ANACONDA

Mary had to get away from the pool. The water teemed with screaming children, cooing couples, babies haloed in bright yellow inner tubes, floating parent to parent, and the soakers—bald men with flushed red pates and women with round, meaty thighs: a writhing, shouting, echoing, jiggling, sweating mass of humanity. She ducked into the hallway past the game room, where boys crowded around a play rifle, hunting video deer.

The lobby, thank God, was quiet. It was decorated in Montana chic: miles of buff-colored shag, vague watercolors of sunsets over mountains, and animal trophies that were anything but vague: a wolf with its mouth frozen mid-howl; a wolverine, its mouth shellacked into a permanent, pointy-toothed snarl.

She flipped open her phone, dialed her son. Mom, she whispered after the beep. Just checking in.

The wolf's mouth frozen in a howl. *That's a metaphor,* she was thinking.

Stop it, she told herself. *You're here to get away. Stop that.* She got up to get a magazine at the gift shop. She was at the register with *O,* studying the headline: "Start a New Year! A New You!" when Rachel walked in.

Rachel! She cried.

The two of them embraced, delighted at this unlikely meeting at a hot springs resort in February. Rachel owned a bakery in Helena, on the other side of the Continental Divide, making whole-wheat loaves shaped like stepping stones, then moving on in the '90s to baguettes.

You're buying *that?* Rachel pointed to the magazine.

You caught me, Mary blushed. I'm not in the mood for *The Nation.* It's been a long winter.

Tell me about it, Rachel said.

Mary paid up and the two of them walked into the lobby, where, under the velvet lips of a trophy moose, they hugged.

Let me look at you, Rachel said. You look tired. Their friendship blossomed in a Yellowstone County jail where they'd been incarcerated in 1979 for chaining themselves to the fence of the Western States Coal Plant. They'd stayed up all night talking about why they'd come back to Montana from eastern schools, something about mountains and family and unrequited love, until the red-haired prostitute snarled, we're so happy you're having your little heart-to-heart, but why dontcha shut up so the rest of us can sleep? You know, Rachel snapped, why don't *you* shut up. The woman blinked at her, but said nothing else. Mary admired Rachel's ability to say the thing that just needed saying.

I'm beat, Mary said.

The two had seen each other over the years at Mary's occasional openings, where she sold the collages made from baby bracelets, daguerreotypes, and pieces from 1960s board games like Monopoly and Sorry! At their children's traveling soccer games or speech meets, they sought each other out on the sidelines or bleachers, where they compared schools, children (Rachel's two daughters, Mary's son), marriages (each slyly thinking hers was the better one), and whose hair greyed the most (Rachel's; Mary, as her grandmother said, "dipped" hers).

Rachel peered around Mary, as if she were hiding something. Where's your family?

In the outdoor pool, Mary said. I can't take the cold.

Or the noise, Rachel said, fingering her braid.

They nodded.

Simpatico, Mary thought. They were always like this—

picking up the threads of their friendship as if they'd just seen each other the day before.

They sat in overstuffed chairs by the fire watching blue flame embrace the artificial logs. Above them was an elk, a sixteen-pointer, its black nose stiff. There was something divine about meeting up with Rachel with her bright eyes and sharp way of pulling the world into focus, even in this carpeted lobby with its glass-eyed animals.

You've heard about me? Rachel's round glasses fogged. This year's been a train wreck. She described the blankness in her mother's eyes, her face empty as a potato. She described the moment when her mother turned to her and said, Rachel, you were always such a nasty little girl. Rachel turned to Mary, her eyes two bright black beads. Then you know the fuck of it all? She gripped the wide arms of the chair, her fingers whitening.

What? Mary said.

She died, Rachel said. Just like that. No I am sorry, please forgive me. No I've always admired you. Just—Rachel snapped her fingers—*gone.*

Shit, Mary said. You did everything for her. She was thinking there must be a lesson in this story, a lesson about what to let go of, what to hold on to.

No lesson. Rachel shook her head. Her laugh was a short, painful bark. She was telling Mary how in the end, she thought she hadn't done enough. She'd been called in as the relief sister, in the last hour, after the other two had thrown up their hands, exhausted. She hadn't forgiven her mother the bitter years between them, the blade of her mother's judgment about her, with her leftwing politics, loudmouth demonstrations, wild hair and unshaved legs. Particularly, Rachel said to Mary, the unshaved legs! I think she could have forgiven everything else.

Rachel sighed. I suppose we want our mothers to love us even more for our rebellion.

Mary pulled up the zipper on her jacket, although it was nearly seventy-five degrees in the hotel lobby. She scooted down into the chair. She was cold, always cold. *I had a feeling,* she said. She told Rachel how she was teaching part-time at the Bitterroot Montessori school, teaching five-year-olds finger-painting of all things—when her son called. On the phone, she could hear sounds in the background, panting, scraping sounds. Butt-dialing, everyone said, and laughed. But he didn't answer when she called him back. *I had a feeling,* she said. She ran home, tearing through the streets of Hamilton, thundering down the rickety stairs to the basement where she found him standing on a chair, a rope around his neck. Her voice broke in two.

Oh Jesus, Rachel said. Jesus, Mary, Mother of God.

It's okay. Mary said. It's okay now. *It was a girl.* She wrapped her arms around herself. We're seeing doctors. He's on meds. She could feel her voice as it filled the front of her head, pressing against her nose, hurting, and then settling again at the thin words: *It was a girl.*

Neither one could remember who suggested it or why but suddenly they had to move. They piled into Rachel's Subaru, Rachel at the wheel, Mary in the passenger seat, the two of them moving away from the shingled resort with its green waterslide slithering like an overgrown serpent into the outside pool, past the petting zoo of overweight goats and the llama with Bette Davis eyes.

I feel like we're running away, Mary said.

Because we are, Rachel said. We most definitely are.

As Rachel drove Highway 84, a snow-swept grey road between two barbed wire fences, a straight line in a landscape of straight lines and square acres, dominated by a brick smokestack, she talked about her sisters. She talked about how they scooped up the china, crystal, jewelry, even rolling up the oriental carpets after the funeral. Unbelievable, she said. The body wasn't cold in the ground. But, she turned her head and looked at Mary. Right before Mother died, she lay back, closed her eyes, and suddenly, there is that strange quiet, after the noise of the heart monitor and ventilator, where, I swear to God, it was her soul leaving her body.

Snow tires snicked along the snow-packed road beneath them.

Maybe that's what death is, Rachel said. Just a strange quiet.

Maybe, Mary said. She wondered where her son was now. She wondered if her husband had remembered to give him his pills. She groped in her purse for her cell phone. Shit, she said. Shit, shit, shit.

What is it? Rachel turned to her.

My cell phone, Mary said. It must have slipped out of my pocket in the lobby. I should go back, Rachel. I can't lose my phone. I can't lose contact.

He'll be fine, Rachel said. She patted Mary's leg. He's with your husband, right?

Mary had to make herself breathe. Right, she said. You're right. He's fine. He's with my husband. What a luxury those words—he's fine—tossed off in how many conversations. Each measured word a stitch holding her together.

I shouldn't have said that about my sisters, Rachel said.

You're my friend, Mary said. We have to say that stuff. We'd go crazy if we didn't. What she wanted to say to Rachel was this: after clattering down the steps, Mary stood before the basement door, resting her hand on the doorknob, when before her eyes rose an image of her son's face as she had seen it on the sonogram: his eyes closed, his face round and perfect, the face of an angel.

When my mother died, you know, Rachel said, I realized that I am now the end of the line. There's no one protecting me. My dad's dead. My sisters are assholes. It's sobering. I haven't been able to talk like this all winter, Mary. All year. Maybe many years.

. . .

You know when your kid tries to kill himself, it's like someone puts you in a box, Mary said. You put yourself in a box. You and your husband. You and your kid. Careful, careful, careful.

The two of them were silent.

Did you bring your cell? Mary said.

Rachel handed Mary her phone.

Mary exhaled, not realizing she'd been holding her breath. She flipped the cover and texted her son. *Pills?* A white circle began spinning on the screen with the message: *searching.*

Mary told Rachel how her son, always a goofy, friendly boy, had gone strange as an adolescent. He wouldn't answer simple questions, his glances grew furtive before he disappeared behind his bedroom door where, in minutes, she would hear the flat, digitized voice of his game, *War Zone: Enemy gunfire at point zero, lock and load, attention, lock and load.*

Searching, still searching, the phone said. She tried the number again. The circle whirled like a merry-go-round. Her stomach knotted. If she had to, she could ask Rachel to stop, and find a pay phone. She could call the resort and have her husband paged. She looked at Rachel. And somehow, Mary couldn't give in. At least not yet. She remembered the two of them, walking up the long roads to the ranch houses, dogs barking, circling them, Rachel knocking, the two of them entering barebones kitchens with the cracked linoleum and large freckled coffeepots, telling the ranchers and their wives how the coal companies would try to trick them, sending in friendly men in cowboy hats, boots, and jean jackets, who would try to get them to deed over their land for pennies on the dollar.

She forced herself to breathe out the fear icing the backs of her arms, her throat, the panic that grew at the sound of a door closing behind her son as he headed downstairs to the gift shop or the game room with a handful of coins.

They passed the steepled Hope Lutheran Church and the

large brick Our Lady of the Saints. Rachel kept driving the car through spear-tipped rod iron gates. At the start, the road was dark, snowy, lined by pine trees. They kept driving, following the narrow road as it wound around and began to climb the hill.

It looks icy, Mary said.

Four-wheel drive, studded snows, Rachel shrugged. We'll be fine.

Mary flipped the phone open again. *Searching, still searching.*

As the car snaked up the hillside, the ice thickened. The landscape suddenly opened out, hillocked with snow. The sun burst out from behind a cloud and shone so bright it was hard to see. It was a sea of graves: tall obelisks, giant family stones engraved with births and deaths of mothers, fathers, sisters, brothers, paupers' graves lain flat on the ground, the dead from mill collapses, mine fires, black lung disease. The graves were decorated: red poppies from veterans' organizations, small garden plots with dried brown bachelor's buttons, faded red plastic roses and carnations, silk sunflowers. There were American flags, Montana flags, Irish flags, Canadian flags, fluttering, fluttering.

There're more people buried here than live in town, Rachel said. She steered the car on a road that wound through the graves.

Dead from 1918. Spanish flu, Mary said, her voice dark with knowledge.

As the car crept along, the two of them read out interesting markers. Mary Louise Poole, Our Mother, Typhoid Fever. Thomas McKinney, Ancient Order of Hibernians, 1896–1950; Don McKinnon, To the Big Hunt in the Sky, 1923–1965.

When they reached the top of the hill, they could see hundreds of graves, seventeen thousand, Rachel learned later, and below them, the town of Anaconda, with its rutted dirt streets, tire shops, the two roads: one leading into town, one leading out.

Rachel turned off the car. They sat, listening to the engine tick.

Across from them was another hillside covered with hundreds of graves, small and white. The ground was bumpy as if the bodies were pushing up against the earth.

That's Childland, Rachel said.

Mary's heart lurched. All of those children. She paused for what seemed like an appropriate time. I wonder, Rachel, if we shouldn't get back.

Rachel started the car and put it in gear. Tires spun, turning and whining. She put the car in reverse and tried backing up. No luck.

Shit on a brick, Rachel turned the ignition off. We're stuck.

We know how to get out of this, Mary said. We're Montana girls. She got out. Bracing herself against the car, she went to the trunk to retrieve a scrap of rug from Rachel's emergency supplies—outgrown mittens and hats and snow pants.

She put a rug under a rear tire for traction. Okay! She shouted. Put it in first.

The wheels spun and threw the rug into the lap of Victoria Kruzek's grave, Blessed Lamb. The second time, it landed on Lucas Phinney's stone, RIP. The third time, it landed on Edward O'Sullivan, Father and Provider.

Mary crept back into the passenger seat. She dug in her wallet, pulled out the auto club card. When she called, the phone miraculously worked.

Where are you? The dispatcher asked.

We are located in a graveyard in Anaconda, Mary said. Where are you?

Denver, he said.

Go figure, Mary said. We can't call our family twenty miles away, but we get a dispatcher in Denver.

There was a pause. It shows me there are three graveyards in Anaconda, the dispatcher said. Which one are you in?

Which one are we in? Mary asked Rachel.

Rachel shrugged.

The two of them laughed.

Rachel stepped out of the car, holding on to the edge so she could stand on the ice. She looked up the hill and down. Tell him it's the one on the hill, she said.

It's the one on the hill, Mary said.

The Uphill Cemetery? The dispatcher said.

That's it, Mary said, looking at Rachel, who was laughing, the two of them suddenly besieged with that infectious, unstoppable, almost painful laughter. It's the Uphill Cemetery.

The dispatcher curtly told them someone from Kruziak's towing was on his way.

The sky darkened. Temperatures were dropping. Snow began to fall.

How much gas do you have? Mary said. Irritation fell like a shadow across her.

A quarter tank, Rachel said. Unless this guy forgets us.

I really have to call my son, Mary said.

Okay, Rachel said. She put her hand on Mary's arm. I'm sure he's fine.

Do you know—Mary looked at her, her voice sharp—how many times people have told me that when, in fact, he was not fine. He was not fine at all. Those words have no meaning for me.

Hey, Rachel handed her the phone. I'm sorry.

This time there was service. Mary could hear ringing. There was a click and then his voice: Hello? Hello?

It's Mom, she shouted. Mom! We're stuck on the ice in the Anaconda cemetery and we're getting a tow. The Uphill Cemetery, she said, smiling at Rachel.

Hello? Hello? her son was saying. She could hear him say to someone, presumably her husband, I think its Mom, but there's no talking. Hello? Hello? He said, exasperated, and the connection was cut off.

Well, Rachel said, you know he's okay.

Mary snapped the phone shut. Why did we come here anyway? I knew I shouldn't have done this. I knew I shouldn't have left, Rachel.

I'm sorry, Rachel said. I just wanted to run away.

I know, Mary said. The windshield blurred. I did, too. I'm just so incredibly afraid.

Rachel put her hand on her arm and they sat there.

. . .

Evening was coming on. The gravestones glowed white in the light of the moon, the carved letters barely visible to the two women in the car. From below, the lights of town pricked the dark, one after one, filling the two of them with yearning.

Lights shone at the bottom of the hill, then gradually began to get larger and brighter. It was the tow truck, a large white four-wheel-drive pickup with the name Kruziak's Towing on its side, moving steadily toward them. The truck stopped fifty yards away from them. A door opened and a tall man with thick white hair and high cheekbones stepped out and walked the rest of the way to the car. He was dressed in a striped, grease-stained jumpsuit with his name stitched on his breast pocket: Edward Kruziak.

Rachel rolled down the window as he approached.

He bent down and looked in at the two of them, smiling.

Okay, ladies. Whose bird-brained idea was it to go grave robbing in February?

Guilty, Rachel held up her hand. She explained how they wanted to see the graveyard, they had such an interest in Anaconda, how it was so old, once the state capital, and they wanted to come up and see the graves, and they didn't realize it was so icy. And then they got stuck.

He smiled. There was a rakish gap between his front teeth. *Crazy women, what were they thinking?* Mary could see the thoughts crossing his mind, then answering himself. *I know— they weren't.* She already felt herself part of a story that would pass down the polished surface of a bar.

Paperwork first, he said. Then I'll get you young ladies on your way.

He held out his arm for Mary. She opened the door and stood. He escorted her back to his truck. He was wearing corks, logging boots with spikes in the soles, that gave him traction on the ice. He was a handsome, stately man. In the cab, where the heater was blasting, she handed him her auto club card. He pinned it to a clipboard, wrote out the date, time, and the nature of the incident. She signed the invoice. Your handwriting, he said, reminds me of my grandmother's. As they walked back to the Subaru in a path lit by the headlights, their shadows stretched out on the ice ahead of them. She held his arm, feeling how steady he was, how unwavering.

He walked her to the passenger door, opened it for her, and helped her sit down.

Thank you, she said.

He walked back to the driver's side of the window, and waited as the woman who lost her mother rolled down the window. She looked up at him from the driver's seat, her dark hair collaring her face, her eyes wide.

You gonna head straight home to your families after this? he smiled. No more visiting graveyards?

No sir, she said. We're headed home.

Now, girls, he looked at both of them. Do as I tell you and you'll be unstuck. Put it in neutral. Take off the brake. Then steer.

The woman who lost her mother shifted into neutral and took off the brake.

He put his shoulder against the window jamb and began to push. Little to the right, he said. She turned the steering wheel accordingly.

He looked out at thick white slab ahead of them.

You can't fight ice or you'll stay stuck, he told them. You have to work with it. You have to put the car in neutral and glide.

How easy it all was. He put his shoulder to the window jamb again. As he pushed, they felt the car float forward as he walked them to the gravel road where they would be able to drive back down to the hot springs resort and their waiting families and the stories they would tell again and again about their crazy mothers and the time they ran off to get stuck at the graveyard in Anaconda in February, but for a brief moment, it was so peaceful, just the two of them, together in that dark car, their hands folded, the man's steady breathing beside them, as they glided forward on that moonstung ice.

III

BALLET AT THE MOOSE LODGE

You could read a town, Deborah's mother told her, by watching
the way the women shopped the Harvest Sale. Some picked,
some pawed, some plucked, but everyone moved faster as they
neared the sale racks: linen dresses at 60 percent off, rayon
blouses for one dollar, fifty cents. At the dramatic reductions
table, women combed through the stacks of slacks and summer
shorts, and as others arrived, they grew frenzied, shedding
castoffs like snakeskins.

Take the professor's wife, for example, her mother said.
Every season, she bought a suit, straight off the rack, full price.
She was new money. The doctor's wife, old money, with her
three-story colonial on Squaw Creek, but she never paid full
price for anything—she was, her mother said, "constitutionally
cheap." Wives of schoolteachers, gas station mechanics, and mill
workers came for once-in-a-lifetime outfits: graduation suits,
mother-of-the-bride dresses.

Then there were the shoppers who defied categorization, the
ones who bought the oddest things, like the polka-dotted swing
coat that hadn't sold in two seasons because it was simply too
high-style for Bridger—*imagine wearing a coat like that when
you're trying to start your car at twenty below,* Deborah heard one
woman say to another—the very coat a woman was buttoning
to the chin as she pivoted from side to side, studying herself in
the mirror.

The woman was, of course, Miss Sophie.

Miss Sophie wore the polka-dotted coat for the next two
winters, subzero temperatures be damned. Deborah knew this

because her mother enrolled her in the Sophie Blix School of Dance. Her mother said it would give Deborah something to do besides working at the store after school or moping around the house, but deep down, Deborah suspected her mother looked at it as a business investment—as a way to keep in touch with the doctors' and lawyers' wives, who didn't invite her to their bridge clubs or symphony guilds, who didn't welcome a divorcée into their ranks.

Miss Sophie set down her purchase on the counter and smiled at Deborah. "How old are you?" she said.

"Twelve," Deborah said.

"So nice to help your mother," Miss Sophie said.

As if I had a choice, Deborah thought as she wrapped the coat in tissue paper and put it in a bag featuring a woman with a "wasp" waist, large hat, and the logo: *Nora's for the Smart Set.*

"This will look lovely with your complexion," her mother said as she punched the register keys, *ching-ca-ching-ca-ching* and the cash drawer popped open with its rows of currency, orderly as teeth.

Lay it on, mother, Deborah thought as she handed Miss Sophie the bag.

. . .

They were always there in the doorway during dance class, the men from the Moose Lodge, dressed in oil-stained jumpsuits or black workpants held up with suspenders, silver lunch pails in their hands. They gathered to watch the girls practice—pliés, jetés, ronds de jambe—watching as the girls hopped about like so many pink-legged crows, until Miss Sophie moved to the record player to start class. Then they lumbered off down the hallway to the bar to escape sore fingers and aching joints in the dark camaraderie of beer and whiskey, Hank Williams and Conway Twitty.

One night in late November, after the men had moved to the bar and the girls had warmed up, Miss Sophie sat on a folding chair and gathered the girls around her. They sat, their feet pulled to their crotches, flapping their legs like wings. Miss Sophie said they were going to be in the spring arts festival and, to make it a success, everyone had to take two classes a week. Polly, the philosophy professor's daughter, had a solo highlighting her lovely arms and deep pliés. Denise, whose father owned half the town, had a solo featuring pas de chat and springy jetés, or jumps. Susan, who was the only one of Miss Sophie's protégés whose parents weren't on the town's social register, had a solo featuring a number of pirouettes. Her mother was a beautician with high, teased hair; her father wore coveralls and pumped gas. The other parents greeted them heartily, as if to underscore their differences.

After the lesson, Deborah told her mother she was going to have to take two lessons a week. Her mother said, "Well, there's a money-making scheme if I heard one." She nodded, her face bitter. "Good God."

"But it's the arts festival!" Deborah said. "It's a good thing."

"We can't," her mother said as they hurried down the wind-scraped sidewalk. "I can't afford another lesson."

This was supposed to signal the end of the conversation, but when they slipped onto the frigid seats of the Volkswagen and her mother shifted angrily into reverse, Deborah pressed on. "I can't dance in the festival if I don't," she said, looking at her mother. "I'll be the only one."

She didn't know if this was true, but she figured it could be. What's more, she loved the idea of marching into her high school in pink tights and a leotard, no longer a student, but a dancer.

"Good God. You think I'm made of money?" her mother asked as they crept down the dark streets, past the courthouse, the library, and the dress shop. Her mother glanced at the darkened window with its mannequins in eerie shapes of women standing, feet turned out. "I've got to change the display," she muttered. "Women shop windows."

"Please?" Deborah persisted.

Ice crunched under tires.

Her mother turned swiftly into the driveway of their small white bungalow. "Miss Sophie doesn't pay the bills," she said and pulled up the handle of the emergency brake with a grinding certainty. "I do."

. . .

"My mother says I can't take more lessons," she told Miss Sophie the next Tuesday. She looked over Miss Sophie's head at the sepia-toned photograph of her, standing en pointe, braids circling her head, from the Rotterdam School of Ballet, studying the froth of her tutu, as foreign as foam at the edge of the ocean.

Miss Sophie gently slipped *Swan Lake* back in the record case. She looked at Deborah. "I can't have the corps practice one day in the week," she said, pronouncing "the" like "da."

"My mother can't pay for more," Deborah said. Her face grew hot.

Miss Sophie sighed. Deborah imagined that she was thinking about how she suffered in this roughshod town, where concerns about money outweighed concerns about art. She pinned her eyes on Deborah, thinking.

Deborah waited, listening to the burble of TV from the bar, the rumble of men's laughter, the clunk and slide of glass on wood.

Miss Sophie fingered her temples as if she were rubbing out a headache. Maybe, Deborah thought, she *was* the headache.

Deborah looked away from her face and up at the star hanging from the ceiling in the middle of the room. The star, lit from within, featured a picture of Little Curlyhead, the Moose mascot, a tousle-headed, gap-toothed boy, his hands pressed together in prayer. He was perched at the edge of bed, the covers turned down. Deborah noticed a stone cathedral in the window behind him, one tower higher than the other. *Mooseheart*, the picture said. It made her think of something wrapped in butcher paper that her neighbor, a hunter, had given to her mother after her father left. When she asked her mother if she liked him, her mother pursed her lips and laughed. *Ed? Oh my God, no. I cut him off at the pockets.*

"Why don't you work for extra lessons," Miss Sophie said, finally. Her *work* sounded like *verk*. "Clean, sweep, dust, mop the bathroom. Understood? This will be our secret pact. In the war, I paid for ballet with potatoes—one potato a lesson—" Miss Sophie leaned closely into Deborah's face. "Remember, art redeems."

"Thank you," Deborah said, thinking *pact*. A secret pact. "Thank you. Thank you so much."

* * *

Deborah rose at nine and walked across the bridge, where the autumn wind sliced through her as she walked through the sleepy downtown, past stores where shopkeepers were slowly moving about, opening their window shades and tills and sweeping a thin sprinkling of snow from the sidewalks, readying themselves for the shopping rush at ten. She smelled the warm breath of coffee at the Florence Hotel coffee shop, the sour smell of old beer and the stink of disinfectant by Eddie's Bar.

She got the broom and rags and ammonia from the janitor at the Moose, a florid-faced man who had mangled an arm in a logging accident. He watched her as she swept the room, his long shadow slanting across the floor and she smiled, and turned her back to him, hoping he'd go away, only to see him again in the mirror, smirking as she polished the glass. She was relieved to clean the bathroom, to know that that word, WOMEN'S, would force him to stay behind.

The only other person she saw was the liquor store deliveryman, who, in his brown delivery suit and cap, wheeled boxes of Jack Daniels and Lewis and Clark gin around her as if she were a piece of furniture.

She was relieved when the older girls arrived at ten-thirty: first Susan, who came at least an hour ahead of the others to practice pirouettes, sweeping her foot to the side, back and then turning, once, twice sometimes three times, her face grim when she stumbled. When she spoke, which she rarely did, her sentences were short and clipped, making it clear that while the two of them may have working-class parents in common, they would not be friends.

Denise and her mother came in on a cloud of White Shoulders.

Polly came last with her ragged jeans and pony-tailed boyfriend, who took one look at the girls in their leotards and pink tights, whistled, and then slid out the front door, the janitor glaring behind him.

Deborah was given a small part at the concerto's opening. She stood in fifth position, moving her arms to the front, then to the sides as if she were opening a gate. Her part was minimal—she knew it—but as she moved her arms in an elaborate port de bras, her hands floating through space, the music soared above, around, and through her. As she watched herself in the mirror, it was as if her body was a separate land, foreign and beautiful, the music trumpeting her across lush green mountains.

Then the rehearsal was over and she peeled off her leotard and put on her jeans and sweater and parka in the bathroom that would be filled later that night with the women of the Moose, drunk and respraying their hair, putting on lipstick and fastening loose stockings to garters.

. . .

November 1, All Souls' Day. Deborah's mother insisted on visiting Deborah's grandfather's grave, tucked underneath the linden tree in the graveyard just over the railroad tracks. It was a small Catholic cemetery filled with an assortment of gravestones, some large winged angels, crosses, and headstones tilted this way and that, overseen by a statue of Mary.

When he'd died, it felt to Deborah as if the surface of things had thinned. Then, eight years later, the family thinned out even more when her father left, after her mother had discovered he'd been seeing his secretary. He moved to Kalispell and started a new law practice. After the divorce, Deborah saw him and his new wife two weeks every summer at their cabin on Flathead Lake. Father and daughter became shy and awkward around each other, picking at their food in restaurants, talking to one another like strangers. Occasionally, he'd try to bridge the distance between them by saying incomprehensible things to her like, "You're becoming a woman now, Deborah," pronouncing "woman" like "woo-man"—and the tone of his voice making it sound like womanhood were a condition of great delicacy, cave-like and smelly. She preferred it when they didn't talk.

After he left, her mother became tethered to the dress store and Deborah out of sheer duty, but it was as if someone, somewhere, had let the stove go out. Her mother became tight-lipped. Even her idea of fun was fierce, like when she'd say to Deborah, "Girls to the movies!" and splurge on a small popcorn Deborah didn't dare refuse.

Deborah touched her mother's beautiful red wool coat, clothes her one indulgence. "You miss your father, Mom?" she said.

"Of course," her mother said brusquely. She traced the frosted gravestone, her finger heating the ice and clearing a small patch. "Like you miss yours."

The air thickened between them. This was as close to talking about feelings as they ever got.

"Do you think your Dad still feels his shrapnel wounds?"

Her mother's face looked away. "Things like that go away."

"What goes away?" Deborah said.

"Old wounds," Deborah's mother looked at her. She opened her mouth but no sound came out.

"You look like you are about to say something."

"I was going to say, we'd better go before we catch our death of cold."

· · ·

Miss Sophie, was short, stocky, wore glasses, and had hair the color of coffee. She had thick, round calves and turned-out feet. But Miss Sophie had style: her handmade leather shoes; her fingerless gloves. She made shocking pronouncements. *"Pictures at an Exhibition,"* she sniffed, when Deborah named her favorite piece of classical music. "Mussorgsky? When the world has Dvořák?" Miss Sophie had a violinist husband, a Dutch accent, and a nervous breakdown every spring.

She told them to avoid desserts, to scrape fat off their meat, to strive for the thin, sculpted dancer's body. Not their own. She told them art survived, not the values of their small town where cowboys tied their horses up in front of downtown bars, where mill workers drank hard after morning and evening shifts and professionals convened in bridge parties and church groups.

She also taught them about fate. Deborah learned from Miss Sophie that she would never—no matter how many lessons she took, no matter how high her jumps or deep her pliés—become a dancer because of the shape of her body. Her torso was too long, her legs were too short and that was the end of the story.

She talked about suffering—which they, as teenagers, thought they knew about on a daily basis. *Suffering?* she'd sniff. *You think you know suffering? Suffering,* she said, *is when you think potato water is soup. Suffering,* she said, *is hearing cries in the night and falling asleep. Suffering,* Deborah looked back at her. *Suffering is wishing your mother would laugh.*

At each rehearsal, Miss Sophie yelled at them. *Straighten your backs! Suck in your stomachs! Round your arms! Look like dancers, not Butte hurdy-gurdy girls! Smile!*

. . .

As the festival grew closer, Miss Sophie's stories came faster and faster—stories about how the bombing of Rotterdam stopped ten blocks from her house; stories about the hunger winter she'd survived. Deborah learned quickly to keep Miss Sophie's stories to herself—when she repeated one of Miss Sophie's potatoes-for-ballet-lessons stories, her mother rolled her eyes and said, "Good Lord, what is she telling you girls?"

During one December rehearsal, she lifted the needle from the record and said, "Remember, girls, people are not what they appear." Her *what* sounded like *vat*.

They looked at one another, confused.

She walked past them, the floor creaking under her feet. "One day I walked past a bombed-out church—nothing but a pile of bricks—and there is a Nazi officer. You know what he's doing? Playing Bach," She whispered. "A Bach fugue. Played by a Nazi."

Miss Sophie walked over and put the needle back on the record. Standing in a long line, the corps stood in fifth position, opening their arms out, then to the side, then up and over their heads as Susan spun pirouettes across the floor.

Miss Sophie stopped the music again.

"Germans—" Miss Sophie pronounced *Germans* like *Chermans*—also saved my life."

They stood, eight of them in fifth position, waiting for the story's end.

Behind Miss Sophie's voice, they could hear the men at the bar laughing, the shouts from the football game on the television set, the ring of glass against glass.

"I lived only because my neighbors, Germans, left potato peels for me in their garbage cans. Potato peels for soup."

She pronounced *soup* like *zup*. "They could have been killed for that."

Miss Sophie put the needle back on the record, and violins and horns and clarinets sounded as the girls spun into lopsided pirouettes.

. . .

Deborah arrived early to clean before the Saturday practice, but as the months progressed, she rolled out of bed later and later and her cleaning became more slapdash. She hurried to finish before the older girls arrived, running a rag down the barre, hastily swiping it across the mirror, as the janitor stood in the hallway door, muttering, "Hasty, hasty." Even Little Curlyhead's face looked disapproving as he stared down at her from above his prayer-folded hands.

At the end of class, Miss Sophie stopped her.

"You must clean," she said, her eyes sharp. "Remember that, Deborah. It is our pact."

"Yes," Deborah said, stung. She stayed late after the practice that night, swabbing out the toilets, shaking gritty cleanser into the bathroom sink and sweeping in slow arcs around the large room, watching herself in the mirror, Cinderella in tattered jeans, as the light waned and the voices in the bar swelled. As she watched herself move around the room in the long mirror, she wondered what it would be like to hear the whine of planes. She pictured herself running through the streets, her face turned, beautiful with fear.

The janitor watched Deborah as she ran the dust cloth along the barre, wiped the mirrors clean and swept the floor, slowly moving the broom across the large empty room behind her. She was relieved when he disappeared into the bar, where she heard a vacuum run, but then he was back, resting his bad arm on his push broom and looking up at the star of Little Curlyhead.

"You know," he said, looking up at the plastic star, "The

way you hear them talk about Mooseheart, you'd think it was a fucking paradise."

She kept sweeping. "What place?"

"Mooseheart," he said—jabbing his elbow at the picture of the boy in the star hanging from the ceiling. "But I'll tell you a secret, kid. The place is just a goddamn jail." He looked at her. "See that kid up there on the star? Know what he's prayin' for?" He laughed, a low, bitter sound.

"I don't know," Deborah answered, wondering just how soon someone else was going to get here.

"He's praying, dear sweet Jesus, get me the hell out of here." He bent over his broom and laughed, tears squeezing out of his eyes, his belly pressed against his striped, snap-front cowboy shirt.

. . .

When Polly arrived at rehearsal, late, as usual, with her boyfriend in his army surplus jacket, they were disheveled and red-eyed, and they soul-kissed right in the middle of the room.

Everyone stared, speechless.

When they pulled apart, he looked up at the star of Little Curlyhead and said, shaking his head, "Fuckin' A." Then he walked out, leaving in his wake an unsettling whiff of the sixties.

Polly went into the bathroom to shed her more dangerous self.

When she reentered the room in tights, a leotard, and ballet slippers—and in the wake of an amazed silence—Miss Sophie looked at her and said, "You're late."

Polly put her leg up on the barre, stretched her torso over it, touched her hand to her toes, and looked at herself in the mirror. "Hey, sexy," she said to her image in the mirror.

A titter swept around the room.

Stoned, Deborah whispered with the other girls, their voices reverent. *Stoned,* Deborah thought to herself as she peeled off her leotard and tights, tasting the word's hard, sharp sound as if it could rent a tear in the tired scene before her—the half-naked girls, the scratched mirror, the dim bulb hanging from a cord above.

. . .

When Deborah walked into the hallway of the Moose Lodge, it was packed. The costumes had arrived in time for the dress rehearsal and so had the mothers. Everyone except her mother, who was, of course, working. There were mothers hovering over daughters, pinning up stray hairs, adjusting skirts, making last-minute repairs, the air pungent with hair spray.

When the makeup and buns were done, the women crowded into the auditorium to watch Miss Sophie open the costume boxes. The room grew quiet, interrupted only by the burble of the television and occasional snort of laughter from the bar next door. Miss Sophie brought the first cardboard boxes, carefully taped, that had arrived from San Francisco with the logo "Ballet Works of San Francisco" in a clean serif type. The costumes had to be ordered from San Francisco because, of course, no store in town would carry something so ephemeral, so beautiful, so wildly impractical.

Miss Sophie took out a penknife and carefully, tenderly, cut the top of the thick cardboard box, the knife rasping as she pulled it across the top. Then she made a careful cut along the tape that held the flaps down.

She looked up at the mothers, the dancers. "Are you ready for this?"

"Open it! Open it!" one of the mothers cried.

She plunged her hands into the dark recesses of the box: this one delicate, white, and shiny, embossed with a deep pink logo that said "Ballet Works of San Francisco." Even the name seemed lofty: *Ballet Works.* Miss Sophie held it for a minute, so they could all admire the box. Slowly she lifted the lid to reveal a bed of carefully folded pink tissue paper, tied with a shiny white ribbon. Miss Sophie carefully pulled the ends of the ribbons.

Some of the dancers now were bounding. One girl was shaking her hands. As Miss Sophie parted the tissue paper, its whispers seemed to spread to the mothers and daughters who gathered around. Miss Sophie plunged her hands in and pulled out the first tutu: its satin bodice beaded with tiny white pearls, the skirt a froth of netting.

Oh, Dorothy's mother said. And the sound echoed the room. *Oh. Oh. Oh.*

· · ·

They debuted the piece at Whitaker, Deborah's dreary brick high school, everyone trooping into the bathroom with bulging ballet bags and starched buns, several mothers in tow. Deborah walked through the polished gymnasium with the Whitaker Redskins stenciled on the floor and the folded up basketball hoop. The place looked smaller to her, as if she were coming back from her future to visit her past.

In the bathroom where she changed for gym, she pulled on her leotard and tights and tried to sit still for Susan's mother, who smoothed rouge on her cheek and outlined her eyes with black eyeliner. When she was done, she put Deborah's hair in a bun, slicking it to her head with hair spray, her movements deft, professional. Then she stood back, appraising her.

"You're darling, Deborah," she says, her smoky voice low and conspiratorial. "But in the future, don't wear your hair back. Your ears stick out."

Deborah stood with the other girls in their blue tutus and skirts, the soloists bunched together like doves, all of them jiggling and talking, listening as voices were spilling into the gym, feet clunking across the bleachers, the principal's voice calling out for quiet. The festival chairman announced them, Sophie Blix School of Ballet for the 1975 Bridger Arts Festival.

Then, one after the other, the girls followed Miss Sophie out of the locker room and into the gym.

Deborah stood with the corps de ballet, all twelve of them in fifth position. She looked out at the bleachers, at the sea of faces. She could see several of her teachers, smiling. The principal was settling in with a look of bored amusement. The PA system crackled. She could feel her schoolmates' eyes on her, on all of them, as she and the other dancers stood in fifth position, their backs straight, their arms curved in a simple port de bras. In just a few moments, they would erupt into movement, into turns and jumps and leaps accompanied by an intricate architecture of notes. She felt the seriousness of their undertaking, the thrill that, as the first triumphant notes of the Brandenburg *Concerto Number 2* galloped across this shadowy gymnasium smelling of wax and sweat, her life in this winter-weary town with its haves and have-nots would be suspended just for a moment, and she would be transported by movement into boundless possibility.

Then, just as Miss Sophie looked at them to see if they were ready, holding the arm of the record player over the spinning black vinyl, Deborah saw her mother slip into the bleachers, nodding toward the other mothers, her red lips pressed tightly together. Her mother, who said that morning she wasn't sure she could get away from work. Her mother pointed the brownie camera straight at her.

Click.

Miss Sophie set the needle on the record. They danced, the music spinning out its triumphant notes. As she looked over at the bleachers, Deborah saw the face of Mrs. Clark, with her fine, arched eyebrows, smiling at Deborah, the storekeeper's daughter. As she danced, Deborah felt her rage at this town soften her arms and lengthen her torso until the faces, the gym, the town fell away, her body felt long and lean and beautiful and female with its curved sides and breasts and hips, delicate and strong at once and then she stepped into a pirouette and as she turned, she saw Miss Sophie's face, hang there for a moment, glowing, just a bit too brightly.

. . .

By March, the festival was over. They performed at two high schools and three grade schools around town, accompanied by squadrons of mothers, trooping in as girls, trooping out as dancers, wearing makeup and buns and hair spray, bowing each time to the hoots and claps of children and teenagers just like them.

It was a Wednesday in spring and she was back to her regular life. Life that hung between winter and summer; life that was a steady march between high school, her mother's store, and dance classes.

Ballet class felt tired, aimless, like someone had let all the air out of the room. Miss Sophie took her place at the record player. Dark rings hung like half moons under her eyes, her hair flew out from the combs in her head. She looked over the class, wearily, then put on *Swan Lake.*

"My God," Polly whispered. "Does the woman have any other music?"

Miss Sophie turned to stare at her. Her eyes filled with tears.

"This is your thanks?" Miss Sophie ran a hand through her hair. Her eyes looked muddy. She looked at her feet, cleared her throat.

There was a scrabble of voices from the television in the bar, the dark clunk and slide of glass.

Miss Sophie looked at them and said, in a strangled voice that all of them could barely understand, "Let that be a lesson." She didn't say for what. Then she put her coat on and walked out the front door. They stood at the bar, listening to the whoosh of the front door closing. It seemed to seal something inside the room.

The speaker crackled. There were voices from the bar.

Deborah and the other girls waited five minutes, waited for Miss Sophie to come back in, to say it was all okay, to put the needle back on the record. Finally Deborah said, "I think she left."

Finally, one by one, they sat down, waiting for their mothers to fetch them.

Susan's mother was the first to arrive. "Where's Miss Sophie?" she said sharply.

"She left," Deborah said.

"Oh, dear," Dorothy's mother said. She looked at Polly's mother and the other mothers and they all knew what this meant. One of the mothers was dispatched to see if they could catch up with Miss Sophie and get her to the hospital.

But it was Deborah who caught up with Miss Sophie as she was walking to her mother's dress store. She hurried up through the slushy streets until she came up alongside her. At first, she wasn't sure Miss Sophie knew she was there.

"Miss Sophie?" She leaned into her, looked into her face. "Are you okay?"

"Go home, Deborah," Miss Sophie said.

. . .

Deborah walked into the grey streets, the smoke from the mill settling over the town, shrouding the mountains, the buildings, the streetlights, and the tall clock in front of the jewelry store that kept time over the vague streets. Her limbs moved in slow jerks. When she got to her mother's shop, she knocked at the door and her mother let her in.

Deborah's mother took one look at her, cupped Deborah's face in her hands and tilted it up. "What is it? What's wrong?"

"Miss Sophie told me to go home," she said, her voice flat.

"Why?" she brushed the bangs out of Deborah's eyes.

"I don't know really," was all Deborah could muster. "I think she's sick." She jerked her head out of her mother's hands and stared at the worn carpet.

"Oh, forget about that woman," Deborah's mother put an arm around her shoulder. "She puts on such airs." She pulled up a chair in the back of the store. "Here—sit here while I close up."

Deborah sat and stared out the front window to the street, watching the blur of red and yellow lights as cars and passersby—shoppers, storekeepers, mill workers—headed home, just another Wednesday in March. She saw the plastic arms of the mannequins glisten, a curved hand here, a bent elbow there, with their pointy breasts and narrow smiles. As her mother pulled back the ornate arm of the cash register and the cash door shot out and sang—*ca-ching*—and numbers appeared in a glass window, Deborah saw the dark shape of a woman appear in the window, a scarf wrapped over her head, her face white, indistinct. The woman leaned into the window, slowly scanned each outfit, then her eyes softened as they settled on a suit of red wool, the streetlights burnishing the planes of her face. She leaned in closer to look at the price tag. Then she straightened up, shook her head, and moved on.

BRIDGE NIGHT: A FAIRY TALE

Who, she thought, would kiss her awake?

It was bridge night. Elizabeth's parents and the Thompsons were sitting in the living room under the chandelier with the crystal globes. They were sitting in proper bridge formation around a card table, like points of a compass: Bill Thompson on the south side, his partner, Elizabeth's mother, to the north. Elizabeth's father, Ted, sat on the east by the card shuffler. To the west sat Peg Thompson. At their elbows were bridge tallies decorated with colored leaves and leaf-shaped dishes of bridge mix and candy. They were drinking coffee and eating her mother's torte, made of graham crackers and chocolate pudding, having what Peg Thompson called "a Methodist evening"—their little joke—because Methodists didn't approve of playing cards or drinking coffee, but by the early 1960s, no one really cared.

Elizabeth stood at the edge of the bridge table eating butter mints and watching the grownups sort their mysterious cards— the deck was edged in silver and decorated with blue birds—as they turned up spades and diamonds, sinister one-eyed jacks, and lonely queens. From the other room, Elizabeth heard the sounds of guns and hoof beats as Dale, the Thompsons's sixteen-year-old son, watched "Bonanza" on the black-and-white television set.

As she scooped up a third handful of candy, her mother rested her hand on Elizabeth's. "Enough," she said. "Time for bed, kid."

Elizabeth said good night and pulled away from the table with great sadness. Peg Thompson patted her on the cheek. Her dad gave her a playful swat on the bottom.

As she headed up the stairs, she sat on the top step to spy on the living room. Her father leaned back in his chair, his cards fanned out in front of him, one leg crossed in front of the other.

With an eyebrow cocked, he was asking Bill Thompson, why, if the state could elect a Republican governor—why couldn't the whole damn country?

Bill, the history professor who reminded Elizabeth of Abe Lincoln with his stiff formality and cold hands, said slowly, "The Republicans ran right into the ghost of FDR, Ted."

Elizabeth tried to imagine Republicans running into ghosts.

Peg arranged her fan of cards with great formality. "Well, at least our state was its usual schizophrenic self." She plucked out a card and shoved it somewhere else. "Republican governor, Democratic house." She snapped her cards face down on the table. "You gotta love it."

Elizabeth's father crossed the room and stood in front of his record cabinet. He opened it, running his hand down the spines, and gently lifted a 78 out of the dark cabinet, slipping the record out of its sleeve. Elizabeth knew exactly what it was: Glenn Miller's "Chattanooga Choo Choo." Her father loved big band music and kept his 78s in alphabetized rows that she was forbidden to touch. He told her the musicians' names as if he were passing on to her some kind of secret code—Tommy Dorsey, Count Basie, Artie Shaw—and his greatest love, Glen Miller: "In the Mood," "Pennsylvania 6-5000," "Stairway to the Stars." As horns, trombones, and trumpets began their ebullient swing, he stood still, directing the speakers, his face flushed, beyond reach.

Her mother leaned over and spied her, still perched on the stairs. "Go to bed, Elizabeth. I know you are up there."

Elizabeth took one long look at that room with its oriental rugs, the shining piano stacked with music, her father directing the record speakers, Peg scribbling something on her bridge tally, then she trudged up the stairs to the dark landing.

Her mother followed her to make sure she went all the way to her room, opening the covers to her bed like an envelope, patting them around her, then she kissed her and told her *sweet dreams*.

Words were replaced by wind, freight trains along the river, the neighbor dog, barking, always barking.

At night, Elizabeth made up stories. There were loud bangs from freight trains in the Milwaukee rail yard below the house. Elizabeth imagined gun battles, two men stalking each other alongside the freight trains, gunshots, bodies curling in the dust. Someone had found a bum once, dead, in the ditch below their house. A lost prince, of course, who had been coming to find her, to have her let her hair down and join him to run away, but instead was caught in the deadly thicket of thorns around their house, like so many princes before him.

She was nine, in bed, in her red flannel nightgown. Now her father was playing "Tuxedo Junction." She heard the rise and fall of laughter as her parents played cards. Something seemed to tap itself into her brain as she listened to the patterns of their voices: the bursts of laughter, the pockets of silence, followed by the nervous welling-up of conversation.

"Deal, would ya, Ted!" she heard Peg cry out.

"I'm hurrying, I'm hurrying, Peg," her father laughed. "We're not all as quick as the Butte Irish."

Elizabeth's mother laughed, a nervous sound.

There was a creak of shoe leather on wood.

Cloth rubbed against cloth.

Eleanor's heart froze.

She waited, pinned to the bed. Her bed had a rounded headboard in which, during a nap once when she was five, she scratched a story with the butt of a toy gun, a story about a little girl who climbed over a tall mountain on her way to her grandmother's house.

. . .

The door creaked open. The voices downstairs grew louder. Peg said, "Damn you, Ted, don't you dare trump my ace!"

He is standing in the door, his body dark, outlined in light from the hallway, the thatch of hair illuminated. "I came to say good night."

"I said good-night," Elizabeth said.

"This is your room?" he whispered. He took two steps inside the door, stepping from heel to toe on each foot very slowly. He tiptoed to the window. "You can see the trains from here."

"I know that," she said. "Tell me something I don't know."

"The Milwaukee Railroad," he said. "They call it the Silk Train because it carries Chinese silk from Seattle to New York."

"So?" Elizabeth said.

"So, we could walk down there and hop that train and in a few days we'd be in New York. That's so."

"I don't want to go to New York."

"I do."

"They bang together every night." Elizabeth said.

He smiled. "They call that coupling," he said. His teeth were very even. Very white.

The ratcheting of a zipper. How he wanted her to touch it and she didn't want to, but she did, too, and the head of it was smooth, the rest of it bumpy, reptilian. Never tell, he said. Just like a spell.

Never, never, never.

What she remembered was how quietly he slipped out the door. And the next time, how quietly he slipped in.

. . .

No. That story wasn't right. Unlike the Goose Girl at the back door, like she'd imagined, she was the ragged princess at the back door. Nearly dead with cold, she was lighting matches to keep warm. A king looking out the upstairs window saw her unbinding her long chestnut hair and recognized her. "She is no mere goose girl," he said to the others. "She is a princess. Look at her fine fingers."

She crawled in an iron oven, the one owned by the witch, and here, she told another story, this one about the boy who comes in her room and makes her touch him until he shudders, but she can't move, because her parents have so many troubles—the aunt who shot herself, the grandmother in and out of the mental hospital—and there they are in this circle of light, laughing. With these words she, the child, would tap her wand and this bubble of laughter and friendship and happiness would disappear and they would be back to their usual diet of pain and grey and cold dinners, so instead, she decided to heal herself. As she says all this to the iron oven, it answers, "Thou hast spoken thy doom."

. . .

There are other bridge parties. Elizabeth in her nightgown, Dale's hands sullenly shoved in the pockets of his letter jacket. She'd go upstairs to her room and he'd part for the television, while the adults made coffee and settled around the bridge table laughing, and she'd lie in bed and listen for the squeak of leather on wood. How it became like a penance, a spell, some grim endurance. They went through the Nixon years. Watergate, the beginning of Johnson's years in the White House, then Dale went off to college, and Elizabeth started babysitting.

. . .

Stop. The script must be rewritten. The scriptwriter was menopausal and weepy and we had to fire her. This is the correct story. The princess walked up from the tracks to the back door. She knocked. No one answered. She knocked again.

This time she decided to go in. Everything was just as she left it forty years ago, frozen in time: her father, mother, Peg and Bill Thompson asleep at the bridge table, her father holding his bridge hand, her mother easing a slice of chocolate torte to the white Spode Prairie Rose china. Peg Thompson's pencil poised over the bridge tally, even the ticks on the dog are sleeping. There, at the foot of the stairs, is Dale. His foot on the bottom step, his hand on the banister.

In this version of the story, Elizabeth kissed the nine-year-old girl. There is no prince. Are you kidding? This is the twenty-first century. The nine-year-old screamed and the sleeping people came to life. The mother threw down the server, and the Spode flew to the floor and shattered. The father cried, "What the hell —?" and jumped up and hit his head on the chandelier, and broke not one, but two crystal globes, before he ran to her rescue amid the glorious sound of breaking crystal. Peg blinked as she turned her head about, looking at the candles sputtering to life, the flies stirring in the window casements. Her father comes thundering down the stairs and there are angry words among the adults and the Thompsons whisk their boy home and punish him soundly.

. . .

But, alas, that is mere fiction.

Elizabeth saw Dale twenty years later at his father's funeral, which was held in the Methodist church in Bridger. After the tributes and prayers, a group of old men known as the "Past Dues" sang "How Lovely Is Thy Dwelling Place," their voices wobbly with emotion. Bill Thompson was a well-respected man, a pillar of the community, with his civic duties and a long career at the university.

After the service, she stood in line to pay her respects.

He was a middle-aged man, overweight, dressed in a blue jacket too short in the sleeves. Her mother told her he lived in

Spokane. She wanted him to be a car salesman, so she was pissed when her mother told her he was actually a reporter.

A reporter? She thought. With a commitment to convey the truth?

She would shake his hand, tell him how sorry she was for his loss, see if there was a flicker, a shade drawn down across his eyes, any registration of what had gone on between them.

He looked at her, fingering the button on his jacket. There were still comb marks in his grey-blonde hair. "Where are you now?"

"Helena," she said. She wanted to go on and say, "I jail child molesters. I cut their balls off." Instead she said, "I'm a prosecutor." She shook his hand and took pleasure in the spider-like finger of hairs combed across his bald spot.

His eyes widened. He turned quickly to the woman behind her in line. "Mrs. McSweeney! How nice of you to come. My father was such a fan of your singing."

She went on into the reception, drinking thin punch and eating cake that had spun sugar frosting, the kind that made her stomach turn.

· · ·

One more story. Fiction, yes, but who cares about genre at this point.

Elizabeth arrives at her old room, painted blue, with the large Renoir print of the girl in the rowboat on the wall. She is there to wake her nine-year-old self. She sees herself lying in bed, her braids brown ropes across the white pillow, her round freckled face. She stands over the girl, clenching her fists, and roars, two bitter tears rolling down her face. When they touch the girl's eyes, her eyes flutter open and become clear, and bright, and blue, and she can see as well as ever.

Elizabeth lifts the girl gently out of the bed and carries her down the stairs, past Dale, still asleep, his foot poised on the stair, his hand on the banister, to the living room where her mother, father, and the Thompsons are there, asleep, the brambles growing around them, and lets the girl see them one last time: all of them, kings and queens, and hearts and knaves, trumps and no trumps, before she carries her out the front door and into the waiting world.

GOOD BONES

The diet started in June, after a family vacation in Vancouver.
Her family traveled with the Dalys, who liked to travel and liked
to cook. She remembered the Butchart Gardens, the Empress
Hotel, the green ribbons of Canadian highways through a kind
of thick, sickening haze of food. Chocolate-covered pretzels.
Cookies. Gum she and Sally Daly blew into wobbly pink bubbles
for one another, laughing until they got lost in the laughing and
when they finished, Emily felt exhausted and sad. She looked
down at her thighs spreading and sticking on the plastic car seat,
and longed to feel hungry again. At night, as her mother and
Mrs. Daly pulled wet packages of hamburger and carrot-raisin
salad from the van refrigerators, Emily watched her brother Billy
walk off to the ocean's edge and wished she were walking away
from the talk and heat to the cool whir of the surf but she felt
pinned to her tree stump, as if she were the anchor that held
the circle of people around the campfire, and if she left, things
would float apart.

When they got home, Emily ran for the bathroom as soon as
the Volkswagen rolled to a stop in the drive, her mother calling
behind her, "You've got to help carry things in."

She locked the door, stripped off her clothes and looked at
herself in the mirror: the breasts staring out, blind, the hips
curving like her mother's, the thighs widening out like hams.
She grabbed the roll of fat at her waist, and pinched it until
there were angry red marks, excited even for the bad news. Then
she stepped on the scale.

Afterward, she carried in more than her load, running her suitcases up and down the stairs, running clothes to the washer, running sacks to the bedrooms. She made herself move like she was being chased, until her mother brushed her bangs from her moist forehead and said, "You excited to be home?"

"You're a thirteen-year-old dervish," her father said as he sorted two weeks of mail at the kitchen table. "You make me tired just watching you."

One hundred and twenty-seven pounds. Emily could feel all of it. She looked in the hall mirror to see the thighs widening out like hams. She wanted to take small knives to cut the extra fat from the stomach. "Lard," she said out loud, feeling the waxy ugliness of the word, the way it coated the tongue, and she could feel something harden inside her.

. . .

The next day Emily ate a fried egg and toast, her last regular meal, and walked ceremoniously downtown to the cool dark of Woolworths to buy a diet book. She passed up the lunch counter, empty except for a few early shoppers clutching rattling sacks and drinking coffee, past the candy counter, piled with dry-looking fudge. She lingered at the eye shadows for a while, then shook herself back to her purpose, laid out a quarter for a Dell diet book, *A New and Thinner You,* and went home, resolute.

She calculated lists of numbers—calories used, calories needed, calories she would from now on consume. She found these additions and subtractions comforting, clean, like a blueprint for a giant machine. She did not cheat on portions, she was as mean to herself as possible, which gave her a stinging kind of satisfaction. Soon she had great lists of numbers. A sample menu. And then it was time for lunch, and she resolutely faced 245 calories of applesauce and cottage cheese.

By the end of June, she had lost six pounds. She felt sleek and strong. She had taken herself in hand. She was hungry all the time.

Emily didn't like tennis, and swimming turned her hair green, so she settled on running and exercises: thirty sit-ups, pushups, side-kicks, jumping jacks, and her favorite, humiliating leg lifts called fire hydrants. The routine did not vary for five months. Each night she put on her tennis shoes, checked her watch and ran for twenty, maybe twenty-five minutes, pushing herself until it hurt, and beyond, pushing herself until she imagined she could feel a bonfire of calories raging in her stomach, lighting her ribs, her body fooled and turning on itself for food.

· · ·

Emily started to bake. Not to eat sweets, but to offer them. She enjoyed mixing the thick doughs, hearing the wheezing sounds of the mixer, and smelling the rich, buttery smells wafting out from the oven. She started with cookies, simple cakes, but now she was getting fancier, fashioning tarts and layered apple strudels. She had never eaten one crumb. She was hungry all the time.

For her father's forty-fifth birthday party, she followed a recipe of her grandmother's that her father talked about for as long as Emily could remember. Her mother had never made the cake. It was a white cake dribbled with bittersweet chocolate that her grandmother made especially for her father, especially for his birthday. Handwritten on a recipe card in dainty, looping strokes, it was even called "Teddy's Cake."

"It's my cake!" her father exclaimed, as she walked slowly toward him in the darkened room lit only by the flickering birthday candles. He looked at her mother. "You made my cake!"

She shook her head. "Emily made it."

Emily wasn't sure but his face fell a bit, then he turned to her and said, "You remembered honey! You remembered your old daddy's favorite cake."

She set the cake down, and he blew the candles out and gave her a big kiss on the cheek. When she served the pieces, she noted how the three layers held together on the plate, how dramatic the dark chocolate looked against the white frosting, and she was happy until her mother noticed she wasn't having any. This was the part of every meal Emily hated.

Her mother looked at her, her fork poised above her cake. "Can't you have just a little?"

The way she said it, all sweet and warm, made Emily want to cut a big slice right down the middle and eat it all at once, just to please her, but she didn't. She couldn't.

"Really Em," her father said. "Can't you have just a bite?"

Emily hated this. When she refused, as she always did, her parents got angry, and visitors thought she was strange. She said it was because she was on a diet. She said it was because she didn't like sweets. "But you're so *thin*," they'd say, and she hated the way they'd look at their plates and back at her as if she could absolve them. She wanted everyone in the world to eat, to eat for her, and she was angry when they passed up dessert.

Emily pointed to herself with the cake server. "So sorry. I apologize to you all." She looked at all of their faces looking up at her. "Cannot do." Then she took a big, stagey bow, and her mom laughed, and Emily knew she was off the hook for one more night.

. . .

Her friend Sally wrote from Hawaii. She had been to a luau, eaten coconut (at least a thousand calories a slice, Emily thought), and she had a boyfriend, Desmond, who made Sally feel "like a real woman."

. . .

On a warm evening in July, Emily walked around the house listening to the sounds—the rustle of paper she always associated with her father, the rise and fall of her mother's voice who was in the kitchen playing Sorry! with Billy. Over the swinging half-door to the kitchen, Emily could see the top of her head. She heard the rattle of dice and her mother said something she couldn't hear. Billy laughed. A stab of envy shot through her at his easy way around her mother, the way he charmed her and she let him alone.

Emily stopped at the hall mirror and looked at herself. Up close, things looked encouraging, a little more flatness along the belly. From far away, a discouraging bulk. She imagined cutting herself out of herself, like a giant paper doll, taking scissors and snipping off the bulge at the thighs, the stomach. She wanted to carve this excess from herself. By August, she willed it gone.

. . .

Emily was down to 115, a breakthrough, the morning her mother cut off the top of her soft-boiled egg and said to her, "Guess what Emmy? I've decided to make you my summer project—I've decided to make you a dress."

"Great," Emily said. She hoped her voice didn't betray her. Their family had a basement full of her mother's projects: curtain panels; an unfinished, pink-checked dress for Emily; a half-upholstered armchair. Emily associated her mother's projects with mouths full of pins, the late night pounding of the sewing machine, cold suppers, and her mother running around the house exclaiming, "Don't these colors look *delicious* together?"

Nevertheless, Emily was measured and whisked off to the fabric store. Her mother hovered about her, trying to interest her in pleated skirts or jumpers. "You'll like them," her mother said fiercely. "They're *classics.*" Emily fought for the empire-waist mini. To her surprise, she won.

Home, lunch somehow made it to the table in the breakfast nook, jumbled with cookbooks, school ribbons, and bills stacked in a corner, and Emily ate to the cool sound of her mother's scissors slicing the strawberry-dotted fabric.

"You look good now, Emily," Emily's mother said. "You must be about done with your dieting."

"Just ten more pounds," Emily said.

"Five," her mother said.

"Ten," Emily said to herself. She looked at her mother's sandwich longingly, and wondered how long it would be until she was hungry again. Fifteen minutes? A whole hour? It was all so temporary. Her own plate painted with a snow-covered bridge and decorated with a few curds of cottage cheese. She wondered where this bridge was, and how old it was. She wondered if any of the boards were rotted, and if anyone had ever fallen through it into the ice-blue river below.

. . .

Emily's father had taken to kneading the bones in her shoulders and saying, "I just want to get you down and force feed you like a goose." He'd pantomime stuffing great wads of bread down her throat. Then he'd tousle her hair and smile, "But you're too damn stubborn, Em. Too much Sullivan."

. . .

Sally wrote from Hawaii. "What we have to do, Em, is decide on our personalities. When you go to high school, you have to have a personality. I have decided I will be loud and adventurous. Ha, ha, ha, laughing all the time. I'll wear pink lipstick and I plan to do a lot of riding around in cars. How 'bout you, Em? What will you be?" "I'll be," Emily started to write her back, "I'll be," but she couldn't go further.

. . .

It was the first week of August, Emily had no tan, and she had reached a plateau at 113 pounds. She was lying out in the backyard, trying to get sun. She had been here fifteen minutes and it seemed like two hours. The smell of the grass was suffocating. Hard, pinkish apples hung from the tree. She looked down her at her stomach. It was flatter, and she could see the soft points of her hips. Beautiful, soft points. She wanted hollows.

. . .

She was reading "Can This Marriage Be Saved?" which made Emily wish she were married, where there were answers for things. She would be good at it. She was good at organizing things, cupboards and cooking, better at it than her mother who was always piling up bowls that didn't fit together, and letting the bottoms of her cupboards get sticky with honey, and never clearing out her household products, so Emily had found old oils and liniments that her grandmother had used.

The neighbor, a single thirtyish woman named Grace Childs, came out her back door with a lawn chair in her hand and iced tea in the other. She had on a blue striped bathing suit with a red sash she described as "gay" and Emily could see broken veins in her legs like small shooting stars.

"Mind if I join you?" Grace asked as she settled herself in the lawn chair and started to rub her legs with oil.

They were silent a minute and Emily could hear the grasshoppers buzzing and the distant whine of a lawn mower.

Grace slapped a mosquito on her leg. "You're really svelte these days, Emily. Do you know that?"

"Thanks," Emily said. She wouldn't have dreamed of asking Grace what svelte meant.

"I probably ought to cut down myself," Grace slapped the side of her thighs.

Emily silently agreed, and said, "It's hard."

"Of course, men like a little something to hold on to," Grace said and looked down the top of her thick Dacron suit. "Don't tell your mother that. She doesn't remember what it's like out there." She shifted in her chair. "They're always after one thing and one thing only. You have to watch out, Emily. You've got good bones."

It was the nicest thing Grace had ever said to her.

"Unfortunately, you've also inherited the Sullivan legs, just calves to feet." Grace sighed as if this pained her. "Like He left out the ankles as a joke."

· · ·

That night, Emily slid her knife under the chicken skin, carefully lifted it to the side of her plate, and cut the meat from the bone. She diced it into small pieces, and began to eat, chewing twenty times before she swallowed.

"Are you going to eat that chicken or dissect it?" her father said.

"Emily eats like a scientist!" Billy cried.

"You could use some willpower yourself, Ted," Emily's mother said. "Take a look at your plate."

"Yeah, Dad," Emily looked across the lazy Susan that Billy was spinning to her father's plate loaded with chicken, potatoes, and twice-buttered bread. "Do you really need that bread?"

"No," he said. Then he deliberately lifted the slice to his mouth, bit, and looked at her, unrepentant.

Emily felt a hook of disgust. "If you cut off the chicken skin, you cut out 100 calories," she said.

"Yes, Ted," her mother said as she stopped mid-kitchen, holding a skillet of chicken grease. "You could just start there."

"Look," her father said, petulant. "I'm not going to cut the damn chicken skin off my chicken. Or stop buttering my bread. I work all day and I'm tired and now you want to take my food away!"

"Please! Please! Don't take my chicken!" Billy cried in a high falsetto and held his arms around his plate.

Emily's parents laughed, but the tension still quivered in the air between them.

When her family had finished dinner and left the kitchen, Emily cleared the table. She brought the plates over to the counter and shut the kitchen door. She listened for voices. It was quiet. Then she hunched over the counter and began to devour what

was left on the plates, picking at the tiny scraps of meat still
clinging to the bone, and crunching the gristle between her teeth.

. . .

One evening when everyone had gone to the band concert, Emily
put on a miniskirt and a tight-fitting top, and she went into her
parents' room and looked at herself in front of the full-length
mirror. She weighed 110 pounds, and she wondered what she
would look like ten pounds thinner. She put on a long strand
of pearls of her mother's, rouge, and some dangly earrings. She
held the necklace out from her body, and watched herself in the
mirror as she danced slowly, shifting her weight from one foot to
the other, the way she'd seen Twiggy dance once on the TV. She
put her head back and made herself laugh, as if a man had just
whispered something in her ear. She pursed her lips, and sucked
in her cheeks. She liked her face in the dim light.

"Boo!"

She started, and looked up to see her brother watching her in
the doorway.

"I thought you were at the park," she said. She felt stupid.

"It was boring," he said, "So I came home. Why do you have
all that stuff on?"

"None of your business."

"You'll look just right on Halloween. We can set you on
the front porch with the pumpkin." He mimicked a dangling
skeleton. Then he cocked his head and looked at her sharply,
"How come you're so skinny?"

"I'm reducing," Emily said carefully. "I was overweight, now
I'm reducing."

"No," her brother said. "You're bony—Maroney!" He ran out
of the room and she could hear him all the way down the hall
to his room, repeating in a sing-song, "Bony Maroney, Bony
Maroney."

. . .

Emily stretched her legs out in the claw-footed tub, watched the bubbles rise up, and felt the warmth course through her body. She liked the way her flesh curved and hugged her limbs. Five more pounds and she'd look like a model.

Someone knocked on the door, and Emily's mother walked in and stopped.

"Emily Sullivan, my God!" she gasped.

"What?" Emily looked up at the ceiling for spiders.

"I can count all your ribs."

"So?"

"What do you weigh?"

"A hundred and twelve." Close enough, Emily thought.

"You don't weigh a hundred and twelve. Get on the scale."

"Mom!" Emily slid down into the water, hoping the bubbles would cover her. "I'm in the bathtub."

"Now!" Her mother said, and gripped her wrist.

The bathwater sloshed as she stood up and she got on the scale without drying herself. She could feel her mother's breath on her back.

"My God!" her mother gasped. "Oh, Emily!"

"Five more pounds," Emily said, wrapping a towel around herself.

"No!" her mother said. She stood looking at her, then she unzipped her pants. She looked down at her bare stomach, sucked in her breath, and pressed her hands against the sagging flesh. Then she sat on the toilet and looked up at Emily, sighed, and said, "Why are you doing this?"

. . .

Billy was making gagging sounds.

Emily looked at her own mound of corned beef and thought he had a point. It was disgusting looking. And 400 calories a cup.

"Oh, come on, kids," Emily's mother said. "Your father loves corned beef hash."

"Goody for him," Billy said and smiled at her mother so she didn't get mad. He plunged a fork into his fried eggs and broke the yolks. "Dam is breaking!" he said to Emily like he'd said a hundred times before. It was their old joke.

"Dam's breaking!" she yelled at him as she cut into her own eggs, and as the yolk broke and ran, a huge sadness swooped down over her.

"Ted, do you know how much your daughter weighs?" her mother asked as she walked to the stove for his coffee.

"About like a cement truck," her father winked at Emily.

"Ted, I'm serious," her mother said.

"What now?" he sighed.

"She weighs 106 pounds. One hundred and six pounds! She looks like a death camp victim!" She shook her potholder at him. "We've got to do something, Ted. This is serious."

"Oh, Mary Susan," he said, pressing the last of the hash onto his fork. "It's just a phase."

Emily took advantage of this little conversation to take her plate to the sink. She'd slip around the corner, feed the hash to the dog, and then wash off her plate and load it in the dishwasher.

"You eat every last bite of that young lady," her mother called.

Emily looked to her father.

"Obey your mother."

"It tastes like dog barf!" Billy cried as he forked some into his mouth.

"Eat!" her mother said.

Emily looked at her and started to eat the mound of corned beef hash mince by mince, separating out the little white pieces that looked like fat. Her mother cleared the table. Everyone went off into the house. She sat at the table eating until the sun went down, until the neighbors put out the lights, until the crickets started to sing and her father came into the room and threw what was left away. "You're something, Emily," he said, and shook his head. He did not smile.

. . .

She began having nightmares. They came like great waves just as she was drifting to sleep, rolls of sensation that pinned her to the bed and threatened to engulf her, to swallow her up. She was too small to resist. She would tell her arm, "Move arm," and the arm could not move. She would tell her leg, "Move leg," and the leg was lifeless as stone. She dreamt about rooms of giant furniture, where she was tiny underfoot. Sometimes she even called her mother to her bed, crying. She was scared enough not to feel silly. Her mother would sit at the side of her bed as Emily lay down again under the light summer blankets, and her mother would smooth the hair away from her forehead and say, "What are you worried about, Em? What's running around the old noggin?" and Emily sometimes felt it was the first time her mother had talked to her in months. She wanted to tell her about the dreams, about this great tide of fear that washed over her and she was drowning in it like an animal washed into a century it was not meant to survive. She felt so lost at times, it was hard for her to speak. Her mother would leave when she fell asleep, and she'd wake up late in the morning, exhausted and sweating.

. . .

"Desmond had deep brown eyes, and he let me feel his thing," Sally said, and she sunk her teeth into an ear of corn.

"You felt his thing!" Emily said. She and Sally were finishing the picnic she'd planned. Only 350 calories, she'd counted every one of them.

"We did more than feel it."

"You did more than feel it!" A ball of fear wadded up in Emily's stomach.

"Emily," Sally dangled her corn from her hand, "I told you he made me feel like a woman."

"Well what's *that* supposed to mean?"

"Do I have to *explain?*" Sally had been talking like this ever since she'd gotten back from Hawaii. She finished her corn and looked at Emily. "I'm still hungry."

"You want more?" Emily said, and she looked at Sally's empty plate. So Sally was tan and she had a boyfriend and she'd had sex, too. She also had thighs.

The garage door creaked open and Emily's mother walked across the yard carrying more hamburgers, corn, and the petit fours Emily had spent four hours on that morning.

Sally looked relieved. "Thank you, Mrs. Sullivan," she said, and reached for a hamburger. She took an enthusiastic bite and a little meat juice dribbled down her chin, and she said to Emily, "Maybe I'll go on a diet now I'm back."

"Just cut out butter," Emily said. "People butter everything."

"Yeah, I know," Sally said. "But it tastes good."

"But people put butter on their bread, on their meat, on their vegetables. It's such a waste!" Emily was getting heated.

Emily picked up the pan of zucchini. "You take a perfectly low-calorie vegetable, like this zucchini here, put butter on it, and you've wasted calories! *One hundred* calories! Things taste good without butter. Vegetables are just fine without butter. Butter is fat! Butter is grease! Butter disguises!"

"Emily," Sally said and looked at her sideways, "it's just butter."

. . .

About the end of August, about the time her grandmother Ruth was due to arrive from California, Emily noticed when she turned sideways in the hall tree mirror, she narrowed into a straight line. The bones in her elbows were bigger than her upper arms. She had cheekbones now, too. Naked, she could see shadowy hollows in her hipbones. Sometimes, if she looked at herself in a dusky, forgiving light, she was almost beautiful.

. . .

Emily was walking downtown to the library, to Woolworths to check out the make-up, and then to the department store to try on clothes. It was her new sport. She loved the way the lined wool skirts slid easily up and over her hips, the satin linings whispering, the way Flora the saleswoman at Bridger Mercantile clucked her tongue and said, "What are you now dear? A size 5?" She liked to imagine herself in these new clothes on her first day of high school, her golden plaid skirt brushing her legs, her perfectly matched sweater just nipping her waist as she strode down the hall to her homeroom, laughing.

She came blinking back into the sunlight, empty-handed, when she saw her eighth grade teacher across the street, and she ran after her, excited to show Mrs. Delaney her new self. Emily touched her on the shoulder, but when she turned around she looked confused, and then she put the palm of her hand on Emily's cheek and said, "My lord, girl, have you been sick?"

. . .

Emily's mother came to her door and told Emily to move into the sewing room. Just like that. Her mother said she wanted to repaper Emily's room. "Well, what if I like the old paper?" Emily said, her hand on her hip. "It's just for a while," her mother replied. "But it's my room," Emily said. "It's my house," her mother said.

Emily carried armloads of clothes sullenly through the halls, and gave her mother dark looks.

"C'mon Em, you'll love it," her mother said. "It's got little white flowers on pink, your favorite color! It's very feminine."

"Gross!" Emily thought to herself and she could feel it rising, the old blind rage, but she didn't do that now, she had stopped fighting with her mother. Emily looked at her mother and thought, "I hate flowers." Then she went into the sewing room, and shut the door. Hard.

Her mother redecorating *her* room, with *her* Beatles posters and her mirror painted with a nail polish peace symbol, while she was stuck in the sewing room with lots of pins, old patterns, and a dressmaker's form.

She threw her clothes on the floor and stamped all over them. "You'll love it," she whispered. "It's got little white flowers." She sat on the bed and stared at the molded form of a woman's torso. She hated it, too. Something about the way it was just there, no excuses, its thick waist widening out to blunt, shelf-like hips, the breasts stuck out as if to say "obey me." She jabbed a pin in the stomach. A breast. She smiled to herself. Then she stuck pins in the y-shaped depression at the top of the legs.

. . .

By the end of August, she stopped laughing. She couldn't figure it out. It was like a great cloud of seriousness had settled on her. Her father would be telling jokes at dinner, or Billy would stick cold spaghetti down her back, even the Laurel and Hardy movies they'd show on the family projector wouldn't do it. Sometimes they even had the opposite effect—she'd cry at these sad attempts, fraught with love and misunderstanding, that always failed. She started reading old novels about Southern families, separated by the war, that ended with big, tearful reunions, and she'd cry herself to sleep. She couldn't figure out why she felt so bad when she was beginning to look so good.

. . .

The morning she stepped on the scale and weighed 96 pounds, she was filled with a vague disappointment. She couldn't say why.

. . .

Labor Day weekend the family went up to Lost Lake for what Emily's mother called the "last hurrah." Emily's father had been planning the menu for three days, and when he showed it to her, printed in his tiny pinched handwriting on the long legal paper, Emily felt tired, as if she had to start figuring out how to avoid all this food on the spot.

He looked into her face and said, "We'll have corn on the cob, we'll have chicken, and, if you help pick the berries, we'll have your favorite huckleberry pie."

She wanted him to stop pleading with her like a big dog. "Looks kind of fattening, Dad," she said.

"You used to love huckleberry pie. You used to eat three pieces at a time. Em," he said softly, "can't you let up?"

She went upstairs to pack. When she got to the landing, she turned and looked back at the kitchen, and she wanted to whisper, "I *hate* huckleberry pie," but when she started to say it, her throat lumped up and the words wouldn't come.

Later, up at the cabin, Emily and her mother and father were sitting out on the deck watching the camp robbers eat the last of the morning's pancakes, when they heard a shout from the lake. Emily's dad started up from his chair, and they looked out and saw Billy out in the rowboat, holding up a great big cutthroat trout.

Her mother and father clapped and shouted congratulations that echoed across the lake: "Billy-boy! Hoop-hoop hurray!"

Emily watched him row to shore, and walk up the path holding the fish by its gills.

"Let's get the camera!" Emily's mother said when he reached the deck. "I think it's the biggest fish I've ever seen out of Lost Lake." She got up from the chair and the screen door banged shut behind her.

"Nice catch, Billy!" Her father looked into Billy's face to be sure he had his attention, "This is a cutthroat trout, *Salmo clarki.*"

Billy looked at them all and clasped his hands over his head like a champion. Then he picked up his fish and said, looking levelly at all of them, "I'll go gut my fish now."

Emily's father looked after him as the screen banged shut behind him.

"We could cook it tonight," her father said. "You know, roll it up in cornmeal and fry it."

Her mother picked up a broom and started to sweep the steps.

Emily went into the front room where a distant song crackled over the shortwave radio, then to the kitchen where Billy was repeating the names of the organs as he gutted his fish.

"Mr. Trout had a fly for lunch. Wanna see?" he said, walking toward her with a long string of pale, slimy guts.

"No!" she said. "That's disgusting."

"Wanna wanna?" he said. He started to chase her, holding up the guts. "Pretty, lovely fish guts."

"Billy! Get those gross things away from me," she said.

"Wanna?" he said and put them close to her face.

"Stop that!" she said and she slammed the screen door, and walked down the path, carpeted with tamarack needles, to the lake. She stood for a minute by the rowboat, looking out to the glistening lake. She was breathing fast, and she felt like she was going to cry. Because Billy held some fish guts to her face? She dragged the rowboat back into the water, the paddle banging against the side, and she stepped in and pushed herself out into the water.

The lake was quiet, and she didn't care if they thought she was copying Billy. She was just tired of the noise. She could still hear their voices, she could hear them over and over as they echoed across the lake, and she could hear her mother say, "Where's Emily?" and father answer, "In the outhouse I think." She rowed quickly out of sight. "Te-ed," her mother called. "Where'd Emily go?" and her voice bounced from one shore to another, "go, go?" then their voices rose up together, rippled over the water and into the cattails, "go, go?" They looked toylike and fragile and they were looking in the wrong direction. A rush of loneliness came over her like that night her mother had sat on her bed and Emily had wanted to tell her about the waves of fear and the rooms of giant furniture, but she hadn't been able to find the words.

She stood up. The boat was unsteady, shifting from side to side as the water slapped wood. "Over here!" she called. She waved. She saw her father tap her mother's arm, and point to her. "In the boat—alone," she called, and she listened to her voice skip across the lake, *own, own.*

Emily watched her dad put his hand up to shade his eyes as he looked from the dock out over the lake, then he pointed and said, "There! Mary Susan, she's rowing," which to Emily in the boat sounded like *"owing, owing."*

A breeze ruffled the water. She picked up the oars and began to row slowly toward shore, as the water continued to echo their voices, *owing, owing.*

ETIQUETTE

The skillet rang as I slammed it on the stove and started to cook the onions. Maurice was in the hospital dying. My boyfriend Sam hadn't called. I was twenty-three, unmarried, and back in Bridger, Montana, my hometown, living with my great-aunt. The onions sputtered as I shook salt over the pan.

"As I was saying," Auntie May shouted to me from the next room, "Maurice was crazy about me, writing me letter after letter from Nicaragua, sending telegrams. And telegrams were expensive in those days. And on Valentine's Day once, when we were courting—isn't that today, Eleanor?—he rode horseback to the Theta house and stopped under my window and sang."

"How wonderful," I shouted back. I opened the mushroom soup and dumped it, wiggling, in the pan.

"And when the housemother came outside to chase him off," she continued, "he apologized, handed her a bunch of hothouse roses to be sent up to me, then he turned around and galloped down Arthur Street."

"What a character," I said, turning the heat up on the burner, hoping the sizzling would drone out the sound of her voice. My boyfriend was in Alaska, doing God knows what—he sure as hell wasn't calling me—and I didn't want to hear about flowers or songs under windows.

As I carried the salad into the dining room, she looked up at me. "And you know what he sang?"

"How about dinner?" I said, smiling for all I was worth.

"'Let Me Call You Sweetheart,'" Auntie May warbled, swaying back and forth in time to the music.

"Aren't you hungry?"

"Let me call you sweetheart, you belong to me."

"Don't you want to come to the table?" And don't you want to stop singing? I thought as I laid out silverware and napkins and the crystal goblets that tinkled and sang what sounded like love songs.

She stopped and watched me from one of the ladder-backed chairs that lined the dining room. "Water glasses on the right," she said.

"The right." I moved the glasses. "Of course."

"Oh, there I go again, getting in your way." She put her hand over her mouth. "I'm sorry, Eleanor. It's just that you need to know these things, dear—how to give a dinner party, how to set a table correctly, where to put the name cards and the salad forks and the wine glasses—they just don't teach these things."

"No, they don't," I said. I don't have use for them, I silently added, in the cabin in Alaska where Sam and I forked our dinners out of a crockpot.

"Well, they should," she said, standing up. "How in God's name will you know what to do?"

"I don't," I said, still smiling. "I don't know much at all."

"Well," she said, brushing off her skirt. "I guess etiquette is about as outdated as I am." With an angry wheeze of her stockings, she walked off to "freshen up," but when she came back, she was all smiles.

I brought out our plates and sat down.

We were silent a minute, listening to the whap of snow gusting down the mountain behind the house, waving the dark branches of the larch trees.

"Stroganoff," she said, looking down at her plate. "You're quite a cook, you know, Eleanor. You really know the way to a man's heart."

"Hmm," I said.

"Would you like to say the blessing?" she asked.

"Go ahead," I said, pointing my fork at her.

She bowed her head. "Bless this food and this company to thy service," she prayed. And get me out of here soon, I started to silently add but stopped when her voice dropped and she whispered, "Please bring back my Maurice." She kept her head down. There was only the sound of the windows rattling.

I touched her arm.

She palmed her hair. She put her hand on mine and looked up at me, her face grateful. Then she leaned across the table and whispered, "Eleanor, dear? Just one little thing...."

"Yes?"

"Never point."

. . .

Auntie May's grandfather had come from Iowa to Bridger, a small mountain town cupped in the high reaches of the Rockies, on an immigrant train near the turn of the century. He set up a bank, built with stone hauled by train from the Missouri River, and like all professional people in town, he distanced himself over the years as much as possible from anything distinctly Western. On Saturday nights, when ranch hands and loggers left the wheat and the cattle and the big-timbered woods for the Main Street bars, the men of my family gathered to discuss investments, smoke cigars, and compare new cars—Model A's, hooded Buicks, and later, sleek Thunderbirds. The women served lime "bombe," with aprons over dresses stitched up by dressmakers, who came to live with the family twice a year. When they weren't busy serving up dessert, they headed up committees to improve the symphony or the theatre or the library, and prided themselves on gardens. Not vegetable gardens, for they bought their produce from a truck farm east of town—but flower gardens of iris, dahlias, and heavy-headed daffodils. No one lived anywhere else for the next four generations.

. . .

My Great-aunt May and my Great-uncle Maurice Dietrich
were the grandparents I never had, and as a child I worshipped
them. Witty, urbane, and adventurous, they were the most
cosmopolitan of the lot. My great-uncle was a Spanish professor
at the university and my great-aunt served gallons of tea and
pounds of "dainty collations" to charities and women's clubs.
They also traveled. They traveled a world I knew only through
the presents they brought me: flamenco dolls, Mexican tea sets,
a Viennese music box. As they aged, their bridge clubs grew
smaller and their trips got shorter and closer to home, and
finally, they did not travel at all.

One morning, a week after I'd returned from Alaska, my
mother and I stood knocking at the Dietrichs' back door when
we heard a tapping sound. We turned to see Auntie May at the
living room window, clutching her robe. "Something's wrong,"
my mother said. "She's not dressed."

That afternoon, Maurice went in the hospital, and I moved in
with May. As she napped on the living room couch, a velvet affair
some ancestor won in a poker game with Louis the XIV, I waited
in her dressing room. As the house slept—no radio playing, no
TV droning—I hung my things in a cedar-lined closet where
clothes were organized by season, shoes were placed in shoe racks,
and gloves were stacked in a violet-scented satin box.

I looked out the window. Some snow obscured the hedge in
a veil of white. I wondered how long I would have to stay here.
When I came home at Christmas, the agreement was this: I
would stay in Bridger for a month, then Sam would join me. We
would move out to Seattle. We would start again. Then Maurice
fell and broke his hip.

A passing car hissed through the streets. I wondered where
Sam was at this exact moment. I thought of the tiny cabin with
the leaky roof I'd left, of Sam rising each morning to start the

wood stove, of the green streaks of trees through the Visqueen-covered window, of mountains white and pointed as sharks' fins. I wondered why, when I'd gone to Alaska to escape my family, I'd come back. Why we weren't getting married. Why I didn't know what to do about anything.

. . .

Suddenly, as I sat on a needlepoint chair in this home of seven-course dinner parties, gloves worn up to the elbow, opera glasses and libraries of classics bound in leather and worn from use, I felt protected, as if my life could just stop outside the door.

. . .

When I heard her hands moving across the coffee table for her glasses, I brought out the tea.

She patted the couch next to her.

"Tell your Auntie May all about your fiancé," she said, leaning close to me as if we were going to plan a "spree," her word for adventure. "Don't leave out a thing."

What could I say? That we once met at coffee break in the cannery fish house and made love among the silvers? That in Kenai we once fought so loudly the neighbors called the police? That Alaska was a place of heartbreaking beauty, where I was miserable and where Sam wanted to live forever? "He's fine," I said.

"You're a brave little thing with your beau away." She put her teacup on the coffee table. I watched the heat cloud the marble.

"I'm surviving," I said. I wondered if Sam was sleeping with anyone else. I tried to picture her. Tall, blonde, and thin. No, dark, voluptuous. And laughing. Always laughing.

"I imagine you must be missing him."

"Yeah, it's hard," I said. A redhead. And she loved to hike.

"You're lucky," she said. "Your life is all in front of you."

"I know," I said. The idea filled me with dread.

We were quiet. Then she shook her head slightly, and said,

"When Maurice was in Nicaragua, Mother said, 'See other boys, don't pine.' But I'm afraid my heart was smitten! We wrote the silliest love letters." She looked at me and laughed, short and sure. "We burned them all when we got married."

"I'd be horrified if anyone read ours," I said. My latest letter ended, "What the fuck is going on?"

"Of course," Auntie May said, lifting her chin, "I didn't just moon. I taught rancher's children. And we had singing parties like you and your friends. And at the end the men would bow and sing 'Good Night, Ladies,' and off they'd go in their buggies!" She waved off the invisible buggies. Then she stopped talking and looked into my eyes as if she could see things. As if she knew the first night I met Sam, I got into bed with him dressed in a flannel nightgown and he pulled it off, laughing, "What's this?"

She pointed her chin at me. "Always leave them asking for more."

. . .

We were watching the evening news when the phone rang. I answered. It was Sam.

"Hey!" a voice shouted. "What's up?"

"I'm taking care of my Auntie May," I said, and lowered my voice, "and getting lessons in etiquette."

"Great!" he said. In the background, I heard people calling his name. People were always calling his name. Sam was boisterous, and insistently happy, and he was always surrounded by friends. The phone squawked as he put his hand over the receiver and I could hear him yell, "Shut your yaps, guys!" Voice muffled, he said to me, "Hey, sweetheart, do you know what day it is?"

"Yeah," I said. "February 15. I knew what day it was yesterday, too."

"I'm sorry," he whispered. "Don't be mad, Elly. Please? Will you still be my furry valentine?"

I remembered the first time he called me "Elly." I had despised the nickname as a child, but somehow he made it seem charming. "Okay," I laughed. "I'll be your damn valentine."

"That's better," he said.

"Who are you with?" I could hear a jukebox playing "Knights in White Satin."

"Carol and Mitch, Paul, Gary. We wish you were here at the Chum. I wish you were here. I really, really wish you were here."

"Well," I said. "I'm not."

"C'mon, Eleanor . . ."

"Do you really?"

"Really what?"

"Miss me?"

"I miss your voice. Your hair. Your thighs. Your breasts. Every nook and cranny of you."

"I can't wait till you come down, Sam . . ."

"Well, that's kind of why I called."

Suddenly it all made sense to me. The two weeks he hadn't called. The call from the bar. He didn't want to give me bad news alone.

"Money's good, Eleanor," he said quickly. "I'll just work a couple more weeks on the rig, and just think, I'll be loaded next time you see me."

"Whenever," I said and I could hear the plastic crack as I slammed down the phone.

. . .

On the fourth step, May stopped. "Did I tell you about Claire?"

"Yes," I said. "Ready to keep climbing?"

She turned to look at me. "Funny, I don't *remember* telling you about Claire."

"You did," I said. I was in no mood to hear about Claire Duchane, the granddaughter of May's best friend, who always made my life seem like a nice try. Once Auntie May wrote me

169

at camp, "Don't worry you didn't make High Honor Roll," her lacy handwriting contorted because she was under the dryer at the beauty parlor. "There's always next year!" She enclosed a clipping listing those who had made it. Claire's name was circled.

"She's working at a lawyer's office in Seattle, making lots of money, but the best news of all is—guess what?"

"Up we go, Auntie May," I said.

She didn't budge. "The best news of all is Claire's engaged. Isn't that *wonderful?*"

I flushed in the dark stairwell and gripped her elbow. "Claire's quite a girl," I said and tried not to push her up the last four steps.

At the top of the stairs, she rested on my arm. "Don't get old, Eleanor."

"Okay," I said. "If you say so."

We walked into the cypress-paneled bedroom, where the twin beds were covered with chenille spreads. Facing the wall behind her bed, Auntie May began to peel off her clothes. She seemed to grow smaller as she took off layer after layer—the pink knit dress, slip, padded bra, full-length girdle, and the thick stockings she slowly rolled down from the garters—the foundations no woman of her generation would be without. I turned to the other wall and in seconds, peeled off my shirt, jeans, underwear.

A storm was blowing in. The spruce trees creaked in the wind, and I could hear the ticks and sighs of the house as it settled in the cold. I wondered how we must look to someone passing on the street. Two naked women, sixty years apart in age, facing opposite walls. I wondered what she looked like naked.

"Eleanor, dear, can you hand me my nightgown?" She continued to face the wall, embarrassed.

I handed her the nightgown, and looked out the window to avoid seeing her. And there she was, rippled in the old glass. Her arms over her head, the nightgown slipping down over her back and buttocks, pink and smooth, glowing in the lamplight. Only her breasts looked old and thin on her bright skin.

I quickly undressed and got into bed. The blankets were heavy and warm. My arms were stiff at my sides.

Auntie May turned off the light.

There was an awkward silence. A dog barked in the distance.

"Maurice always kissed me before we slept," she whispered.

I thought of getting up. And later, as if this was a movie I could stop and reshoot, I saw myself rising from the bed and bending over her, her white hair curling across the pillow, her near-sighted eyes searching my face as I kissed her.

But I lay perfectly still. She sighed and turned over. I listened to the swish of snow falling, and I wondered if it was snowing in Alaska, if Sam was watching sled dogs from the Arctic, if he was in bed at this moment. And with whom. The wind was muffled, larch branches tapped against the window, and I was almost asleep when I heard the dry whispers of May's prayers.

· · ·

Two nights later, Auntie May went to visit Maurice in the hospital. I went to the Noose, a sleazy bar on the wrong side of the tracks. "The Noose?" my friend Sally Denise said when I invited her. "Are you sure?" "Please," I said. "I need an Auntie May antidote." She came.

As the band began to play, "You're a Man, I'm a Woman, Hold My Hand," I said, "I don't know, Sally." I stirred the pink clouds of my tequila sunrise. "This particular car might be spinning its wheels. Sam's staying in Alaska."

"Well," she said. "It's all how you look at it. I mean the poor guy might just be trying to get you guys a stake. You got to have a stake, Eleanor."

"I know," I said. "But if he really loved me, he'd leave that damn state on the next plane. He didn't even remember Valentine's Day."

"Oh, Eleanor, write me a romance."

"Okay, so I'm unrealistic," I said. "And you're right. Here the poor guy's working his ass off on a big stinky oil rig so we can make a go of it. And I'm crying in my beer."

"There you go, kiddo," she said, patting my arm. "Cheer up, it won't be long."

. . .

The waitress came to our table with drinks, a skinny, frizzy-haired woman whose face had settled early into impatience. "Tequila sunrise and a whiskey ditch, girls. From the guy at the bar in the white shirt."

We nodded at the bar. Three men in white shirts nodded back.

"I mean, where would I ever find someone like Sam?" I said. "Someone who'd bring me breakfast in bed? Who'd bike over to my house balancing a plate of pancakes from the school cafeteria on his handlebars? Who'd make me laugh when I got all worked up about my future?"

Sally was about to answer when a tall man with a pear-shaped belly whispered something in her ear. "And why the hell not?" she said, and went off to dance.

I lit one of her cigarettes, and thought about the letter I'd just gotten from Sam. It was sweet, cajoling. I wondered if this meant he was sleeping with someone. I took a long pull on my whiskey and felt the liquid warm my throat. No, I wasn't going to think that way anymore. Sally was right. I'd been underestimating Sam. I'd been selfish, grabby, needy, all those things I hated most in women. No. Sam and I were good together. We were going to Seattle, and we were going make it.

A man whispered in my ear, "What's a beautiful girl like you doing in a place like this?"

He called himself Danny D. We slow-danced, and he held me so tight I could feel the metal snaps on his shirt pock my belly. When I tried to move away, he nuzzled my ear.

"Lonely tonight?" he said.

"Lonely?" I said. "Who's lonely?"

The band burst into "Ace in the Hole," and Danny D. broke away from me and started to dance, bending backwards, wiggling his hips, punching the air with his clenched arms. He looked at me with a determined, glazed look in his eyes—as if I had vanished, as if I were only the dimly lit air.

I went to find Sally Denise, desperate. As we left, I looked back. People stopped dancing and formed a circle around Danny D. Someone started clapping. "Gator!" a man shouted. "Go for it, buddy!" As I walked out the door, I could see Danny D. in the middle of the shifting crowd, bending his back to the floor, his eyes on the mirrored ball that glittered and turned in the smoky light.

· · ·

Auntie May was asleep on the couch when I got back. I stood, wavering, at the doorway, watching the blue light of the television flicker across her. Her right cheek was pressed flat against the velvet, and her face looked sad. I covered her with a blanket and was making coffee, spilling grounds around the kitchen, when the phone rang.

It was my father. He didn't make it, he said. Maurice is dead.

I looked from a corner of chipped plaster in the phone nook to Auntie May, still curled up on the couch. "Oh, God, what do I do?" I said.

"Let her rest till we get there," he said, and hung up.

I put my head in my hands and listened to the tiny explosions of the coffeepot. Auntie May sighed and turned over.

"Eleanor?" she said drowsily.

I brought her tea. She warmed her hands around the cup,

the rings slipping around the thin fingers. The phone rang again. I prayed there had been a mistake, some mix-up of names. It was Sam.

"Sam! It's you," I said. "It's you," echoed back at me. The connection was bad. As I whispered, "Something's happened," Sam's voice came booming through.

"Surprise!" Sam said. "I'm coming down in a week." His voice was full and sure.

"A week?" I said. "A week?" the phone echoed. Suddenly I didn't want to tell Sam about Maurice. I didn't want to hear it echoed back at me, the words thick and slurring over the static, and most of all, I didn't want to hear the way Sam would warm it and shape it and make it his own. "It's not a good time, Sam."

He didn't hear me. "I just hiked Crystal Lake," he said. "'Member where the eaglets screamed all night? Where you said you hated Alaska, set up a tent across the lake, and went fishing naked?"

"I caught a dolly varden and a cold." I smiled and picked plaster from the wall. "Look can I call back? Something's happened." "Happened," the phone said.

"I need to see you," he said quietly.

"I've got to go," I said, and gently set the receiver in its cradle.

I got some coffee and sat down next to Auntie May on the couch.

Auntie May cupped her hands around her teacup. "Sam?" she said.

I nodded.

"He misses you, dear."

"I think so," I said, surprised.

"How I missed my Maurice!" she said, touching her heart. "While we were down in Nicaragua, he'd be out with his crews, traveling up and down the coast for weeks looking for mahogany, and me home with my tea and my piano and my pet monkey Julio."

"Auntie May, tell me about Claire's wedding plans." Talk about something else, please, I thought.

"I played Chopin, Mozart, and all the old songs we used to sing, 'Buffalo Gals' and 'Danny Boy.' The night they thought he'd drowned, I played them all night long. I played every piece of music I knew, then I started again, and when they brought him, shouting, down the street, I was playing 'Green Grow the Rushes, Ho!' for the seventeenth time."

I stared into my coffee cup.

She looked at me and said, "When he walked in the door, I pulled the cover down over the keys, and I never played again."

It was quiet outside, no cars, no wind, and in the dark living room, her words seemed like tiny stitches holding our universe together.

. . .

When Dad told her, she held her head high and angry and she fixed her eyes on him, then something broke and her chest caved in and she shrunk down in the chair and began to smooth her dress, over and over. "We've got to make arrangements. We've got to call Paul, Sarah, Babe," she said, naming people who had been dead for years. "Papa had many friends."

"May," Dad started.

My mother put her hand on his arm. "Let her talk," she said.

. . .

Auntie May talked on about her father's death, about the satin-lined casket and some limping pallbearer. Then she began to tell stories. In a rushed monotone, she told one story after another, stories about her father that became stories about Maurice that become stories about herself, like one door opening after the next.

I watched the picture above her head, an elk standing in a dark forest, lifting his antlered head to a distant call.

When everyone left, I helped her over to the couch. We sat down. She stopped talking, and stared in front of her. There was a sound of water. A chinook had blown in, and the icicles were dripping.

"We didn't know when he'd arrive," she said out of nowhere. "Mother didn't know what to do about the invitations. Finally we just left the date blank."

I knew she was talking about Maurice. I'd heard this story before. "When did he come?" I said.

She didn't seem to hear me. "What an uproar!" she said. Then her face pulled in around something sad. "But you know what? I didn't know if he was coming at all."

I looked at her. "But all those letters?"

"What letters? He only wrote me twice from Nicaragua." She looked at me as if she couldn't figure out who I was. "I thought I'd teach children the rest of my life. I was an old maid and he was my last chance." She wiped her eyes.

Suddenly I could see her mother, fiercely organizing the wedding, marshaling about the proud little Montana town ordering cakes and violinists, and, late at night, Auntie May lying face down across her bed. "You must have been terrified," I whispered.

"Then he called from Big Timber and we filled in the date," she said quickly as if she'd swept up a mess in a dustpan.

. . .

Her mouth began to make dry clicking sounds. "There was a string quartet and a hundred guests. A hundred guests! And Mother never forgave Maurice for putting out his cigarettes in her vases."

"May, drink some water," I said and handed her a sweating glass.

She took a sip and set it down. "My dress had a six-foot train," she said. "Cream satin with pink silk rosettes and a six-foot train. I was a slip of a thing then!"

"I bet you're exhausted," I said. I remembered Sam had called, years ago it seemed. He was coming. I couldn't remember when.

She looked up at me, her eyes unfocused. "He walked in the door and said, 'Well, old lady, it looks like it's about time.'"

I held out my hand and said, "Let's go to bed, Auntie May. It's been a long day."

She was silent for a minute, then she said softly, "A six-foot train."

I sank back down on the couch. "How old were you when you got married?" I asked.

"About your age, dear," Auntie May looked at me appraisingly. "About forty-three."

. . .

Auntie May declined rapidly after Maurice's death. She was becoming very hard of hearing. One afternoon when she woke from her nap, I told her I was going to change the bed and she began to shout, "What's that? What are you saying? Speak up, girl!"

I took a deep breath. "I'm going to change the bed," I shouted back. I swung her legs to the floor and slipped my hand under her back. She sagged in my arms, but finally I got her to sit at the edge of the bed. The sheets stunk. She had been incontinent since yesterday.

"Okay," I said. "We're going to stand."

I tried to stand her up.

"You're hurting me!" she said petulantly, and sat down again.

"Two's a charm," I said. "Let's go!" and, half-supporting and half-pushing her, I got her to stand up. She wobbled, but she was up, when suddenly—it must have been the phone that startled her—all I knew was that her legs buckled and she was putting her hands out to the floor, and all I could do was to grab her armpits to brace her fall.

She lay at my feet.

"You clumsy girl," she whispered over the ringing phone. "You stupid, clumsy girl. Haven't I told you a thousand times to be more careful?"

"I'm sorry," I said, "I don't know what happened." I helped her to her feet. I wondered who was calling. *Hang up,* I silently pleaded. *Hang the fuck up.*

"Don't you sass me," she hissed. "Don't you ever sass me, Maria."

Today I was Maria. Over the past four days, I had been Sarah, Babe, Mosey, once I was even Mother.

The phone kept ringing.

"I'm going to walk behind you to the armchair," I shouted over the jangling. "Start walking!"

"One more word, girl," she narrowed her eyes, "and it's coming out of your pay."

When May was in the chair, I ran to answer the phone, my head pounding with its high, insistent bleating, but she grabbed my sleeve.

"Maria," she hissed, "obey me."

Blood rushed to my face and in the overheated dressing room stinking of urine and old age, where the phone rang on and on, I turned to her and yelled, "I am not Maria!"

She looked at me, furious. "Listen to me."

The phone kept ringing.

"No. Listen to me. You know what? I am not Maria. Or Sarah. Or Babe. Or Mother," I yelled. "I'm Eleanor. Got that? Eleanor. Your great-great-niece. You know the one who doesn't really have a fiancé or a career or, when you think about it, much of anything."

"Shush," she crooned.

"Eleanor," I said.

She put a finger to her lips and searched my face with her cloudy eyes. "Shush," she said. "Hush."

Blat, blat said the phone.

"Now sit there," I said, my voice softening. "While I answer this goddamn phone."

I ran to the phone, and put my hand on the receiver and felt it vibrate the palm of my hand. I couldn't believe what I'd done.

The phone quit mid-ring.

. . .

While Auntie May rested, I went up to her upstairs bedroom and sat on her bed. There was a miniature painting of Marie Antoinette over her bed, her white hair piled stiff and high atop her head.

It was warming outside, and the world was slick and drippy, and from the window I could see bare spots in the lawn, places where the snow had melted and the old grass was exposed, grey and lifeless, and there were patches of dirt in the tulip beds. I dialed Sam's number.

"Arco, twenty-eight." Pipes clanked and machinery roared in the background. I wondered what time it was in Kenai. Who was living in our shack. What day it was.

Sam came to the phone. "Eleanor?"

Words rushed up toward my throat then stopped up. I couldn't say anything.

"Eleanor, is that you? C'mon, who is this?"

I said nothing and instead touched the smooth, cool surface of a china figurine on the bed stand. It was a man and woman waltzing, the woman in a long, ruffled gown, the man in court attire. He held her out from him like a prize, as if she might break or fly away. I noticed her tiny slippered feet, her thin fingers, how her lace-edged petticoats dipped and flared as she turned, then I heard a click and static and the operator droned, broken connection.

. . .

Mom's bracelets slid down her arm as she took off her coat. After Auntie May fell, she wouldn't eat, wouldn't drink, she'd just nod to the toast or orange juice, then lay her head back down on the pillow. I had called Mom and said, "Help."

"First we need to change the sheets," Mom said when she arrived. "It's ripe in here."

"Gotcha," I said, unrolling my sleeves.

She rolled Auntie May, still sleeping, to one side of the bed, lifted off the sheet, and repeated the process on the other side till the bed was stripped. Auntie May stirred, but didn't wake up.

"Where'd you learn this stuff?" I asked.

"Around," she said and shook out the sheet until it billowed white into the dimming room. Watching her long arms moving quickly over Aunt May's sleeping form, I realized that I hardly knew my mother. I had done everything to live my life differently from her—finishing college, running off to Alaska— and I had always looked with scorn, with an angry pity on what seemed like this small life of hers, this washing, this cooking, this quiet ability to help someone.

Auntie May opened her eyes.

"Would you like anything?" Mom asked.

Auntie May just looked at her.

"She's thirsty," Mom said.

I went to the kitchen for orange juice.

When I came back, Auntie May touched Mom's sleeve and said, "I messed my pants."

Mom helped her to the bathroom, and I scrunched down in the chair, listening to the tap running, the towels snapping, the voices rising and falling, echoing against the tiles, Mom's voice low, smoothing, Auntie May's wobbly. She was calling Mom "Babe." Mom ignored it and answered, "Now let's get you washed up."

Auntie May came back into the bedroom talking about her gardening plans: azaleas, in the front. Snowdrops, lily-of-the-valley, anemones.

I turned back the sheets and handed Mom the orange juice.

"You do it," she said, and handed the glass back. "Just remember. Sit at her side and help support her."

I put my free arm under her neck and along her backbone, and tilted up Auntie May's head.

She closed her eyes for several minutes, as if watching something inside her. Then she leaned forward. I put the edge of the glass between her lips, and in the grey afternoon, motionless as winter, where it seemed like nothing would ever change, Auntie May looked up at me. It seemed, for a minute, I could see beyond the room, beyond the near-sighted blue eyes and far into her, and then she blinked. I tipped the glass. She drank.

IV

SCRABBLE

Netty rested her glasses in her lap, but she didn't put them on. She liked waiting to bring her world into focus, she liked to be damn good and ready. It was startling, that moment of sudden clarity, when the black mailbox and the oak tree and the Dainty Bess tea roses emerged from a blur of color. It stunned and saddened her.

While she waited, her past visited her: Her husband, Thomas, who bowed to the ladies, his waist like a hinge, and held out his pinky finger when he drank tea. Who respected her and bored her and died quietly at fifty. The hairdresser, Mavis, who permed her hair orange once. The neighbor woman, Marla, who came to the back door, holding out the red-streaked palms her husband pressed on the stove when his supper was burnt.

There was Olivia. The petunias made Netty think of Olivia: the sweet, peppery smell of the wide-faced flowers that spilled over the window boxes and onto the porch where Netty would see her today for the first time in fifty years.

Olivia putting petunias into red clay pots, tamping down the dirt while she trilled, "I-i-i-t's summertime!"

Olivia pulling her yellow hair into a bun as she flitted around the two-room schoolhouse where they had shared a teaching post, scattering hairpins in her wake, calling, "Netty, have you seen my papers?"

Netty, whose papers were in the satchel at her side, waited in their only armchair. She had sighed and said, "Your papers are where you left them last night."

"But I've looked everywhere!" Olivia cried, circling the room, faster and faster, slipping on her dress, damping down the stove, hopping on one foot then another as she put on her shoes.

Netty thought about letting her get a notch more frantic, but they didn't have time: they had lesson plans to review, bullied children to comfort. She walked across the room, picked up Olivia's papers and handed them to her.

"You really have a gift for finding things, you know? You really have a knack," Olivia said. "Can you button my dress?"

The most unfair part was, when they arrived at the schoolhouse, Olivia looked cool and lovely as if she'd just bloomed on the spot. Her pupils all loved her.

Netty, they feared.

She pushed her feet to get the porch swing going again, and remembered the morning she decided to see Olivia. At the kitchen table, she'd had a vision of her life splitting apart, like great chunks of ice shearing off a glacier and bobbing out to sea. Olivia was on one of them saying, "I like *delicious* colors. Yellows and reds."

Fifty years, Netty told Marilee, her daughter, in the middle of breakfast. Fifty years is long enough. Long enough for what? Marilee said. Long enough to hold a grudge, Netty answered. Didn't someone say if you forgive people you belong to them? I guess, Marilee said, and handed her the toast.

. . .

The station wagon sailed into the drive and minutes later, Marilee came out on the porch, saying something about the children's swimming or was it tennis, something about good weather and luck.

Netty didn't say anything. She no longer answered things that didn't need answering. Age boiled all things down to basics, and she couldn't say she minded—she'd always thought life was a bit too embroidered at Marilee's, with the endless lessons and meetings.

Marilee squared her shoulders. "I thought you might want your cross-stitch."

Netty took it, but she had plans for it. She was going to leave off "home," which would bother Marilee almost to tears. "Mother!" she'd whine, "God bless our humble?"

"Put on your glasses." Marilee thumped the black leather case on the ice cream table. "You need your glasses, Mother. You can't see anything."

Netty put her hand on her daughter's. "That is the point."

Marilee started as if she'd been shocked. "You must be excited," she said, then she hurried across the porch with small quick steps, almost a jog, the boards sighing under her feet.

Excited, Netty thought, and she felt a longing burn through her like smoke.

As she settled her glasses on the bridge of her nose, and the muscles in her eyes sprang alive and anchored her in the present again, the moment returned and arced through her heart. The moment Olivia stood at the door of the hospital room, her hand fluttering to the hair at the nape of her neck, and she whispered, "Frankie and I are going to be married."

. . .

September 27, 1928. The wipers whispered, *on-ward, on-ward,* the hymn Netty's mother practiced each week for church, the chords echoing around the upstairs rooms, thin and mean-spirited. Netty loathed it, but she couldn't get it out of her mind.

She shifted on the cracked leather seat to look outside. It was an early storm. Snow swept from the green, unmown fields to the base of the Bitterroots. The mountains were shrouded in black-bellied clouds, but every once in a while a peak appeared, sharp and pointed as a tooth.

Olivia wanted to take the bus together, to make an entrance—
Olivia liked entrances—but Netty insisted on traveling alone. She
liked to mark big passages of her life alone. She had graduated from
college and now she was going to support herself and her mother
by teaching in Elk, Montana, with her best friend, Olivia. When
Frank finished law school, they'd marry and settle in Bridger.

She thought of Frank, of the wind rippling his taffy-colored
hair last July, when they rode horses at his ranch up Ninemile.
She had never ridden. He gave her a lead-footed sorrel that hung
its head and shuffled the path after Frank's restless bay. When
they came to a meadow, Frank stopped and turned around in
his saddle. "Are you sore, Netty?" he asked as she plodded up
beside him. "Do you want to stop?"

Netty looked at him. His eyes glinted back at her from
behind his rimless glasses. There was a quickening inside her, a
pleasurable dropping down, and she shivered and banged her
heels in the stirrups. She kicked again, and the horse's legs began
churning through the oat grass until the black-eyed susans
blurred into streaks of yellow. She kept galloping toward the
dark line of forest.

"Netty!" Frank said when he caught up with her. "What's got
into you?"

She nudged the horse on.

Frank's laughter floated out behind her. "I don't know if
Bones is ready for you!"

She reined the horse to a stop. "And are you?"

At the picnic later, he pulled her down on the checkered
cloth. Ants swarmed over the chicken bones, the plates smeared
with potato salad. He ran his hand up her leg. She kissed him
and pushed it up further.

· · ·

At the station in Elk, a hardware store with benches out front
and a red metal passenger flag, a man threw her trunk in the

back of his cart. He gave her some blankets and slapped the seat next to him. "Model A's broke," he muttered as they clattered off down the road. The snow thickened, swirling through the apple orchards, whitening the horse's rump, and she was half-frozen when they arrived at the schoolhouse.

She opened the door.

About a dozen children stared back at her. They were dressed in overalls or thin grey dresses and holding buckets, dirty and lusterless as their eyes.

"I thought school started tomorrow?" Netty said to Olivia, who was bobbing up and down, working the pump.

Olivia laughed and stood up. "Welcome!" she said and held her arms out. "We've got the only indoor pump in town."

Netty took over, while Olivia stoked the fire. As she gave them their water, they gave her their names—May, Clinton, Bessie, Thomas Satchel McLeod—till their buckets were filled and they put on their overcoats and stood by the door.

"Do they need help home?" Netty looked at the children. "Do you need help home?"

The children stared back at her.

"I guess not," Olivia said. "They come back every night."

When the children left, Olivia filled a basin of hot water at the stove, and walked to Netty's chair. She knelt down and unbuckled her galoshes.

Netty held her feet up. "Oh, no."

"Put them down."

"They stink, Olivia. They're what you might call ripe. I can do this myself."

"Don't be silly." Olivia put her hand on Netty's leg. "I want to."

"You don't have to."

"Of course I don't," Olivia said as she squeezed the excess water from the washcloth.

Netty looked down at Olivia. Her face grew moist and her hair caught the light from the lamp and flicked gold into the room. She wrapped the cloth around Netty's feet, first one, then the other, and Netty felt the heat as it pulsed and stung and traveled up her legs to her heart.

. . .

She wanted to be standing when Olivia arrived, these things were important. She waited in the swing until 3:00, when Olivia was due, then she waited some more. Olivia was always late. Twenty minutes later, she stood up slowly, her legs burning, and shook out the blue-checked cloth and watched it float slowly over the table.

She was setting out the tea things when the Thunderbird rolled to a stop in front of the house. The brakes wheezed. A harried-looking man in sunglasses slammed the driver's door, checked his watch, then rushed around the car to help the passenger to her feet.

Gravity, Netty thought. It keeps working against us.

The old woman inched her walker up the sidewalk, her white hair, light as cotton, swaying with each step. As she talked to the man at her side, she didn't seem to see the way he kept measuring the distance to the porch and scowling.

Netty clenched the tablecloth as a sour taste rose up from her heart and scalded her throat. She took a breath, set down the sugar bowl. "Olivia!" she cried, "You haven't aged a minute!"

Olivia stopped at the bottom of the porch steps and looked up. "I'm sorry," she said, her voice wobbly. "My promptness, I'm afraid, hasn't improved with age. Just ask my son Larry here."

As she said this, Olivia looked a little to the left of her. Cataracts, Netty thought, and graciously held out her hand.

. . .

"The world," she said to the third graders, "is made up of large bodies of water and land." She rolled down the overhead map, and held her pointer on the blue expanse of the Atlantic Ocean. In the thin January light, dust motes spun to the wooden floor and for some reason this made her sad.

May stared out a fogged window. Clinton drew something he shaded with his forearm, the thick red pencil angling out from his hand. Bessie Fitzhugh looked up dutifully, her eyes coated with boredom and heat and the fact that none of this would matter in a future of children, cooking, and cattle.

"Continents," she said. "Can you say continents?"

As the ragged sounds of their voices filled the room, the children's faces seemed to dim and recede from her.

She was saying, "The seven continents are . . ." when the rushing sound started in her ears and she asked them to keep quiet.

Something was wrong. They paid attention. Why was that interesting? She couldn't read children, that much was clear. Speak with a deep, commanding timbre, her education professor had said. Clap! Move! Startle them!

She clapped her hands. "We are continents!"

Stars floated across the periphery of her vision. There was a banging noise and she was sure the wood heater had exploded and she remembered telling Thomas, the oldest, to check it.

The next thing she knew Olivia was standing over her, wringing her hands, and saying, "Netty, what happened?"

Netty lifted her head and said, "North America, South America, Australia, Africa, Antarctica, Asia, and Europe." Then she shut her eyes and didn't wake up till they carried her across the schoolyard.

That night, Frank sat at the edge of the mohair sofa and said, "Don't go." He had driven down from Bridger to join Netty for the Elk Primary School Cake Walk and Dance. He put his hand on her forehead. "You're warm."

Netty pulled herself up into a sitting position. "I decorated the schoolroom. I baked a cake. I got the orchestra, and by God,

I'm going to enjoy myself."

"Damn it, Netty," he said. "You always push things." He opened the wood heater door, and jabbed a poker at the fire.

The logs shifted.

She said, "You don't understand."

"What do you mean?"

"They'll turn on me."

"For being sick?"

"They've fired teachers for less," Netty said. "And I can't afford to lose this job. Tell me, how would I survive? What would my mother do? What would we do?"

"We'd get by."

"I feel just fine."

"You're too damn stubborn." Frank stared at the fire, his eyes glassy. "You get stuck in things. Like that deer skull we saw up Ninemile."

"I do not," she whispered. "I'm not like that at all." She shivered, remembering how wide-plated bark had healed over the skull so the four-point tips stuck out like bony branches. The deer was probably in rut, Frank had said, charged the tree and got stuck. Netty tried to pull the antlers loose. Don't you think he could pull free, she asked him all the ride home. Don't you think he could make one big jerk and pull himself loose?

Frank looked over at her, the poker dangling from his hand. "If I ordered you to stay home, as my future wife, would you?"

"No," Netty said.

"What about 'love, honor, and obey'?"

"I'd obey you if you were right," Netty answered.

"I'll keep that in mind," Frank said quietly. A log sparked. He turned it over, and the coals flared and dulled in the cold air.

. . .

The pineboard room was bright with crepe paper garlands. Rows of desks had been unbolted from the floor and stacked in a corner, and on makeshift tables of boards and sawhorses, there were nearly a dozen cakes—layer and sheet cakes of vanilla, lemon, chocolate, and spice.

By the door, Davey Doe's five-piece orchestra tuned up. The drummer juggled his drumsticks. The violinist, the man who met Netty at the station, pulled his bow across the strings and a chord rasped out over the room. Men talked about falling apple prices. Women clustered in the center of the room, pulling at evening dresses of velvet or crepe. One woman traced a box step, and when she was done, she looked up and laughed.

Nearby, Olivia was taking dimes for the cakewalk and when she saw Netty, she waved.

In the wake of a thin hush, Netty crossed the room with Frank at her elbow. She held herself very erect, nodding at the children and their parents. When they passed Clinton, a red stain spread from his cheeks to his ears and he giggled and looked away, and she knew it was a good thing she'd come.

They walked to Olivia, who was standing in front of a large chalked circle, sliced up like a pie and numbered.

"Are you sure you should be here?" Olivia whispered.

Netty glared back at her.

Olivia gave Netty a look, then turned to face the room and said, "Shall the cakewalk begin?" No one looked at her. Netty shouted, "Attention!" and her children looked back at her with a familiar mixture of boredom and dull hatred.

As the noise grew around them, she nudged Olivia. "Go ahead," Netty said. "Win me a two-layer chocolate cake with seven-minute frosting." She turned to Frank. "That goes for you, too."

"Are you sure?" Olivia said.

"Of course, I'm sure."

The players took up their positions. Netty looked at the

conductor and as she brought down her arm, the orchestra played, "Smile, Darn Ya, Smile." People began moving slowly around the circle.

As the fiddler's arm sawed up and down, and the cornet player arched his back and tilted his horn into the air, Netty watched, thinking how old she felt. She drew a number from a bread bowl. "Four!" she called. The music stopped and a farmer's wife threw her meaty arms up and walked away, laughing.

As the crowd walked the circle again, Frank winked at her. She looked at his lips. They made her want to kiss him, to do things for him, but there was a look in his eyes she hadn't noticed before. Something cool, distant. "Ten!" she called, and a bow-legged cowboy shook his head, and went outside to spit.

One after one, she called a number, until only Olivia, Clinton, and Frank followed each other around the bleary circle. Between the two adults, Clinton walked the circle with great concentration, never taking his eyes from his feet.

"Well, at least the caller's my fiancée," Frank said.

"But she's my best friend!" Olivia cried.

Frank laughed. "No, I'm quite certain she's on my side."

"Well, you're not married *yet*, Mr. McClure!" Olivia flipped her hair over her shoulders and squared her back.

The crowd hooted.

Frank looked at Olivia, and something in his gaze stabbed Netty. She wanted to net that look and make it come to her. The room grew unbearably hot.

Later, she remembered things in this order. She called out, "Six!" Olivia cried, "Oh, no!" There was a scraping noise, then a scuffling of feet as Davey Doe and the Pioneer Club Orchestra played "Smile, Darn Ya, Smile" for the tenth time that night.

. . .

It was walking pneumonia.

They took her to Bridger Community Hospital, to a
dun-colored room with high ceilings and rattly windows.
She was in an oxygen tent while doctors came in and out of
her room and shook their grey heads at her. Olivia took over
her classes. Frank came when he could, and brought her a
hothouse orchid stuck in a bottle of Great Falls Select. He
brought Olivia up on weekends, and the two of them snuck in
sandwiches and beer.

Netty's mother stationed herself at her bedside,
triumphantly refilling her water pitcher and smoothing the
sheets as if she'd gotten proof of something she'd known
all along. "You're just too proud, dear," she said at one point.
"You've been struck down."

Three weeks later, her lungs cleared, and Dr. Babin had taken
to patting her leg and telling her she could go home, when
her fever shot up to 103. Olivia was visiting and she stayed by
Netty's bedside, putting cool washcloths on her forehead until
Netty told her to stop it, she felt like a sponge.

Olivia folded her hands and was silent. "The children miss
you," she said finally.

"I bet," Netty said. The mention of the children panicked her.
She lifted her head from the pillow. "What about my job?"

"I nearly forgot!" Olivia drew a large paper valentine out
of her satchel and handed it to Netty. It was a red heart pasted
on a doily and filled with stick-like handwriting. "This was the
children's idea."

"I know whose idea it was." Netty fingered the papery lace.
"Thank you, Olivia. But tell me, do I still have a job?"

"You're wrong. The valentine was Clinton's idea."

Chills racked her body before Netty could find out that
Olivia was right, the valentine was Clinton's idea, and before
Netty could find out that the Bitterroot County School Board
had voted to replace her for fear of infection.

Olivia smoothed the bedclothes, kept saying, "Give me something to do. I feel so helpless." She looked out the window at the lights, then her hands. "I know. I'll read you a story. We're doing fairy tales now in second."

Netty was too far away with fever to answer. Olivia burrowed down in the chair and as she began to read, Netty turned her face toward the comfort of her voice.

"And the enchanted bear bore their play in good temper." Olivia spoke in a singsong. "And only when they hit too hard, did he cry, 'Snowy-White, Rosy Red! Leave me my life! Will you beat your lover dead?'"

Several days later, Olivia stood in the doorway of the hospital room, her fingers working loose hairs back into the braids circling her head.

Netty turned to look at her. "Come in," she said. "I won't bite, you know."

Olivia looked across the room at her.

Netty had a thin needle taped in her arm, her brown hair haloed her head, and over the bed, there was a sampler that said, "Healing Begins in the Heart."

Then Netty saw Olivia's open hands and bent waist and the way she strained forward as if she were trying to give something and take something away at the same time.

Olivia's hands dropped to her sides, and hung there. Then she leveled her gaze at Netty and said, "Frankie and I are going to be married."

Netty pulled out the IV. She walked across the room to the window, a single streak of blood coursing the white of her arm, and as she looked out at the town, she remembered thinking how bright it was, how the buildings and trees and people were etched so sharply against the snow, they made her wince.

"Get out," she whispered.

. . .

The memory was like a crystal, and as Netty examined it over the years, its changing planes and colors revealed new, infuriating angles.

For the first several years, she was furious about Frank. How he deserted her, how he took away what she had with him, like that moment where she'd galloped across the meadow, Frank calling behind her, and she kept riding until the sound of his voice trickled away like water, and then she rode further. She had thought about writing him, blackmailing him, killing him. Then she got married.

She saw him only once, in the Bridger Mercantile. It was her husband's birthday, and she was buying him sock garters when she looked up and there was Frank. He paled, threw down the boxer shorts he was holding, and walked quickly away, the floor creaking under his feet, through Men's Everyday and Evening, on to Hardwares and out the door.

Later on, it was their timing that galled her. The fact that Olivia told her while she was flat on her back, terribly ill. "On my *death* bed!" she'd whisper with grim happiness. "Fever of 103!"

But from the day Olivia had stood in the hospital doorway until the time her own legs began their steady arthritic burning and her child had gone grey, Netty knew it was Olivia's treachery that she minded the most.

She'd remember the night she and Olivia lay in their beds, the fire popping and hissing in the stove, talking about how they'd decorate their houses. Olivia described everything from the canopied beds to the pansy-covered shelf lining, when she stopped suddenly. "Can I tell you something?"

Netty sighed, she was nearly asleep.

Olivia walked across the room, her gown billowing white into the dark room. She crawled in beside Netty, her hair fanning across the pillow. "I hit a boy," she whispered.

"That's okay. You didn't mean it," Netty said.

"But I did. He was smarting off, and he wouldn't stop, and I walked up to him and—instinct took over." She turned on her side to face Netty. "The worst thing is, I don't feel sorry. I don't feel sorry at all." She started to cry. Netty put her arm around her. "You're sorry," she said, and Olivia looked at her, her face shining.

It was this face—Olivia's delicate, sweet face with her eyes turned down at the corners—that haunted Netty. *How could you?* she'd wanted to ask that face, when it rose up before her night after night, and the smile turned into a leer and the face laughed, *easy.*

At first, the pain came in stabbing waves, and she'd leap out of bed and burn things: Olivia's handkerchiefs, pictures, lockets of hair. Later, the very syllables of Olivia's name seemed to pierce her heart, in and out, like stitching, till the pain gave way in her later years to a sharp, peculiar feeling of pleasure.

. . .

A year after she married Frank, Olivia wrote her a long letter in her flowery script. She went on and on. "We just didn't expect it," she said. "We just didn't have any idea. Having hurt you is my cross to bear, and I beg the Lord every day for your forgiveness. Please, Netty. Please." She underlined the second "please" four times.

After she read it, Netty folded up the letter and put it in her undergarments drawer. After she closed it, she looked up in the mirror a long time, watching her face go in and out of focus, then she slowly turned the key in the lock.

Each year, she added another Christmas card, first from North Dakota, then Iowa. There were black-and-white pictures of Olivia and Frank dressed in old-fashioned costumes or Santa Claus outfits, then holding one baby after another. There was the grainy color photograph of the six of them, Frank and Olivia, grey and slightly stooped, the children looking apologetic and embarrassed. Each year, Olivia looked more birdlike, and Frank became pale and bloated, as if he needed more and more flesh to anchor him there. Then the pictures stopped, and there were only cheap cards of holly or reindeer and Olivia's lone signature.

Netty had tried to forgive her.

After her husband Thomas died, she went into her dressing room, sat down at her writing table, laid out a fresh sheet of stationery with "Mrs. Thomas Fullerton" on top, and touched the nib of her fountain pen to the paper. She watched the ink puddle. She took out a new sheet. This time she wrote "Dear Olivia," and stopped. She stared at the paper. She wrote "I," then a thin line of ink trailed off down the page.

Over the years, the memory hardened and settled inside her, settled between her and Marilee, who had tried her entire life to shake something loose in her—from the time she was a child and she used to stand on her head to try to make her laugh until these later years, when she chirped about weather and luck. Every time Netty looked at her daughter, it was a challenge: go ahead, show me why I should let go.

. . .

It seemed to Netty that Olivia had been going on for hours about her granddaughter, the little actress, Olivia clasping her hands to her breast, reciting "'See what a scourge is laid upon your hate, That heaven finds means to kill your joys with love!'" Netty had had enough. She stopped talking, and enjoyed Olivia's fumbling conversation and Marilee's bright answers and glowering looks at her.

Then they were silent.

Marilee looked desperately around the table, pounced on the cake cover, and as she lifted it up, the metal rang out dully. "Lemon cake anyone?" she said looking from Olivia to Netty, holding the cake knife in her fist like a gavel.

. . .

They were handing around the plates, the air was filled with the clatter of knives and forks, when the phone rang and Marilee leaped up to answer it.

As Netty pressed the cake onto her fork, she listened to the distant watery sounds of children playing.

"Netty?" Olivia finally said.

"Yes?" Netty answered.

"Why . . ." Olivia looked down at her lap, and then back at Netty. "Why don't you tell me about your grandchildren?"

"Let's see," Netty put down her fork. "Thomas is in third grade. He's fat, he can't run an entire block, and he likes to kill birds. Katherine is in fifth, she's got buck teeth, a sour disposition, quick wits which she employs to . . ." Netty looked at Olivia, "to make her friends unhappy."

The sound of passing cars slid between them.

· · ·

Netty unfolded the Scrabble board on the table, and lined up her letters on the wooden easel. She looked politely across the table at her opponent.

Olivia snapped open her purse, and, to Netty's satisfaction, drew out a large magnifying glass. As Netty might have expected, Olivia started out with words like "ox" and "fan."

Olivia started describing the rest home her son kept her in, the best in Butte (Butte!—Netty thought—the best in Butte!) where they played bridge on Mondays, rummy on Tuesdays and mahjong on Wednesdays. "Mahjong," Olivia said absently, "was Frank's favorite—I think he liked the sound of those tiles."

The taste again. The bilious, sour taste that carved the edges of every day and laced the nights and nursed that other pain, that of seeing what you didn't want to be and then becoming it. Just say you're sorry, she told herself, but words seemed to sprout, unbidden on her lips. "How'd Frank go?"

Olivia paled.

"Well?" Netty blurted.

"Heart." Olivia's finger traced slow circles around the board. She shrugged and laughed. "I always told him, too many steaks and butter pats!"

"Were you there?" Netty said before she could stop.

Olivia looked at her as if she hadn't heard her correctly. Finally, she said, softly, "I used to wash your feet, Netty."

"So you did," Netty said, and her teacup chinked as she replaced it in the saucer.

. . .

This time they did not talk. Marilee swung in and out of the house, watering the flowers, bringing pictures of the children to show Olivia.

Olivia laid out her tiles. "Ever hear anything about Professor Murray?" she said finally. "Remember Teaching Methods II? 'When the attention drops, get out the props!'"

"No," Netty said. She laid out "orts."

"Netty . . ." Olivia started, but she was interrupted by Marilee asking for iced tea orders.

When she left, Olivia said gently, "That was a long time ago, Netty."

"Then tell me what happened." This is the time, Netty told herself. She will tell you what happened, then you will take her hand and say, forgive me.

"Lord, I don't want to dredge up all that stuff. What good will it do us now? It's so far behind us." Olivia fussed with her tiles, finally laying out "hay."

"Far behind some of us," Netty said.

"Can't we just bury—" Olivia looked at Netty. "All right, I'll tell you. One night we were coming back from seeing you, Netty, and we stopped to let some cattle cross the road. We were just waiting, talking about you, Netty, I swear it, when Frank kissed me." A blush crept over her face. She paused. "And I kissed him back."

Netty looked at Olivia. She imagined her mouth forming the words, and she waited for something to well up in her heart, but she felt instead a terrible panic of things giving out, like some essential starch had washed out. She wanted to scream, *Do you know what you've done? Do you have any idea?* and then she wanted Olivia to do something—touch her, say a word—that would release her, restore her.

Instead, she laid out "vortex."

"Please—" Olivia looked at her and stopped.

There was a slight tapping noise as they set tile after tile on the board. Netty was keeping score. She was winning, but not by as much as she'd hoped. Filling in her letters after a turn, she lined up the tiles on the easel. The word popped out, plain as day. No, she told herself. Move on.

Then Olivia gave her a milky smile, and Netty looked at her and laid out the word "betray."

She put her hands in her lap, and waited.

Olivia rose up to hold her magnifying glass over the board, and Netty watched as the letters grew large and ripply in the glass.

Olivia looked at the board a long time, then she sat down heavily and sighed. "You should forgive me now, Netty."

"Eleven points?" Netty said. Her hand drew a shaky eleven in the column of numbers under her name.

"You're being childish." Olivia's voice was quiet.

"Your turn," Netty said.

Olivia rose up out of her chair and gripped Netty's wrist. "Give it up."

Netty stared back at her, surprised by the strength of her grip. She could hear the swing creaking, and the sound of a bicycle screeching in the dirt, then she said in a small voice, "I can't."

"Be like that," Olivia said. Her eyes burned, and she snapped down her tiles, one by one, until she spelled "cake." Then she smiled sweetly. "Triple score."

. . .

Still, as she watched Olivia go down the steps, she wanted to stop her and say, "Remember when they went through our trash?"

One night in Elk, they woke up to the sound of footsteps outside and looked out the window to see two men in overalls and low-slung hats, going through their garbage, tossing bottles and cartons onto the snow. "They're looking for beer bottles," Netty said. "Going to see if we're nipping firewater?" Olivia said. They had collapsed, snickering, on the floor. Then Olivia sat up and whispered, "I'm scared."

Netty pushed her feet to get the swing going again. From the house, she could hear water running and dishes knocking against one another, Marilee saying to her husband, "I wouldn't call it a disaster, but you know Mother...." In a while, Marilee would come out to see if she'd like to watch a little TV before bed. She'd refuse. Marilee would think she was mad at her, but Netty would be too tired to care.

She plucked a dead blossom from a petunia and crushed it in her hand. On the sidewalk, she could see Olivia's back receding, growing small and dim and white. Before she stepped into the mouth of the car, Olivia turned back once to look at her. Her face seemed to hang there for a moment in the dark, bright as a moon, then it was gone.

The sun was setting, and the sky had turned a deep electric blue. The street was quiet, except for the sounds of women's voices calling their children in. She swung her head blindly toward the rumble of the motor, toward the rise and fall of Marilee's voice, and she whispered, "Forgive me."

❧

FRUIT IN GOOD SEASON

It's true, all I wanted was to wander the hills around Hope, Montana, but Aunt Dot raised me to tea parties and ladies' clubs until a ranch hand showed up on our porch with a handful of phlox and said, "A prayer is a whisper from the heart." He touched my cheek and my blood rose up against years of dim rooms where clocks ticked loudly and my aunt crossed her legs with a wheeze. I threw over those mild men, the clerk and the lawyer, with their shiny suits and dime store bouquets. "You're trading a good name, Edie," my aunt shook her red face at me, "for a hayseed and a Bible."

Weeks later, we walked down the aisle of a rough wooden church. My aunt cried as the organist made a hash of the recessional, then we stepped out into the world.

. . .

But my story really began the night Howie rolled over in bed, pressed his flat body against mine and whispered, "Thou shalt propagate."

"Oh, Howie," I said and pulled my nightgown closer around me for my breasts were sore with nursing and exhaustion flooded me.

"Fruit in good season," he said.

"Gabriel didn't sleep," I murmured. "I'm the walking dead."

"The leaf shall not wither," he said. He moved against me, his body still sinewy from the years on the ranch, one long line of tight-bound muscle, except the tiny red teeth marks where the barbed wire raked him.

. . .

"Do you know what it's like?" I said, jerking the covers up. "All these hands at you? Grabbing your arms? Your hair? Your breasts?" All the while Howie is pulling my gown up over my head until I'm naked, my breasts lit by a thin June moon and tight with cold. I pulled my hair around me for warmth. "What it's like to walk streets where the neighbors watch me, where phones rattle before I get home, *Howie Deschene's wife, did you see she wore pants on the street?*"

"Rage, rage," he whispered. There was a hoarseness in his voice I'd never heard those long nights he pulled me under the covers and the world bloomed up from our bed.

"Howie," I whispered.

His eyes went flat. He pulled my hair across my face, pressed me into the mattress.

I tightened my legs, pushed against him. "Stop."

He drove against me, reciting Psalms 2, verses 1 through 9.

I began to float up from myself. I hovered on the ceiling above us, looking down at my hair sheeting the bed, Howie's spine bobbing over me, white as a ghost's. I thought, *Howie* until the pain between my legs stopped, until each letter rose up before me like the skyline of a nameless city. Pines scratched the windows, and as my limbs turned from wood to ice, I heard the lilting call of a wolf and from farther away, an answer.

. . .

The next morning he turned to me, a cold light stealing around the room, the narrow angles of his face hollowed with hunger and a look that said help me. He took my hands. I looked away. He got up and jerked open the window shade, and as it went flapping up, dread rose up in me, then drifted away like smoke.

I got up and started the stove.

In the front room, tight and dark with the curtains shut, I took Gabriel to my breast while Howie shoved one book after another in his satchel, the pages opening and shutting like mouths. "Today we cross-pollinate tomatoes," he said, looking away because nursing embarrassed him. He grazed my cheek, closed the door, and frosted air fell to the floor and crept the baseboards.

I opened the curtains, and Gabriel and I rocked and looked out at Redbow. Clouds chased down the valley, Mrs. Larsen shook out a mop on her porch, and old Mr. Peterson walked his Scotty dogs down the sun-slicked street. Age had frozen his back straight up and his arms straight out, and every day at 9:00, he took mincing steps down the bumpy road, never looking at his feet.

"Well, Gabe," I lifted him to my other breast. "There goes Mr. Perpendicular."

Gabriel reached up for my mouth and grabbed fistfuls of housecoat instead. There was a tingling in my cheek and a stone in my heart, and I could feel myself slipping below the surface of things.

I set Gabriel in his crib, and walked to the mirror to repin my hair. There was the doughy face of a peasant and mud-colored eyes, but as I pulled the hairpins, my hair fell heavy across my breasts and shoulders, and I brushed it until my scalp stung, until it lit the room like slow-burning fire.

I turned to Gabriel. "Look."

He lifted his arms to me.

The sun stole over Teacup Mountain and silhouetted the feathery tops of the ponderosa.

. . .

I took scalloped potatoes to Mrs. Larsen that afternoon, but when I handed them to her, she smiled in a way that let me know I was never to come back. A day later, I tried the Merry Mixers. They played canasta. As they shrieked and howled and plunked down straights and flushes, they looked over at me sorrowfully and said, "You're so serious, Edie, don't you ever laugh?" *Watch this.* I curved my lips in a smile and forced a laugh that sliced through me like glass.

Three days later, Mrs. Delano invited me to the Pioneer Women's Philanthropic and Cultural Society. As her Buick prowled the rain-drenched streets, she patted my gloved hand and told me how much I would like the gals. They're a hoot, she said, just the tonic for a grey spring in Redbow, Montana.

We went to the home of Mrs. Whitely, whose husband owned the Redbow Beacon. The women my age eyed me suspiciously, while the older ones directed things, pouring coffee, staring the group into their chairs. When everyone was seated, I stood up, brushed the skirt of my princess-style brushed cotton A-line, and stared at the windows until the light hurt my eyes. I said, "I am Edie, wife of the science teacher."

"Science," the ladies said.

"I have a little boy, Gabriel," I said and I wanted to add *and a stone in my heart.*

They started discussing a bake sale to raise money for a home for the blind in Billings. A woman across the room was upset because two people had offered to bring yellow cakes, when what was needed was variety. Another woman pulled her skirt over her knees and said quietly that she would bring snickerdoodles, but everyone ignored her. Mrs. Whitely looked at the two women and said that there was room for two yellow cakes, but she was sure Mrs. Fitzhugh would see it in her heart to make a chocolate instead.

I stared at the rug, at the red birds that flew nowhere and blue flowers that bloomed forever, listening to the chatter, to the tick and clink of cups and saucers. Mrs. Delano whispered, "Aren't they a bunch?"

"Yes," I said. A word or a phrase seemed to burn inside me. I wanted to say *I will make kiss-me cake.* I wanted to speak their language, to have them turn and smile at me and look at each other approvingly. My aunt raised me to say the words— coffeecake, meat loaf, black jet for evening—but she had never taught me how to speak in the spaces beneath them. How *there is always dust* means *lonely*, how *I burnt the chops* is *fury*. My hands and legs seemed to grow larger and larger. My stocking wheezed as I crossed my legs, and when I dropped the cookies, they went wheeling across the floor. The ladies paused, and in that silence, something was decided.

"So nice to have you," Phyllis Whitely said, as we left in a whirl of bobbing hats. She did not say *come back*.

On the way home, Mrs. Delano said, "I'm glad you gave us a try, Edie."

"Thank you for bringing me," I said and watched her pink gloves crank the steering wheel. "Can I ask you something, Mrs. Delano?"

"Call me Carol."

"Carol, do you ever—" I couldn't find the words. *What are the words?* I watched her check the rearview mirror, "Do you ever—take care of diaper rash?"

"Good gracious for a minute there . . ." she said, her body relaxed into the seat. "Of course. A couple dabs of petroleum jelly and presto!" she snapped her fingers.

The car rolled to a stop at the curb. I put my hand on the door handle, but I didn't move. The blinkers clinked on and off between us. "What do you . . ."

She unbuttoned her coat, and looked out at the greying street, waiting.

I peeled off my gloves. I twisted my wedding ring around and around. Suddenly I looked at her and blurted, "What do you do when your husband . . . ?"

"Oh, that," Mrs. Delano laughed, but her face looked like I'd caught her naked. "It's his due, honey. We women don't always like it but . . ." she turned around suddenly and grabbed my arm. "You know what I do?" Her eyes were heated, and the cloth violets pinned to her coat shook. "I just lie there still as a mouse and I think about Crazy Cakes. I wonder how one would taste with chocolate sprinkles or butter cream. And I wonder why they work. If the vinegar is what makes the cake sweeter."

. . .

Eight months later, I was sitting in church among the pinched faces of Redbow, hugely pregnant in my red wool coat. The preacher finished his words of hellfire and torment, then stepped from the pulpit to gather the collection plates.

Howie patted my knee, said, "Shall we?" Every Sunday morning of the four years he'd taught science to loggers' children in Redbow, we went down to the clammy basement of the Faith Missionary Baptist Church where we held plastic cups of watery tea and talked about Armageddon with the townspeople: Gertrude Larsen with her pursed lips, Phyllis Whitely with her sugary put-downs.

This time I didn't move. I'd heard something in the words of the sermon, in *sword of the Lord* and *darkness will come upon the earth* I'd never heard before. Instead of the fire that had stirred my blood, I heard cold, sharp words thrown like a mumblety-peg into the circle between fear and infinity. I sat there until the pew cleared, until even Mr. Schmidt, his radar ears quivering, walked to the back of the church.

Howie turned to me, a question furrowing his face.

"You go ahead. I can't do it anymore. I'm not going down for my weekly going over by Phyllis Whitely." I buttoned my coat.

He swallowed, touched my hand and said, "We won't stay."

"No," I said. "You go. They smile at you and talk to you, and then they see big Edie, poor thing, she's just, well, odd."

"Look." He grabbed my arm, his fingers digging into my wrist. "I don't ask much. I ask less and less, a lot less than some, but I'm on the Worship Committee. I have obligations, Edith, and they watch. They keep track."

My face went stiff. I pried his fingers off, one by one, and stood up. He looked straight ahead, erect with God, his face blazing.

"I'll get Gabriel." I said. I turned down the aisle where sunlight sent down bolts of color that blurred on the polished floor into the rough shape of a cross, and I walked through it.

Gabriel squirmed as I carried him from the nursery out into the street, too startled to cry. I kept on walking past the market, the hardware store, the slant-roofed houses, a chinook at my back as I dragged up Snowshoe Hill. I walked until my breath was ragged, until snow slopped over my galoshes, my feet burned with cold. At the crest of the hill I looked back at Redbow, crisscrossed with rivers and houses and the road that led north to wider valleys, and I began to scream.

. . .

At dusk, Howie let me come in, fry his pork chop, nurse Gabriel to sleep. Then he picked up a coffeepot and banged it down on the counter.

"Take a good look, Edie," he said, sweeping his hand across him to indicate the sink piled with dishes and the crumb-coated floor. "Look at your life." He looked at me from a great distance.

"Well, you're a fine one, banging coffeepots, and bellowing like a bull," I said. "But I guess it's what you do best."

His face blazed. "You should talk, Miss Runaway," he said. "Where am I going to find you tomorrow? Libby? Think you'll hop a freight to Drummond? Why confine it to the state? Think you'll head off to Tacoma for a few days—just for a break?"

"Who told you I ran away? Miss Phyllis Knows-Everyone's-Business, or Mr. Schmidt Hears-Everyone's-Business? Does anyone in this town have anything better to do than meddle?"

"These people are nice people, Edie. You don't give them a chance. You don't talk to them, get to know them. You just give up. You gave up on this town from the day we came."

"That's not true," I said. "And can I help it if they don't like me? Can I help it if they don't invite me back?"

"Even if they did," Howie said, and he put his hand on his hip and smiled. "You wouldn't go."

He was absolutely right, which infuriated me. I headed for the door. He got there first.

"Kneel down," he looked into my eyes. "Kneel down and ask forgiveness."

"I'm not ready for begging. Or forgiveness."

"Get ready," Howie said, for his was not a religion of compromise.

He led me into the bedroom. We knelt on the cold linoleum, and he pressed my hands together, called, "Punish us Lord for Satan has entered our hearts!" His voice lashed the dim air, his eyes burned, and I knew, as far as he was concerned, the fight was over.

. . .

I vowed the next morning to do better: no running away, no teetering piles of dishes in the sink, no roving dust balls. Moving quickly in spite of my bulk, I tore down curtains and washed them, beat rugs, dusted shelves, scrubbed walls, moving like a dervish through the rooms, while Gabriel stared at me through the slats of the crib, squealing and waving his arms when I walked toward him. The first night, when Howie walked in the door, he kissed me, and sent up thanks. But after I painted each room, after four days of moving drop cloths to eat, and sleeping in cold rooms, he got impatient.

"Don't you think you've done enough?" he said. "Can't you stop now?" He leaned over Gabriel and wiped his nose with great ceremony. "We'd better finish now. This is making him sick."

But the truth was I couldn't stop, and each time I neared the end of a task, a small panic would grow in me until another arose to take its place. When I thought it would alarm him if I painted again, I got it in my head to build a fruit room.

I pictured looking at my shelves, groaning with huckleberry and raspberry jams, chokecherry syrup, butter beans, dried venison, and the hulking crocks of sauerkraut. Instead of the individual jars, instead of berries we'd picked up Lost Creek or the deer Howie shot in the Cabinets, I thought that the collage of purples and reds and greens would tell me there is a design. And if I didn't like the pattern, I could rearrange it.

In the root cellar, I nailed up shelves, hammering one sweet-smelling board after the other, stopping only to touch my stomach and wipe my forehead. Gabriel clapped his hands at the ring of metal on metal, reached toward spiders crawling up lacy webs, toward mice scurrying off to dark corners.

A day later, Howie came flying home with a hardware store bill in his hand. "Edie, you've spent $54 on supplies. $54! Do you know how much money that is? That's half my wages. We'll barely make the house payment!"

"Let me use up what I have," I said quickly, figuring I had enough to finish the shelves.

"No," he said. "Stop." He looked up at me sideways. "Promise me?"

I looked at him across the room, and said in a small voice, "I'll try."

"Put it here." Howie held out his Bible.

I placed my hand on its grainy cover and said, "I promise," and hoped that I meant it.

The night he came home from Prayer Circle, I was lining up cans of tomatoes and green beans next to my preserves, on shelves that smelled sharp and clean as sawdust. I lined them up neatly in rows, the green beans after the peas, the Spam next to the sardines, and in the silvered moonlight, the cans glowed like bullets. The room was thick with the smells of dirt and tin, and I held my belly, singing, "Jimmy crack corn, and I don't care." I kept singing until I could feel him behind me, until I could smell the tang of his soap and feel his breath warm my neck.

He whirled me around and said, "You have broken your promise."

I knelt down on the cold dirt floor, knowing it would never help. He looked back at me and touched my cheek. "Edie," he said, his eyes shining, "what is inside you?"

. . .

Something was coming over me, a kind of heaviness in my bones. It's the housecleaning, I told myself, it's the baby dropping down, pinning you close to the earth so you won't go off. I took to my rocker and asked myself questions about Howie.

I wondered about his religion. I used to believe in its torments for the ungodly, its gifts and trials—the way it drove Howie's backbone straight in those early years. It was a bracing faith, black and white, no milky forgive and forget, like my aunt's. Now what I heard behind the words was rattling.

I remembered those early mornings in Bozeman, when Howie'd go to school, and I'd watch him lope down the street in his red plaid jacket, a farm boy taking the world straight on. I watched him till he disappeared, then I slipped our wedding 45s out of their dust jackets, lifted the arm of the record player and set them in place. I closed the curtains and fixed myself a foamy bath, and as I floated, I listened to the scratchy recording over and over again. As Pastor Salmonsen rumbled, . . . *this mystical union,* I slipped underwater. My cheeks filled with breath, my hair swirled around breasts Howie touched, and I came up gasping when he said, covenant.

I went over everything: Howie's first job in Malta teaching rancher's children, then Redbow. The day he'd gotten the job, he came home holding the letter over his head and said, "The Lord has spoken." "What did he say?" I said. "Redbow, Edie. He's calling us back to the mountains," he said, for the prairie made him nervous with its openness and constant wind.

Truth was, the longer I tried to think of what was wrong between Howie and me, the mushier my mind became. Too much meanness, I'd think, then answer, *the day he climbed Teacup Mountain to pick a handful of black-eyed Susans.* Too much silence, *then camping in the Swans where we talked by a moon, Howie stroking my hair, saying, dream, dream.* Neglect, I'd say, but I had answers for that, too.

But when I thought of him coming home, coming home in two years, ten years, his flattop greying, his back slightly bent, his face setting, growing stern, and this new child, another child to dress and feed and love and betray, a leaden feeling coursed down my legs and I thought I would die.

I packed Gabriel and the belongings I could carry, and I walked up over Snowshoe Mountain. I picked my way slowly, past wet bushes and larches looming dark and shadowless, to the Oxtail River where the deer were fawning and chickadees were nesting. In a large meadow, I staked the tent, built a fire. The spring sky was pale and cool but cloudless, and I nursed Gabriel and put him to sleep.

For three days, I stayed there, watching a shy sun whisk across the grasses, the moon still owned the sky. *Darkness will come upon the earth.* I listened to the river murmur go back, go back, and once I got as far as packing up again, when I thought of Howie's hands. Big, rough, patient hands unlocking the door, cutting his meat, pouring the water for tomatoes, pressing together in prayer, folding back the covers on the bed. How in spite of his religion and its fiery visions, the hands took each thing and weighed it and measured it to some exact dimension that was Howie's own.

Red-tailed hawks wound the sky. The deer floated down to the river at dusk.

. . .

He walked up through the wide-spaced larch, and I watched his face change, as relief replaced worry and anger replaced relief.

He peered in the tent where Gabriel held his toes, gurgling. He walked toward me, the weeds rattling. I was perched on a stump, at the edge of the river. He stood over me, and said, his voice tight and low, "What are you doing?"

I didn't say anything. I couldn't tell him about his hands, or about the visions I'd had of watching Mr. Perpendicular walk his dogs to his death, of rocking into an old woman in that front room in Redbow, greying into stone. I said, "I had to."

"You had to?" he said. "You take my son and run off in the hills and get half the town worked up and make me sick with worry and all you can say is you had to?"

"Yes," I said.

He slapped me.

I pushed myself up. I was so big now it was difficult to move, and I went to stand in an apron of tree shade.

He came toward me.

"Get away from me," I spit. "Don't come near me."

"I'm sorry," he said. He started to cry. "I'm sorry."

"*Sssss,*" I hissed.

"What have I done, Edie? I work all day and I come home tired and find the front door wide open, and you're gone."

I just stared at him.

"Please, Edie," he said coming closer. "I forgive you. God forgives you."

"No."

"We'll work it out. We'll get a different house. Go to a different town. How about that, Edie? We'll go someplace you like better. Someplace where people are nicer. Where the country is open like you like it. And we'll have a new baby, Edie. Think of it. A new little baby to love and hold and take care of."

I began to cry. "But—"

"Don't you love me, Edie?" he said, fixing me with his eyes. "Well? Don't you?"

I couldn't say it. I couldn't say anything. My hands fingered the wide-plated bark, and I wondered if it ever dropped off in a fierce cold.

"Well, then, what is it?"

"Everything's got tramped down, Howie," I whispered. Suddenly I felt limp, as if his words had pierced something and vital fluid leaked out.

"Let's go home now, Edie," Howie said gently. "Take my hand. That's a girl."

His hand was inches from me now, palm up, and his long, rough fingers were curved and trembling.

I gulped, hung my head, and took it.

. . .

Aunt Dot brushed my hair as I sat in bed. Howie had called her when I'd run away, and she'd come to stay until the baby was born.

"You have beautiful hair," she said, smoothing it down my back. "The color of chestnuts."

"I want to leave him," I said. "I didn't know that before, Dot, but I know it now."

"Hush, hush," she said, pulling the brush through great fans of hair that crackled and fell back down my back. "It's just baby-jitters, Edie. You had them last time."

"No, Dot," I said. "This is different. It's Howie."

"Shh!" Dot said. "Your beautiful baby will hear."

"No, Dot," I said. "I want a divorce."

"That's enough." She threw the brush on the bed and wheeled around to look into my face. "Do you know what it's like to raise a child alone? Someday I'll tell you all about it. I tried to talk to you about Howie before you got married, but you'd have none of it. 'I know what I'm doing,' you said. 'I know perfectly well.' You chose your bed, dear, and now you've got to make the best of it."

"I'll do it alone."

"And how, I'd like to know? With a high school degree? You don't even have beauty college, Edie. How do you plan to raise and feed two children and pay the rent? Tell me that? I had Daddy's money. You don't have anything."

"I'll waitress."

"Don't be a fool. What would you do with your children? Sit them in a booth in the corner to draw? Howie's put a good roof over your head, Edie, he's a good father. Maybe he's not what you bargained for, you're no great shakes either, kid, not speaking to the neighbors, running off all over the country."

"Do you know how to get a divorce?"

"I brook no more of this, Edie Deschene. Get off the bed, wipe your son's nose and make Howie supper, and don't say anything again."

"Please, Dot?"

"I said *no more.*" She drew her fingers across my mouth like a zipper. "Keep it here," she said, tapping my heart. "This is your own."

. . .

The days stretched on between us. Rising each morning, Dot fixed the breakfast, I fed Gabriel, Howie sighed and left out the front door and came back each evening to a dinner served up with Dot's chatter. I spent my days in the rocker, watching the sunlight move down and up the mountain, whispering to Gabriel, "We are going somewhere green. Warm. Somewhere there's big, white horses."

Howie grew quiet. His face became flushed and tight as if he were always keeping something back, and some nights after dinner, he'd walk down to the basement, where he'd sit next to my rows of preserves and read his Bible. Other nights, he went to the church, to prayer circles and foundation boards, coming home long after I'd gone to bed to kneel on the cracked linoleum of the bedroom and whisper his angry prayers.

"Enough!" I shouted one night, and threw the milk across the kitchen and watched it shatter across the floor. "I can't stand this."

Gabriel began to cry.

Howie looked up at me, sprung. "What is it?" he said.

"This infernal silence," I said. "Say something."

"Please clean up the milk," he said.

I knelt on the floor and mopped up the milk. Dot picked up Gabriel and rocked him, saying something about Mrs. Hansen across the street, about what a lovely woman she was despite her rude children.

I sat down and put my hands on the table and stared at him. "Tell me. Tell me what you hate in me."

"The things we hate are often the things we love the most," he said and cut the meat from the bone of his pork chop.

"Don't be so goddamn wise," I said. "You hate something. I can feel it."

. . .

Dot excused herself, saying something about how the green beans needed watering. Howie watched her walk from the kitchen and out the back door. Then he whipped his head around. His face was bright red.

"Have you had enough? Are you trying to get me to give you the punishment you have coming from other quarters?" He calmly rose up from the table and looked down at me. "This is in your hands, Edie. I can punish you, but you know it's up to you."

"What's in my hands?" I shrieked. "What?"

"You know," he said. He went slowly around the kitchen, shutting the windows. He raised his hand. "You know."

. . .

Dot brought me dinner in bed and brushed my hair out and told me I looked like a princess and he came early to bed that night. I stared out at the moonlit garden, barren except for the beanstalks dried around their stakes, and knew I'd pack the suitcase and leave when the house was asleep. I knew I'd steal across the back lots and up Teacup Mountain and walk west. I'd keep walking until I reached some farmhouse where a kind, wide-faced woman in a red apron would open her door and take me in. She would take me to a back room with high, sloped ceilings and she would let me sleep there, sleep for ages, with only the sounds of the wind in the larch and the far away laughter of birds. I would find this place. I knew it. I touched Howie's back and he turned to me in sleep, and I cradled his head against my stomach, stroked the long line of his jaw till he turned.

. . .

My water broke long before the sun rose, and the contractions came fast and hard. Howie packed me off to the two-room hospital, where he sat outside my room, reading his Bible, moving his lips as if he were dreaming.

I was groaning. I didn't let them give me ether, and the nurse thought I was odd, but I believed this baptism of pain would bind my baby and I. That was before things came unhinged. Before the doctor leaned in close and pain cornered and played with me like a cat.

To keep things in focus, I looked at the picture across the room. It was of a young girl opening French windows to cherubs gathered outside. In the wash of grey, she reached out to fat, curly-headed babies as if they would take her away. I watched that picture for hours as the doctor swung in and out of my room, the nurse mopped my forehead, murmured *Push, push*. Pain blanketed me. The lower half of my body looked like some distant mountain.

"Let us help the pain," the nurse kept saying, her round freckled hands fluttering around me like birds.

The girl in the picture said *no*.

The doctor came in, checked my pulse, said, "Time to knock you out."

I kept saying no. He didn't seem to hear me.

The girl in the picture said something. Tears trickled down her cheek. I tried to get up to hear her, when the nurse pressed a button and people rushed in to hold me down, and the nurse said, "Slug it out, Mrs. Deschene."

The girl was moving her lips, but I couldn't hear her above the clanking noise swelling up around me. I shouted, "Quiet." The girl cried harder, and I heard the cherubs singing something so sad and beautiful it made my skin crawl, and when the clanking stopped, the thin, sweet voices sang, delicate as lace, "Heigh Ho, Nobody's Home."

Something sharp stung my arm, and the room went black.

The nurse came in after I woke, a big smile on her face. "Look what I have, Mrs. Deschene," she said, slinging a tight-bound bundle under my chin. "A beautiful baby girl."

I looked into the screwed-up, purple face, the blue eyes that didn't yet focus and put the covers over my head.

"Mrs. Deschene," the nurse said, her voice cold, "Sit up and take your baby girl."

"Take her and leave," I said.

"Yes, Mrs. Deschene," she answered, her voice flat, and I knew it would be all over town.

I lay still until she closed the door. Then I rang the aide and sent her for scissors. I struggled out of bed, my groin was numb and huge, hanging like an udder.

I waddled to the mirror. My face was grey as putty, but as I undid the clasp, my hair fell down across the pale gown, catching the light from the window and shining copper down my back. As Miss Cindy chattered about babies, their fingers and toes, I cut my off my beautiful hair, hunks at a time, until it

tufted around my head like straw. Then I laid back in bed and
called the nurse.

She walked in and gasped.

"Now," I said. "Give me my baby."

She returned, holding my girl as if she hated her, and right
behind her came Howie, his eyes widening.

"Howie," I told him. "We'll call her Grace."

· · ·

I steal out of the house to speak my story to the dirt. Thick with
thistles and crabgrass, it is warm in my hands. I yank weeds
till the bed is clean, till my hands bleed, but the noise inside of
me continues. I plant daffodils, tulips, snowdrops, and crocus,
and think of their small uplifted heads, their slender, voiceless
throats. How after five years, they will go blind and stop sending
up blossoms. I slice an earthworm, and the two halves wriggle
away. Two round tubes of flesh, each with six hearts, move off to
start separate lives, and a voice sings, *our daily bread.*

MEMORIAL DAY

They were buried beside the railroad tracks, these MacLeods and Biggerstaffs and Charbonos who in 1860 rounded the weary bend of what the Indians called the River of Awe. They built a town they called Bridger, then they rested, forever. They rested under skies that purpled with dusk or oncoming storms and chattering cottonwoods that shook down leaves in a graveyard so big it had streets named Yew and Hope and Eternal Glory. They slept and played pinochle, and at night they listened to the rasp of crickets and the coupling and recoupling of trains, except for the restless ones who gathered their bones and hopped slow-moving freights headed west.

The McGuires lay there, too. Fierce Scotch-Irish, they came west from Chicago for the sake of their boy who'd sickened in the stench of the stockyards. There was Edward, his gentle wife Corrie, and three children: the daughter who married well and ran countless committees, the son nicknamed "Dandy," and the baby who died at delivery because the doctor was drunk. They rested easy in lives well lived, except for Corrie's sister, Sarah, who claimed that the shift and crash of the trains kept her from God-given sleep, and her brother, Simon, who drifted south to Boise.

Today there were no games—no last minute bets or retreats or card-slamming victories. Today everyone waited: husbands for wives, sisters for brothers, babies for mothers. Even those who had been here for decades waited for a prayer sent earthward, even a plastic flower. The air was tense with listening.

No one said anything about the tapping of a small girl's shoes as they ran across the McGuires' flat marble gravestones. ("Who wants to spend a fortune on a monument to death?" Poppa McGuire always said, and all the family agreed except Dandy, who insisted on a weeping angel for his wife.) For most, the patter of footsteps was like the sound of a welcome rain.

No one complained except Sarah, who winced at each footfall and said, "It's going to be awful." "Of course not," said Corrie. "It will be lovely." "Lovely?" Dandy cried, "It will be lovely?" "Lovely," Corrie said, and her voice was firm. There was a rustling above them. "Lilacs," Corrie whispered. "Smell that perfume." "You don't know what it's like Corrie!" Sarah cried. "Don't start," Edward said, scowling. "Can't we make this nice for once?" Sarah went on anyway. "They always say kind things about you, Corrie, and some years they squeeze out a tear, but not for old Sarah. They just flop down a tulip, and laugh—and I nearly went blind embroidering those runners for Jimmy! Remember the cornflowers in five shades of blue?" "Of course, dear," Corrie said. "Jimmy's wife put them out every summer for company." "Maybe I wasn't easy," Sarah said. "But once, just once, I wish someone would say, 'Now Sarah—there was a fine woman.'" Just then the baby woke up and her mouth opened and shut in a soundless cry. Corrie held her, and hummed, *rock-a-bye.*

. . .

The footsteps stopped. There was only the rumble of an idling switch engine, then a murmur rippled down through the ground. Corrie lifted her head. "Jimmy?" Edward said. Corrie nodded, and said in a rush, "Look at his face, Edward—how sad it is, how heavy with the world. If I could just—" "Let him be now," Edward said. "He's a man." "Just warm his cheek in the palm of my hand," she continued. "Well you can't, Mother," Dandy said. "'Cause you're dead. Gone. Forgotten." "Keep to yourself," Edward said. "Just because your heart's locked tight, doesn't give you license to break your mother's!"

There was a banging of cans, the thudding of more feet, and someone calling "Rrrrruhee," though it was hard to hear clearly through the earth. Corrie clutched Edward's arm. "Don't worry," Edward said. "She'll come." "She's got so much to remember—" Corrie said. "Do you honestly think she'll forget you for the Lady Pioneers of Erudition and Charity?" Edward said. "Who cares if they come?" Dandy said and tossed his head. "It's the same every year—they stand above you, say your name, and someone dredges up some idiotic story, but honestly, do we have to go through this forever? Do you really think things can change now? Better to extinguish hope, Mother. Face facts. May's never going to get on her knees and ask for your help." "When has May ever forsaken your mother?" Edward cried. Corrie began to shake. "You bled me dry, Dandy McGuire," she said and looked at her son, but her tears were long gone. "Those years I took care of you, something grew up between May and me and when we entered the same room, things just broke into two like a plate with a hidden crack. You're right Edward, she never forgets me—not a birthday or a Christmas or an Easter, but don't you see? I'm just another item on the list, next to flowers for the church coffee, and napkins for bridge." "Corrie!" Edward slapped his hand on the earth. "May was devoted to you." "No dear," Corrie said, and her voice was hushed. "She was lost to me."

. . .

Something slammed shut with a chunk.

Sarah trembled.

"May's here," Dandy said, ringing with triumph.

"May?" Corrie said.

"May," Edward said and settled in for the duration.

The pattering continued, on out over the MacLeods and

the Biggerstaffs and the unmarked graves of some early horse thieves, then west to the unpeopled territories of earthworms and bitterroots.

. . .

From the darkest part of the yard, Rudy could see her mother and Auntie May on the patio talking. They were talking about flowers, their voices low and echoey. You won't have anything left, her mother said. I don't have a choice, Auntie May said, family comes first. She began ticking off a litany of family names on her fingers, Mama, Poppa, Dandy, Sarah.

Rudy hung her hair on the lilacs, and whispered, help.

Her mother called.

She shook the branch. Violet blossoms floated to the earth. She looked down and imagined they were princes crying, Rapunzel, Rapunzel. . . .

Rudy, where are you? her mother called.

Rudy watched her. Her mother stood up in the garden by Auntie May's kitchen, and looked out toward the darkening yard. Patches of yellow light outlined her bare white arms. In one hand, she held a trumpeting daffodil. In the other, clippers. At her feet, Daniel pushed his truck around a can filled with dripping flowers, saying *rnnnnnn*.

Rudy answered. She shook the branch again, but this time she just watched the lilacs fall. She was tired of Rapunzel. Her hair wasn't long or ropey—it wasn't even the color of gold. She took her hair off the branch and sat down.

The night was watery and sweet, and the grass was damp. She looked at her knees, tensed them, and the folds of skin seemed to smile back at her. She scooped up some petals, and watched them flutter through the greying air to the ground. She tossed handful after handful. She loved to watch them falling.

Her mother came toward her carrying a coffee can, and in the dimming light her movements seemed liquid and slow.

When she reached the lilac, she began snipping off clumps of flowers and putting them into the can. Rudy watched the leg planted in front of her. Her mother's calf looked white and cool as stone. Rudy touched it. It was warm. She could feel the muscles bunch as her mother stood on her toes. Her mother said, go find your brother.

She ran to the front where her aunt was bent over the flowerbeds. At the edge of the yard was a doorway cut in the hedge. Through it, Rudy could see the street outside, where lamplight spilled across the cars and puddles and a cat strolled down the sidewalk. She went into the sweet-smelling doorway. It was dark, and the ground was scattered with needles that looked soft, soft enough for a small girl lost in a forest. . . .

Daniel, she called. She had to find Daniel.

She found him in the backyard where it sloped up and turned wild, where a bear once came down from the mountain to eat apples off the tree. Daniel was sitting on the grass next to a flowerbed, and beyond him stretched a tangle of bushes and saplings too thick and prickly to walk through.

She stood over him, and said, if you stay here they'll find you.

He stared up at her. Who?

They come out of the trees at night. . . .

Stop it, he said. He waved his arms at her. Stop it.

They were quiet.

She watched him tear up the grass between his legs and listened to the metallic whisper of clippers, Auntie May's voice calling from somewhere, We've got to hurry. We're losing our light. Her mother answering, I know. It's going.

She looked down at Daniel, and said, We're going to see dead people.

Daniel waited for her to go on.

She didn't know what else to say. Finally, she clutched her throat, choking, and fell to the ground.

Daniel patted her head and got up. He wandered off. When he came back, he stood over her holding an armful of leaves.

Timber, he shouted.

She shouted, no.

The leaves came tumbling. They were slightly damp and smelled like earth. She didn't brush them off. She liked their weight, their rustly skins. She lay flat on her back and looked up at the stars that looked bright and heavy.

Daniel covered her with leaves till only her face showed. Then he dropped leaves over her face, calling, Bye, bye, Rudy! Bye!

It was black. She held absolutely still. She heard Daniel breathing, a door slam. She wondered if her mother would notice she was gone. If she'd crawl up the hillside crying, my baby, my baby! like Rudy'd seen a woman do once in a movie. Or if she'd start up the car and pull out of the drive and go home as if nothing had happened, while Rudy lay there listening to the engine whirring off down the dark streets.

Rudy where are you? her mother called.

She shot up and stood next to Daniel. They waited.

Her mother was on the patio. She lined up cans of flowers, took off her gardening gloves, pinned back her hair, and opened the screen door. Come in now, she said, this is last call.

Rudy ran after Daniel, and they streaked down the slope toward the lighted patio where their shadows grew long and thin.

In the kitchen, Auntie May pulled down a cookie tin decorated with Indians sitting around a campfire. Their faces glowed with reddish light. The trees beyond were black and pointed. Auntie May held the tin to her chest. First, she said, dirty little kittens must wash their hands.

Their mittens, Rudy said.

Mittens then, her mother said and wiped Daniel's nose with a cloth and said to Auntie May, sometimes it just goes on and on.

On and on, Auntie May said.

Rudy tugged Auntie May's thick red housecoat. She asked to see the dancer.

Dancer, Daniel shouted and twirled, tipping over into her mother.

Auntie May opened the china cabinet. She took out a bottle with a long neck. It was the color of amber. She wound a small knob at its base, and as the tinny music played, a tiny ballerina began to pirouette. Rudy watched her spin, her porcelain legs stretching out as she dipped and turned. Did she ever get tired? she wondered. Did she ever unhook herself from the pin she spun on to run up the bottle and rattle the top, shouting till the crystal rang?

They drove home through the dark, cans clanking and sloshing, lilacs bobbing. As if she knows what it's like to have children, her mother said to the windshield. Pow pow, Daniel said. He and Rudy looked out the rear window. Car lights swung toward them. They began to hum. The engine vibrated through them and wobbled their voices.

. . .

The morning was grey. They drove across the bridge, over a river boiling with snow melt. Past store windows of flowery dresses, houses with sagging porches, humped sidewalks, weed-choked lots, and a graveyard. The wrong one, her father said, Catholic. They drove on down a road, where the fields grew wider and tepee burners breathed black horsetails of smoke, to the shaded graveyard where Rudy's father pulled up the brake. He turned back at them.

Quiet, he said. We must be very quiet.

What was he afraid of? Rudy wondered. She pulled her foot up and tried to see herself in her shoe, but her face just clouded the patent leather.

Children must be good, her mother said. If they are good, they get ice cream.

Daniel started to clap.

Her father put a finger to his lips. Hush, he said.

. . .

The back door swung open and her mother stood next to them. She took her gloves off, and ran her hand wearily through her hair. Help me, she said.

Rudy carried lilacs. She walked slowly behind her father, the can sloshing water on the arms of her coat, and with each step she got wetter. She could not see her feet. When they reached some flat gravestones, her father stopped and looked down.

This is your family, Rudy, he said. Edward, Corrie . . . they are part of you.

His voice was soft and sad, and it made the back of her neck tingle. She remembered the picture on their dining room wall, the wide, wrinkled face of her great-grandmother in its haze of white hair. Something about the way the face peered out from the darkening photograph made her shiver.

Give Corrie your flowers, her father said. Corrie loved lilacs.

Rudy set down the lilacs.

A door opened behind her. She turned to see Auntie May stepping out of her long-nosed car, and Rudy ran to put her arms around her, her hair flying out. Auntie May was warm and smelled like cinnamon. They walked back across the grass to stand next to her father.

Suffer the little children, her aunt read. She let go of Rudy's hand and set lilies on the grave. She said, the baby died because the doctor dropped her.

Rudy touched the cupid carved in the stone and said to herself, the baby died because the doctor dropped her.

Rudy's mother took her hand. Hers were wet and red. She led her and Daniel to a large block of granite, and sat them down. Don't move, she said. It's time for quiet.

Daniel put his thumb in his mouth.

They sat there, watching. Auntie May and her father bent their heads low and talked. Rudy heard Auntie May say, remember Sarah ringing that bell for mother? her father say, died at the tender age of eighty. Their talk ran together and burbled like the sound of water. She turned to Daniel.

Let's dance, she said.

Daniel wriggled in place.

No, she whispered. Dance *wild*. She stood up and twisted, her hair whipping across her face.

Daniel held his arms out. She looked around. Her mother carried forget-me-nots to the faucet. Her father and Auntie May walked down an avenue of trees. She helped Daniel down, and they began to dance.

I'm warning you, her mother called.

They sat down and kicked at the grass.

What's dead? Daniel said.

When they put you under the ground, and you go up to heaven, Rudy said. Like Carmel, our dog.

Daniel slid down and began scratching the ground. I want to see, he said.

She stared out at the trees drooping over the grass. The branches bent down like doorways. Through her coat, she could feel the chilled granite on her bottom, and she brushed herself off and sat down again. She could see her father's back getting smaller as he walked down the road. Her mother wasn't anywhere. Trees rustled. Cold climbed her limbs and spread through her. She got up. Wait, Daniel called. She kept on walking.

* * *

She walked back to the family graves. Grey lumps of rock. They are part of you, her father had said. They were heavy and silent, and something made her want to hit them with sticks. She stood on one. Stamped her foot. Then she ran over them, one stone,

231

two stones, three stones, four, her shoes sliding on the marble and sounding like wind.

Her father and Auntie May walked toward her, waving their arms.

She turned away from them, and crossed a dirt road.

She began to leap from stone to stone, over Biggerstaffs and MacLeods and Charbonos, her mother's voice floating out behind her, Rudy! Honey, Rudy's gone! She wanted to move away from them, from their voices and flowers, and she nearly lost her footing on the red-veined marble where "the mouths of angels" stared up at her foot. Her mother shouted. The panicky sound of her voice made Rudy move faster. She ran to the fence. Trees reached down and brushed the top of her head, and she ran to the corner. Morning glories blossomed and climbed the barbed wire, and she slid under it to the other side.

She stood still. She could hear a whistling and a rush of wind above her. Out of the corner of her eye, she saw a bird startle and fly, its large wings beating the air. Her family looked far away, the size of dolls.

She lay down on her back. The earth was damp, and wet her legs. She thought she heard a noise, a hollow thumping. In the movies, she remembered, Indians could hear faraway horses by listening to the ground.

Grass tickled her nose.

There was a blowing sound.

A cloud floated across the sun.

. . .

It was as if she rose above herself while a great hand pressed down on her body. Her legs tingled. Her heart was getting bigger, as if it were filling with gusts of warm air and someone somewhere were stroking her hair and singing her a lullaby in a voice that was soft and slightly off-key, and she could hear their breath going in and out of their chest and she whispered yes and a great calm flooded her.

It was a lovely, weightless feeling like floating on her back at the lake. From up above, she saw herself curled in the grass in her red coat and black shoes, her hair fanning out. She could lie here forever. Watch people move in and out of trees, cars prowl down dirt roads, trains rattle slowly down the tracks. Hear the airplane, buzzing. The trees whisper her name.

Her mother was running toward her. Even up here, Rudy could feel the rumble of her footsteps, but the harder her mother ran, the farther away she seemed.

Her mother stood over her. Enormous, panting. She said, I told you not to run.

Rudy looked up at her. She told herself, get up, but she could not lift her arm from the grass. Move, she told herself, but her legs would not listen. She was too far away to cry.

Her mother knelt down, helped Rudy sit, and put her arms around her. Through a layer of wool, Rudy felt the warmth of her mother's stomach. She put her head in her lap and held on.

Her mother said, I'm here.

Rudy held on, and after a long while she was back inside herself. Then she pushed away her mother's arms and picked herself up.

Let's run back, her mother said. I'll chase you.

No, Rudy said. I want to walk.

Her mother held apart the strands of barbed wire. Rudy stepped through the fence to the tightly bunched trees where the brambles were thick. She shivered. Then she walked slowly across the wide lawn. It was green with new grass and pungent with the smell of wet earth.

. . .

There was just one set of footsteps now. The faucet squeaked, then went silent.

"Well," Edward said. "Another year."

"Another year," Dandy said. "Another year to pin on some

233

dim hope that things might change, and another year to be deceived."

"A tulip," Sarah said. "A wilted, lousy tulip."

"They're going," Corrie whispered. "They're going away."

A car started and rolled down the road, whining off into the distance. There was the jetting sound of the sprinklers, a meadowlark's ringing arpeggio, the rising chorus of cicadas, and a rumbling, like thunder, from the direction of town. It was almost time for the 5:40 to Pasco, and they knew it would be passing overhead soon, and then moving on.

THE BOY SCOUT

He lay between cotton sheets and his wife adjusted the
morphine drip in the bedroom of the wood frame house he
bought after ten years at the mine. He didn't remember how
he'd tried to make a go of it logging, cutting down Doug firs and
ponderosas, which crashed and bounced down the mountain,
before lying still in great brushy zigzags, before that September
day, his second child on the way, when he walked into the mine
office and filled out a mimeographed application and the dream
began—launched by the steady green river of paychecks—the
house, children, basketball games, graduations, retirement,
grandchildren he took fishing along the Kootenai with its black-
green pools and bull trout that circled and circled.

   He didn't remember when the cough started. Dry, abrupt.
Like the sound of a cupboard door slamming. *Achh!* The lungs
with its areolae like tree roots, flocked on X-rays like the white
Christmas trees his wife favored. As the morphine honeyed
his veins, he forgot about those early promises: Zonolite! The
miracle substance! All because a miner came to Montana,
stuck a candle in the wall of a cave, and the rock came alive,
twisting into hundreds of worms. And then its offspring, soft,
soapy material that was going to make them rich, the workers
trucking ore down the hill into ovens where they cooked it
at 2,000 degrees until it popped into feathery material they
shipped across the country for insulation, shingles, printers'
ink, even yellow, pink, and orange crayons. He didn't remember
how happy he'd been, that winter morning, light filtering

down from high windows, the Zonolite settling over generators and conveyor belts, scudding along the floor—even the name sounded heaven-sent, like progress. When the men—those suspicious Nordic men, with their Lutheran sourness, and barebones existence—teased him about the snow-like substance glinting and sparkling in the air, he laughed and thrust his arms in a barrel of it and pulled them out, his thick arms coated in hairy pink fibers.

He flapped them.

Jesus Christ, Pete Nord said. *You're the angel of Zonolite Mountain.*

A lazy son-of-a-bitch, Mark Lundquist said. If you ask me.

I don't think he can hear me, his wife was saying.

It's hot in here, his daughter answered. Can we open a window?

He didn't remember that the doctor in Spokane looked at his lung X-ray, left the room, and, when he returned, his face was set. The doctor asked him where he'd been working. As the sweetness spread into his cerebral cortex and the chorus of beeps and thumps from the ventilator subsided into a mosquito-like hum, he didn't remember that the doctor said, once detected, it was too late or that the clock on his wall was two minutes behind.

There was a dog barking somewhere. A pressure against his hand. The smell of lilacs from the yard wafting in.

He didn't remember the courtroom where the company president swore, under oath, the company had not knowingly exposed them to tremolite asbestos, the fibers working their way into the lungs of the workers, as well as townspeople, more than two hundred to date, the graveyard taking on the look of a church luncheon with its eternally cheerful silk flowers lined up, row after row.

. . .

He was traveling, traveling down the narrow road that snaked around Bull River, traveling with his scoutmaster, Mr. Edgarton, an odd man, but kind. He'd helped them sell firewood, popcorn, homemade Rice Krispies bars, and fireplace tongs they had forged themselves in Mr. Edgarton's smithy—raising enough money so the eight boys of Troop 45 could attend the World Boy Scout Jamboree of 1967. All of them packed and sweating in the July heat, windows down in Mr. Edgarton's Ford Fairlane, singing "And the Caissons Go Rolling Along" and as dark forests and silver rivers spun by, the boys cried, "Whooo," as they rode up the hills, and "Wheee," as they rolled down. It was dusk by the time they arrived at the navy training base in Farragut State Park on Lake Pend Oreille.

All he could do was stare until his scoutmaster told him to stake the tents or they wouldn't get any sleep that night. It was a town of boys. Negro, Japanese, Jewish boys, boys with freckled faces, shaved heads, boys with strange drawls, all of them moving, talking, jumping, like herds of antelope quick-moving, running and swooping across open ground. Twenty camps, forty-seven troops, twelve thousand boys.

He woke the next morning, sweating in his flannel sleeping bag printed with hunting dogs, staring at the seamed canvas tent. Mr. Edgarton was shouting, *Breakfast, 7:00 a.m. sharp, up and at 'em!* He pulled on his underpants, pants, belt, and his blue shirt heavy with badges his mother had stayed up the night before to sew on—badges he'd earned for fire starting, wood skills, and backwoods emergencies. He climbed out of the tent, squinting. Before him were hundreds of pup tents under the large cottonwood trees at the old naval base where submarines had been tested during World War II. It was as if the war had just picked up again, only the troops were quarter-sized.

Seven days organized around fun. Swimming. Water skiing. Hiking. A Wild West rodeo. They were even on television, and he stood just inches from Jimmy Stewart, holder of the highest scouting award, the Silver Buffalo—who narrated the show about the Twelfth Annual Boy Scout Jamboree. He didn't remember how he had ached to be the Eagle Scout who received the U.S. flag from astronaut Scott Carpenter. Or how new the words sounded here, the pledge he had recited each week in the Lutheran church basement: *On My Honor I will do my best: To do my duty to God and My Country, and to Obey the Scout Law; To Help other People at all times; To keep myself physically strong, mentally awake and morally straight.*

There'd been a Skill-O-Rama where boys demonstrated how to start a fire without a match, how to tan a deer hide, how to make a rope chair, how to build a bridge out of logs, how to navigate by the stars. The Coeur d'Alene, Idaho, troop with their original song based on an old Indian myth about the lake monster, the Paddler. The presentation from Okinawa on the art of cloud watching. The Lewistown, Montana, troop's demonstration of birdcalls: a duck, a goose, a meadowlark, and the clincher—the eerie yodeling loon.

We're sunk, Eddy, his best friend, was saying. *Totally, completely sunk. No way we're going to win that Skill-O-Rama prize. Might as well kiss that good-bye.*

Now, Eddy, Mr. Edgarton straightened his tie for the third time. *Think positive.*

He didn't remember that he was furious with Eddy as he stepped in front of their booth and the crowd hushed as his troop members circulated among them, handing out sample sacks of their magic rocks.

He held out the matchbox, slid it open, and pulled out a wooden match.

Even now, he couldn't remember how the green grass, blue shirts, canvas tents, and white buildings blurred, and he took a breath and the words came straight out of his mouth, bypassing his brain, flying out from some deep cosmos inside him. So many came from towns like his, tough towns, where the dads worked in mills or gas stations or in the woods and moms scrambled to make ends meet and the kids went to school and tried to stay out of trouble, but guess what?

They were all watching the match, waiting.

This rock, he said, *is vermiculite. When you light it, it expands and grows! It makes insulation to heat our homes, ink to print our schoolbooks, crayons for the kiddies. And it makes our town sparkle! We put it in our gardens, on our running tracks, in our pavement.*

The boys were looking away, he was losing their attention.

If you light it, he said, *it burns.*

Fire. Their eyes were on him again. He could feel the crowd's hush as a physical presence.

Rocks don't burn, you say?

He wouldn't remember the pounding of footsteps afterward when the boys ran up to question him: how could a rock do that? What was it called again? Did he have extra samples? What would happen if he lit a boulder and rolled it down a hill, would it light the town on fire? What if he lit large rocks and blasted them at the Russians? All the while, the head scoutmaster was shouting for order, the bugler blowing his horn—they were mounting a podium and they'd won the Special Exhibit, First Prize, Troop 47 from Libby, Montana, Mr. Edgarton holding the trophy, all of them laughing, Eddy slapping him on the back, saying, *Where you get that bunk about how our town sparkles? Man, you're a gasbag.*

As he settled back on the pillows and light striped the sheets, what he remembered was this: the scratch, hiss and *tcchht* as the fire rose from the match. He held it to the rock on the tin pie plate his mother had loaned him and the rock popped, expanded and grew porous as angel food cake and as he looked at the boys' faces—bright, pink orbs— they opened their mouths, sucked in air, pursed their lips and then, in one long exhalation, said, *Wow.*

NEIGHBORING ON THE AIR

One morning in March, Daisy Flick walked into the offices of
KAL Radio in Hamilton, Montana, notes, recipe cards, and
clipped newspaper items in one hand, a coffee cup in the other.
Her two children followed her: Sally, who was three, birdlike and
quiet; and Stanley, five, a chunky, self-assured boy who had the
annoying habit of correcting her and usually being right. She
perched on a leather-covered chair, her children beside her, their
eyes on the lighted sign that read "On Air."

In the sound booth, Rose Boileau was finishing her
homemaker show, "Koffee Klatch," with a recipe for Crazy Cake.
She winked at Daisy as she slid effortlessly into a plug for Dotty
Duncan's hats. "Ladies are lovelier in hats," she said, touching
the smooth brown wave that swept up from her neck. Then she
leaned into the microphone. "Good-bye, my friends," she said.
"Keep your heads high, your smiles wide, and your days will be
brighter."

She set the needle on the turntable and the Singing Pioneers
sang "Tumbleweeds."

In addition to raising four children and helping her husband,
owner of Jack Frost Orchards, Rose Boileau was queen of the
station's four homemakers who were neighboring on the air
with weekly programs of recipes, gossip, and community news.
She'd had her show for nearly fifteen years and two generations
of women in the Bitterroot Valley had grown up learning to
keep house according to Rose. Rose shaped their everyday lives;
she determined what they set on their tables. When the Pac and

Carry, for example, had a surplus of bananas, Rose came on the air with recipes for banana bread and banana cream pie and the overstock was gone in a day.

Each Christmas the manager of KAL Radio sent Rose Boileau a dozen roses. All Daisy got was a card with a picture of a wreath.

But what Daisy envied most about Rose was her ease. Rose sat at the microphone, and recipes, news, and advertisements seemed to flow from her. How did she keep all that in her head, Daisy wondered. How did she move so smoothly from cakes to coupons, from weddings to club news? Daisy could hardly remember what her children had for breakfast, much less the slogan for the Hamilton Merc.

As Rose came out of the sound booth, she touched the cheeks of the children, who looked up at her, terror mixed with awe. "Hello, dear," she said to Daisy in her calm, imperious voice. "I always look forward to your show."

Daisy entered the room, throwing her coat on the floor, her notes on the table. She settled her kids in the corner, promising popcorn if they were quiet. What was it that Rose enjoyed about her show, she wondered, her bumbling delivery? The botched recipes?

She turned on the microphone and looked at her notes.

In large crooked letters, they said: CALVING. SICK COW. CHICKADEES.

"This is Daisy Flick, your neighbor with news from 'My Kitchen Sink,'" she started. Her voice tangled in her throat. She took a breath. "It's calving season, friends. So my husband, like yours, is out there all hours of the night—it's like living with a new baby and we all know what that's like. Our milk cow is still sick and her milk's poor, but we're rooting for her."

She panicked slightly, but her notes steadied her. "A family of chickadees has taken up residence in front of my kitchen window. The mama's making her nest—she seems to be partial to horsehair—and we're looking forward to eggs, aren't we, Stanley?"

Stanley looked like he was about to say something, but she stared him into silence.

"This is probably old hat to most of you out there, but I was a town girl and what I grew up doing was talking. 'Well Daisy,' my husband always says, 'When the good Lord gave out the gift of gab, you were first in line.' 'Well, Henry,' I always answer. 'You got the corner on tact.'"

She went on about the meeting of the Merry Wives Club, the bridge supper at the Klines', and then, of all things, the baby shower for the father of a newborn boy, where, it was reported, his friends played a game of pulling clothespins off a line with their teeth.

Her mouth ran dry; her mind blanked. She grabbed the newspaper clipping about the cat who'd been locked in a kiln at the brick company. "When he was found," she read, "his skin was burned dry as a cracker and his nose was scarred, but he was alive. 'He always was a tough cat,' the owner said."

The advertising. She'd forgotten about the advertising and the manager was always getting after her about that. She plugged the Creamettes sale at the Pac and Carry and finished with an elaborate thanks for the homemaker shows' sponsor: Jack Frost Orchards, "where the apples seem to smile."

Even though they'd heard this dozens of times, her children stared at her as if that were the dumbest thing they'd ever heard.

      • • •

A light rain started up on the drive from town and the children fell asleep in the backseat to the wipers' steady squeak. Daisy drove the narrow highway to the ranch, passing stock trucks and the occasional tractor, until she reached the county line where she turned west. This turn always filled her with dread. Maybe it was the mountains—they were high, jagged, and remote, and they seemed to repeat themselves endlessly, like mirrors mirroring mirrors. Maybe it was the bare stretch of the hay fields and the lonely power line. She'd grown up in Bridger, sixty miles up the road, with orderly maple-lined streets, several radio stations, a large department store, where if you got on well with the saleswoman, she'd keep you in mind on her buying trips. Downtown, there was always the hum and clack of commerce, the ringing of tills, the breathy sound of doors opening and shutting, the people on the sidewalks calling to one another.

The ranch was Henry's dream. After they'd been married several years, his aunt died, leaving him enough to start up a small cow-calf operation. Then the trips to the bank began: for a barn, a tractor, more cattle. They learned everything they could from their neighbors, but they'd lost several cows in the heavy snows last winter and several tons of hay had been ruined by rain. It was then Henry and Daisy named their place the Green Ranch for all the inexperience and money they poured into it.

She pulled up the drive next to the peeling white farmhouse, the midday light slanting across the bare ground. She slung Sally over her shoulder and delivered her to her bed. Then, with a grunt, Stanley. She was loading up the percolator with coffee when Henry walked in, his black hair wind-slicked, his face red, his eyes hollow. He'd been up all night, calving.

"How are the mamas?" she said, watching the small bursts of water at the top of the coffeepot.

"Restless." He dropped into a chair at the linoleum table and began tracing flowers on the oilcloth with a square-tipped finger. "I stayed up with that big heifer, who seemed like she'd go any minute, then the rascal lay down in the straw and slept like the dead. I'm bushed. And I've got dozens of these to go."

"Poor baby," she said, sliding into a chair at the kitchen table. It was strange, Henry up at all hours, drifting in and out of their bed. The other night, when she was up with Sally, who'd had a nightmare, she had the sense that they were all a tribe of night wanderers, roving from bed to bed in the semi-darkness, never really quite sleeping.

"Well, heck," Daisy said. "Look at the bright side."

Henry looked at her, waiting to hear the bright side.

"Tonight, just as you're settling into bed, she'll go into serious labor."

Henry gave her a wan smile and went back to tracing flowers on the oilcloth.

She poured them coffee. Two lumps of sugar for Henry; nothing for her. She'd heard on one of the homemaker shows—was it Rose's?—that drinking black coffee was one way to lose that roll at the waist.

In the hush of children sleeping, Daisy put her hand on Henry's and felt his exhaustion roll over her. He smiled at her, his face tender. When they were alone together, they'd grown shy around one another—a shyness not unlike the days they were dating, except that she wasn't excited by the quiver between them, she was irritated by it. Irritated by what it seemed to ask from her in this rare moment of quiet. Then, at the thin cry from a distant bedroom and the urgent patter of footsteps, the moment was washed away by clean, immediate purpose and she jumped up and poured juice in a cup.

Sally stopped in the kitchen doorway, her hair in clumps, her face moist with sleep, her dress twisted around her thin body. "Mama," she cried. "I hurt."

. . .

By the next week, there were twenty more calves, and, she announced to her listeners, the chickadees had begun sitting on their nest, leaving only for food.

Of course there were no chickadees. In fact, there were pine siskins that fluttered about the ponderosas and never came close to the house, but Daisy thought chickadees sounded better—didn't every ranch house have a cheerful nest of something at the window? These images of fertility, she thought, somehow dignified their life in the white house with the peeling paint.

Of course, the first time she mentioned the birds, Stanley said, as they left the station, that he hadn't seen any chickadees in their windows, he hadn't seen birds at all, but she told him they were magic birds. That kept him quiet for a while.

She talked about Sally's cold. Did colds ever disappear in a house with children? she asked her listeners. Or did they just visit one family member after another until, when everyone was well, they circled back for more. Somehow she had a sense that illness was always around, crouched and waiting for a lapse—wet hair, wet hands, wet feet—to pounce.

She read aloud a letter from a Mrs. McLeod who wrote that what the sick cow needed was wool and camphor around the throat. You need that milk, she wrote, you've got to get her producing.

Sally started coughing from the back of the room. Stanley gave her something to drink, as Daisy had instructed him to, but the coughing deepened until Sally began to gag. Daisy grabbed a record and put it on the turntable—"Night on the Prairie" by Marlene Sue and the Cowbells—then she wrapped her arms around Sally until she grew quiet.

She should have stayed home. Sally had looked pale on the twenty-minute drive in, falling asleep almost as soon as they were out of the driveway, her blonde hair spread across the seat, and the whole time Daisy wondered if she was doing the right thing. Then Rose put her hand on Sally's cheek and told Daisy the new baby aspirin was just the thing for fever—besides sleep, of course, in a bed heaped with wool blankets and clean sheets.

Daisy nodded, stung. It was true. She was selfish. She pushed the kids too much, dragging them into town, to the grocery store, the feed store, and the hardware store until they were exhausted and cranky.

She'd considered asking Rose to sub for her, but she was afraid Rose would do such a good job they'd never ask Daisy back. They needed the $10 she earned, but she also suspected Henry would only be too happy to have her quit. As much as it traumatized her, she needed her show. She loved her show. She loved setting her coffee cup next to the microphone; she loved putting records on the turntable; she loved turning the microphone on and hearing those first few halting words and thinking of the women on the other end: washing their dishes, sweeping their floors, comforting their babies as she talked to them.

She made a deal with herself: if she could do her show, she'd devote her undivided attention to this cold. She'd get up nights. She'd be the soul of patience: playing games and telling stories until Sally slept.

Sally's forehead grew hotter.

Okay, she thought. A few more announcements, then she'd get the kids in the car, get some baby aspirin at the Pac and Carry, and go home. This was the moment where everything shifted, and suddenly you weren't trying to fit the illness into your life, you were suspending regular life to accommodate illness.

· · ·

Back home, she played cards with Stanley while Sally napped. The icicles dripped at the window, the air was pungent with the sharp smell of wet dirt.

"Go fish," Stanley shouted, slapping his cards on the table, his round face gleeful, when Henry came in and stood in the doorway. His face was pale, his eyebrows drawn together.

"What is it?" she said.

"Fish, Mom," Stanley begged. "C'mon."

"One of the Herefords." Henry kicked the doorframe. "She's having a rough time."

She was up, Stanley at her heels. She put on rubber boots and an old coat, looking at the clock, thinking Sally would probably sleep another hour so she had no time to waste. She threw on Henry's old wool coat and helped Stanley into his. Then they trouped into the brilliant April day, the door swinging shut behind them.

The heifer lay in her stall, bellowing, looking piteously at Henry as they walked up. Henry knelt down in the straw, and put his hands up inside the cow. "I can feel the calf, but it's stuck," he said. "I need you to pull while I try to dislodge it."

Daisy thrust her hands inside the cow, groped in the slick, hot flesh, the uterus contracting around her hands, in and out, in and out, until she felt two stick-like legs. "Got 'em," she said.

"On the count of three, pull." Henry looked at her, squinting. "She'll kick, so watch out. Stanley, stand back—the last thing we need is for you to get hurt."

Daisy caught Stanley's eye. He stood at the edge of the stall, staring at the bawling cow, horrified and fascinated, and she wondered, for a moment, if he thought that was what she looked like during birth. And what would she say to him if he asked?

Henry counted to three.

She pulled the thin legs out of the cow, and kept pulling until her stomach hurt and her arms ached. Henry eased the head out, leaping back every once in a while to avoid the cow's kicks. The mother arched her neck, crying, her eyes rolling back until they were nearly white. Then Henry said to give it a rest, the calf was hung up on something.

They straightened up and looked at one another.

"Green Ranch," Henry said.

"Should I get the Parkers?" she said, panting. The Parkers, whose family had ranched in the Bitterroot for three generations, lived fifteen minutes away and Henry had called on them for help once or twice, when his pride let him.

"No," Henry said.

They put their hands on the calf again. She could feel Henry's breath on her cheek, hear him grunt as he knelt, determined. "When she contracts this time, pull like hell."

"You said hell," Stanley said. "That's a bad word, Dad."

"Heck," Henry grunted. "Pull like heck."

"It's okay because Daddy's working so hard," Daisy smiled across the cow at Stanley. "Now help us count. One. Two. Three."

They pulled and the calf eased out.

"It's coming." Henry flushed. "Good job, mama." Daisy thought he was talking to her, but he patted the cow. "Just a few more pulls and we'll have it."

He knows more about this calf's birth, Daisy thought, than he does about his children's.

They pulled again and suddenly a wet bundle slipped onto the straw, followed by a sea of afterbirth. There was a tense moment as the cow lay on the straw, exhausted, the limp calf next to her. Then she was up on her feet, licking the membrane from the calf's nose.

The only sound in the barn was the wet scratch of the mother cow's tongue.

The calf looked blindly toward them, then swung its head back to its mother.

And there was Sally, standing barefoot at the edge of the stall, coughing.

"My God," Daisy cried. She draped Sally across her shoulder and ran toward the house. "Get back inside. You're sick."

. . .

The chickadees, she announced, were still nesting. The male bird seemed to fly back and forth bringing the female food while she sat on the eggs—wasn't that charming, wasn't that the way it was supposed to be? She could tell by the fury of their activity that those chicks would hatch any day now.

She saw Stanley look at her, then look down. Magic birds, was that what he was thinking? Or was he thinking that his mother looked worn as an old shoe?

She was flushed and tired and seemed to be floating above herself, and when she started reading the recipe, "Delicious Broccoli and Corn Casserole," she choked up, thinking of her great aunt, who'd been dead for fifteen years, who always made the casserole when Daisy stayed overnight. Stop, she told herself, straighten up, you can't fall apart now or everything else will. She abandoned the recipe and read a letter from a listener who was concerned about the recent heavy rains—What if the river rose? the woman wrote. What if it flooded the fields and the stock had nowhere to go?

She turned away from the microphone and wiped her nose. Stanley stared at her.

It's okay, she mouthed.

She swallowed, her throat tight. "It's Sally, friends," she said. "She's got a fever of 105; she's coughing. She's wrapped up in a blanket right here in the studio and as soon as we finish neighboring on the air, we are going to the doctor." Somehow saying this made her feel better, more competent. "She'll be fine, and when she's fine, I'm fine."

Daisy could see the blue glint of Sally's eyes from inside the blanket, watching her.

"Thanks to Mrs. McLeod," Daisy went on, "the cow is producing again. And the calves keep coming—even yours truly helped bring one into the world."

She teared again at the memory of the wet scratch of the mother cow's tongue as she licked the calf's nose, then she shook her head clear. "A poem," she said quickly. "We need a poem for this grey April day." She cleared her throat and read from Dawn Williams's *A Cornucopia of Poetry:*

> Face the dawn and know today brings a lovely thing
> For in spite of the clouds and funeral bell's ring
> There is cheer in a heart warmed by a child's giggle,
> A blooming crocus, a puppy dog's wiggle.
> Let us look for treasures in the others we love,
> Let's find delight in blue sky above.

Stanley looked at her, incredulous.

. . .

The doctor listened to Sally's cough, moving the stethoscope slowly across her chest as Daisy waited and Stanley asked questions about stethoscopes. The doctor suggested aspirin and cold baths for fever and wrote out a prescription for the cough medicine. "No pneumonia," he said, the first words he'd spoken since Daisy came in the office. She felt that he disapproved of her somehow—her mothering, her children, her radio show, she didn't know what.

"Cough medicine and lots of bed rest," she repeated as she brought Sally's dress over to where she sat on the examining table, shivering. Daisy was relieved yet disappointed that the doctor didn't name a more specific illness. Daisy wanted the sickness pinpointed, given a name, a long complicated name that raised in others the alarm that she felt.

"A steamer perhaps, to ease the breathing," the doctor said, his hand on the doorknob. He looked at her, his blue eyes sharp, almost cutting, and then he was out of the room.

That night, Sally was up, her forehead blazing, and Daisy held her, her voice bright and quavering with fever, her hands shaky. Sally talked about the cows and her friend Molly and how she went to the store but they didn't have her favorite red suckers any more but the lady said they'd get more soon and could they get some, a special treat for being sick? Daisy rocked her as she talked, feeling her body burn against her like a coal, watching out the window as the wind tossed the thick branches of the blue spruce.

. . .

"I have good news, ladies." Daisy smoothed her blue polka-dot dress as she spoke into the microphone. She'd dressed in anticipation of meeting Rose Boileau. She had wanted to impress her with her neatly dressed—and healthy—children and her fashionable dress. Maybe Rose had command. But she, Daisy Flick, had lightness and she wanted to cram that down Rose Boileau's throat.

But Rose had gone home early to oversee the spraying at the apple orchard.

"The chickadees are hatching," Daisy said, looking at Stanley who was playing jacks with Sally. He didn't look up. "Two eggs have hatched out into the tiniest chicks you've ever seen and we're watching each morning for the other three. The mama and daddy bird take turns going out for worms."

She was telling them about Sally's recovery, when she caught her reflection in the glass. Her face was narrower, carved with lines. She felt an arrow of regret pierce her for the times Henry used to tell her she looked like Myrna Loy with her thick black pageboy and long legs and she'd push him away, laughing. He didn't tell her that anymore. He told her she was a good mother. A great cook.

She passed into a promo for the Jabber Jaws Cafe, "home of the bottomless coffee cup," then went on to club announcements and a few items from the paper. When she was done, she thought, she was going home on this glorious day—the sky a deep blue, the air filled with the wet promise of earth—to clean up the morning dishes and uncover her garden, the beds she'd scratched out next to the house where the crocus and daffodils were sending up slender green shoots. But first, she'd stop at the town playground. The kids had been so patient;

she wanted to reward them. She wanted to see them run; she wanted to see them shouting.

At the park, they spilled out of the car, Stanley heading for the merry-go-round, Sally for the long, twisting slide. She looked pale and skinny in the spring sun, but her cheeks were pink—and not from fever.

Daisy sat on a bench as they played, listening to their piping voices, feeling the sun loosen something inside her, some knot she hadn't been aware of till now, till it was unraveling. It was a long winter, longer here than in town where there were so many more distractions. But Sally was well, Henry had successfully pulled—how many was it? sixty?—calves. And she'd gotten a fan letter today, from a Mrs. McKinney, who said her corn and broccoli casserole was wonderful, despite the fact that Daisy had left out the onions.

. . .

Then it was Stanley. Stanley who had slept the nights while Sally coughed herself awake. Stanley who cross-examined the doctor while he examined Sally. Stanley who amused Sally in the car on the trips to town and chased her around the house while Daisy fixed dinner. That night his fever crept from 100 to 105 and the next night, when it hit 106 degrees, she called the doctor, who advised a cold bath. She stripped him as Henry ran the tub and together they bathed him. Stanley talked about eagles, his teeth chattering, his eyes glassy. How eagles could spot their prey from miles away. How an eagle could swoop down on an unsuspecting rabbit and dig its talons in its back before the rabbit could blink.

The tremulous sound of his voice terrified her.

She wrapped him in a blanket and began to rock him, his arms and legs limp as flour sacks as Henry watched her, silent. As she rocked, she looked down at Stanley's spiky black hair, thinking of how his body—with its sturdy legs, round cheeks, and its healthy, dependable appetite—had betrayed her.

He murmured in his sleep, twisting his head back and forth, and she put her hand on his forehead, wishing she could draw the fever to her, wishing that the forehead beneath her fingers would cool and she could go back to trusting his body again.

Several days later, his fever was still high. She canceled her show and stayed by Stanley's side, reading to him and trying to keep Sally from jumping on the bed. He slept most days, getting up every once in a while to drink some broth or look out the window. His fevered listlessness, his torn-up bed, his damp pillow frightened her. At one point, when Sally was asleep too, she sat at the kitchen table with Henry, numb with fatigue, and looked out at the kitchen and living room. Everywhere she looked was something she needed to do: jelly was smeared on the kitchen table, dust balls collected under the coffee table, clothes were strewn across the floor.

Henry was unusually chipper—five more calves had been born yesterday and the others were doing well—they hadn't lost any yet. Maybe, he was saying to Daisy, their luck was turning. "Maybe we've learned something after all," he was saying. "Maybe we will make a go of this."

She didn't pay attention, she was just listening to the rise and fall of his words thinking how pleasant they sounded, how they seemed to spill from him so easily, so unfettered.

When he stopped talking, he put his hand on hers.

"You know he'll be okay," he said, studying her face. "Stanley's tough."

"I know," she said. Henry's face blurred, and she wished she had his confidence.

"He'll be fine," Henry said. "Mark my words."

At the whirring sound of a car in the drive, she wiped her eyes. There was a knock at the door and when she opened it, there stood Rose Boileau, a pot of soup in her hands. "Chicken soup," she said, as she walked in the kitchen, taking off the clear plastic rain hat covering her swept-up hair. "I put extra garlic powder in it because it is good for respiratory illnesses." Rose looked around the kitchen and the dining room and Daisy's first impulse was to leap up and distract her somehow from the clutter and the dirt. Rose, who looked at housekeeping like a science, a matter of finding the right solutions to problems. Instead, Daisy thanked her, took the soup from Rose's hands, and set it on the stove.

Rose settled herself at the kitchen table. As she sipped her coffee, she told Henry apple prices were falling due to the flood of fruit from the Yakima Valley. She told him how hard it was to get good pickers, although the Indians still came down each fall from the reservation and pitched their tepees along the Bitterroot, though you could never really rely on them—they'd be there one day, full of promises, and gone the next.

As she talked, Daisy studied Rose's hands. They were strong-looking and wound with veins and looked capable of anything—hammering, canning, diapering, picking—and her round freckled face that was so sure of itself, so set with the knowledge of her world and her way around it.

Then Rose touched her on her arm.

Daisy had to keep herself from flinching.

"You look exhausted, dear," Rose said softly. "Last year Janie had double pneumonia and I was up every night for two weeks with her. You feel like life will never be normal again. You feel like you are lost in this sickness—in the coughing and the fevers— and you will never return to normal life." Rose's face softened, and Daisy could see all the fear and confusion and powerlessness that she felt, and she realized this chaos was more frightening than anything for Rose—all her poultices and recipes and advice were simply attempts to stave off formlessness.

"It will end," Rose announced as she stood up, all command and control and efficiency again as she made her way to the door. "It will end," she repeated and the door snapped shut behind her.

. . .

Staphylococcal pneumonia, the doctor said after he examined Stanley, who fidgeted on the leather examining table, the paper crinkling underneath him. We'll have to hospitalize. The hospital? she wanted to scream, but she didn't dare because the doctor would give her one of those icy blue looks and then she would be flooded with guilt.

After she settled Stanley in the hospital, she drove home to pack a bag for him with his flannel pajamas, a pile of books, and some games—then it struck her that she was packing his bag as if he were going off to an overnight with his grandparents in Bridger.

That night the doctor called just after Daisy fell asleep. She leapt from bed when the phone rang three times—their ring on the party line—and as the doctor talked, she could feel her heart knock against her ribs. Henry, of course, was out in the barn.

Stanley's right lung had collapsed, the doctor said. He'd operated to insert tubes in Stanley's chest to drain the lungs. "He's fine, the nurses are taking good care of him," he said, his voice scratchy and distant. "We've put him in an oxygen tent and he's sleeping more comfortably now, so there's nothing you can do."

"I'm coming in," she told him.

She dressed quickly in the dark, speaking quietly to Henry when he came into the house.

"Call," he said. "Call as soon as he wakes."

The ponderosas swayed above her as she drove down the muddy roads, silvery in the moonlight, and she could smell the earth in the fields, pungent, sweet—a betrayal—and as she thought of Stanley, she felt a familiar tingling in her breasts, the ghostly sensation of letdown.

She pleaded with the nurses to let her in the room, and they finally relented. Stanley was asleep behind the plastic oxygen tent and pale, breathing hard. He opened his eyes as she pulled a chair up next to the bed.

She leaned over to kiss him through the plastic.

"I'm in an oxygen tent," he said.

"Does it hurt?" she asked.

"No," he said. "The doctor said the wet air will help me breathe. And these tubes," he touched two black tubes coming out of his chest, "are draining my lungs. The doctor said my lungs have to be drained just like a water balloon."

"I want you to breathe better," she said. She wanted more than anything to run her fingers through the damp hair on his forehead, to rub his back the way he liked but she was afraid to upset the delicate-looking apparatus, so she just stroked his hand. "We have to you to get well, Stanley. We got to get you running again."

He sat up and looked at her, his face grave. "My lung collapsed," he whispered.

. . .

Sally and Henry met her at the hospital the next morning. This time Henry too looked panicked at the sight of Stanley, fragile and wavery-looking in his plastic tent. This time he didn't say that Stanley, sturdy Stanley, would throw this off. Instead, he seemed awkward around his son, asking him how he felt and if he had slept and if the nurses gave him ice cream. Only Sally seemed unfazed by the seriousness of Stanley's condition as she skipped around the room, turning the faucets on and off, shouting, "Stanley is sick! Sick! Sick!"

Rose organized a legion of women to bring in casseroles, and each day at dinnertime a new dish would arrive with the name of its creator written on masking tape. There were scalloped potatoes from Mrs. McLeod. Bean dinner from Mrs. Vann.

Hamburger noodle surprise from the Tennyson sisters. Cards arrived at the hospital and at home, and when she dropped by the radio station to say she didn't think she'd be in for a while, there was a stack of cards there, too. The station manager told her not to worry, and Rose Boileau waved from the booth where she was launching into Daisy's show.

It made Daisy sad to be back in the station, to see the booth, the microphone, the folding chairs—they seemed like the remnants of a life she'd lived a long time ago and that she'd never have again—a happy life sprinkled with small concerns, concerns that seemed so big at the time and so small now, like whether the kids would stay quiet during the show or whether she'd remember to get all the sponsors in.

She and Henry had dinner at the hospital, eating dry roast beef sandwiches and coffee at Stanley's bedside. A neighbor was taking care of the cows; Rose had offered to stay with Sally, but Daisy lined up another neighbor. It made Daisy queasy to think of Rose in her home, amid the dust balls and dirty dishes.

Stanley and Henry were playing checkers, Stanley sticking his hand through the tent to move his pieces, crowing once when he picked up two of Henry's checkers in a double move, then collapsing in a heap of coughing, his head against the pillow, tears squeezing out of his closed eyes.

They put the checkerboard away and she read *Swiss Family Robinson* instead.

That night, after Henry had gone home to Sally, Stanley's temperature climbed again to 106, setting the nurses off in a flurry. She dampened a washcloth and reached into the tent to mop his forehead as he writhed, coughing and twisting the sheets one way, then the next. The doctor came in after a while—called from bed judging from the jumble of his clothes—and his face was grave as he listened to Stanley's chest. He talked to the nurse about increasing the penicillin and the oxygen in the tent, then he turned to Daisy and said, "That's about all I can do, Mrs. Flick. This is not in my hands anymore, you know."

The sounds of shoes clattering and beds squeaking and Stanley wheezing were muffled and distorted as if she were on the bottom of the sea.

She gazed out the window at the dark houses, absently counting the lights. One at Flahertys'. One at Deschamps'. She wondered what the women in these houses were doing at—what was it? 3:00 a.m.? Were they drifting in and out of their kitchens, their living rooms, their bathrooms, moving about, unaware of each other, living this nighttime life that was completely separate, subterranean, a life only glimpsed at times when you were thrown out of your own life and you became aware of its shape and everything surrounding it?

Stanley stirred and turned over to look at her. His eyes were still dull with fever but his face looked less flushed.

"Hey buddy," she said.

"I'm tired of being sick," he said, looking up at the ceiling.

"That's a good sign," she said. "That means you're getting better."

Stanley said, "I see things when I sleep."

"It's fever," she said. "Fever gives you strange dreams."

"The dreams scare me, Mom," Stanley said.

They were silent a minute, listening to footsteps in the hallway, the hushed sound of the nurses talking and the tick and creak of the building.

"Tell me about the chickadees," Stanley said finally.

"Well those little chicks grew big, Stanley," she said. "The chicks ate worms and grasshoppers until they were so big they didn't fit in the nest and the mama bird knew that it was time to teach them to fly, so those birds lined up—little splashes of color against the black branch—and the mama bird showed them how to fly. Then one by one the chicks leapt off the branch and tried their wings. One fell to the branch below. One flew a few yards then had to land. One even fell to the cat in the yard and they all mourned her passing, but they had to go on. With practice those birds learned to fly and soon enough those chicks were sailing around with the best of them, singing, chick-chick-chick-a-dee."

"Mom," Stanley sighed. "Everyone knows chickadees are black and white."

. . .

That night the fever turned. Stanley was in the hospital for another two weeks and then, in no time, he was running about the ranch looking for bugs and gophers. Sally was overjoyed at first, but Daisy knew things were back to normal when they started quarreling again.

At the station, Rose greeted her on her first day back with a bunch of red carnations tied with a matching ribbon and lollipops for the children. The owner too came out of his office to tell her that he was glad she was back—two shows a week had simply worn Rose out.

She went into the booth and settled the children with a stack of comic books, put her notes before her—the advertisements for the hardware store and Jack Frost Orchards, the newspaper clippings about calving season in the Bitterroot Valley. She sat for a minute at the microphone, looking at the table, the folding chairs, waiting for a rush of pleasure. She'd waited so long to be back here. She'd missed all of this, even the announcements for the Methodist Women and the Merry Wives Club.

But she felt empty.

Stanley was well. The pneumonia had cleared up, dwindling down into a cough if he overexerted himself. Calving had gone well—Henry was even talking about buying a few more acres. Her crocuses and daffodils were up; the deer had even spared a few tulips. So what was wrong?

She launched into the recipe for kiss-me cake, an old recipe of her grandmother's, rich with nuts and raisins, then followed up with announcements about engagements, a wedding, and the meeting of the Ladies of the Moose. As she talked, she thought about all the women in town—the women in their Cape Codders and bungalows and ranch houses, with mudrooms and well-scrubbed kitchens, these women with their husbands and their children and their radios tuned to her show as they washed dishes or folded clothes. As she talked, she felt the words skating on top of her: collections of syllables with meaning that were little scribbles on the heap of human existence. As the sound of her voice filled and warmed the room with her news about bridge games and dances, meetings and rummage sales, and something loosened in her chest, like ice breaking in a stream, she thought of her words flying out of this room and over the airwaves, magic birds, linking them all together with their hopes and their sorrows and their near misses.

ACKNOWLEDGMENTS

Anton Chekhov said, "Writing is a long patience." Writing is a long patience in the work itself, in the finishing of that work, and then in the seeing of that work from the typescript to print. Along the way are all those people whom I want to thank for helping me on that long, bumpy, pot-holed road.

I owe my first big thanks to Rick Newby, who first published a story, "Fruit in Good Season," in his wonderful anthology, *The New Montana Story.* I was so honored when he asked if I might be interested in publishing with Drumlummon, as we stood next to the lemonade cooler at the Governor's Arts Awards in June 2015. He is a brilliant editor. I love the fact that four wonderful women helped bring this book into being: my gratitude goes to Lucy Capehart for her brilliant tutu image that graces this cover, DD Dowden for her elegant design, and Dana Henricks and Beth Judy for making me look a lot smarter with their terrific copyediting and proofreading.

These are the editors who published my stories and offered their sage advice: Jennifer Barber, Peter Brown, Allen Jones, Michael Koch, Ronald Spatz, and Willard Spiegelman. My immense gratitude goes to my mentors and fellow writers who inspired me and kept me true: Sandra Alcosser, David Cates, Debra Earling, Kate Gadbow, Dana Fitz Gale, Beth Judy, Melissa Kwasny, Tami Haaland, William Kittredge, John L'Heureux, Beverly Lowry, Crissie McMullan, Deirdre McNamer, Sheryl Noethe, Nancy Packer, Amy Ragsdale,

Annick Smith, Peter Stark, Susanna Sonnenberg, Dave and Sheila MacDonald, Neil and Kim MacMahon, Janet and Kim Zupan. And the ones whose presence are always with me: James Welch, Patricia Goedicke, Ripley Schemm, and Richard Hugo, with whom I fished at Pierce Lake, our family cabin, and caught cutthroat trout galore. I learned a love of Virginia Woolf, Eudora Welty, and dinner table savoir faire from Lois Welch. My road trips and talks with artist Sandra Dal Poggetto have helped me define my aesthetic in regard to the West. A shout-out to the wonderful women of the Rattlesnake Ladies' Salon, with whom I spent many hours reading, editing, and discussing literature. There are so many friends whose warm hearts have nourished me along the way and to all of you, my deepest thanks.

I am enormously indebted to the fabulous writers I met at the Ucross Foundation, where I first assembled this collection, as well as the wonderful men and women at the Virginia Center for the Creative Arts, where I wrote several stories that I used to complete this book. The writers I met through the Wallace Stegner Fellowship at Stanford University were enormously influential in shaping me as a writer, and I will forever be grateful for that two-year period of writing, a heady and terrifying gift. I am also grateful for the Vogelstein Foundation, the Alison Deming Money for Women Foundation, the Montana Arts Council, and the Henfield Foundation for their support.

I thank my family for their love and belief. My parents, Jack and Laura Patterson, my sister and her husband, Cathleen and Michael Morrison, and their daughters, Halley and Georgia, and my brother, John, have supported me as a writer with their good cheer over numerous family birthdays or impromptu cocktail parties. My children, daughter Phoebe and son Tobin, have inspired me with their courage, pluck, and intelligence. Maisey, my dog, has done nothing to help this book along, except to hop in my bed each morning and to issue body-wagging invitations to get outside and walk. And finally, I am most grateful of all to Fred Haefele—husband, editor, friend, lover, and fellow warrior in this long, strange journey. You've been the best inspiration of all.

ABOUT THE AUTHOR

Caroline Patterson grew up in Missoula, Montana, in the four-square Prairie-style house that was built by her great-grandfather in 1906 after he won a case against the Great Northern Railway. She lives there today with her husband and her two college-aged children. In 2006, she published the anthology *Montana Women Writers: A Geography of the Heart,* which won a Willa Award. Her work is appearing in upcoming anthologies including *Montana Noir* (Akashic Books, 2017) and *Bright Bones: Innovative Montana Writing* (Open Country Press, 2017), and she has published fiction in periodicals including *Alaska Quarterly Review, Epoch, Salamander, Southwest Review,* and *Seventeen.* In addition to teaching fiction at the

University of Montana, she has received awards including the Wallace Stegner Fellowship in Fiction at Stanford University, Joseph Henry Jackson Prize from the San Francisco Foundation, a Vogelstein Foundation Award, as well as residencies from the Ucross Foundation and the Virginia Center for the Creative Arts. She is the executive director of the Missoula Writing Collaborative.

Lona Hanson: A Novel
by Thomas Savage
(introduction by O. Alan Weltzien)

Splendid on a Large Scale
The Writings of Hans Peter Gyllembourg Koch,
Montana Territory, 1869–1874
Kim Allen Scott, editor

"The Whole Country was. . . 'One Robe'"
The Little Shell Tribe's America
by Nicholas C. P. Vrooman

Long Lines of Dancing Letters
The Japanese Drawings of Patricia Forsberg
by Rick Newby

Robert Harrison: The Architecture of Space
by Rick Newby & Glen R. Brown

Coming Home
The Historic Built Environment and Landscapes of
Butte and Anaconda, Montana
Patty Dean, editor

Frank Lloyd Wright in Montana
Darby, Stevensville, and Whitefish
by Randall LeCocq

Cass Gilbert in Big Sky Country
His Designs for the Montana Club
by Patty Dean

49499348R00175

Made in the USA
San Bernardino, CA
26 May 2017